Overnight

M. Evans
An imprint of The Rowman & Littlefield Publishing Group, Inc.
4501 Forbes Boulevard, Suite 200, Lanham, Maryland 20706
http://www.rlpgtrade.com

10 Thornbury Road, Plymouth PL6 7PP, United Kingdom

Distributed by National Book Network

First Rowman & Littlefield paperback edition 2014

Library of Congress Cataloging-in-Publication Data Available

ISBN 13: 978-1-59077-446-5 (pbk: alk. paper)

™ The paper used in this publication meets the minimum requirements of American National Standard for Information Sciences—Permanence of Paper for Printed Library Materials, ANSI/NISO Z39.48-1992.

Printed in the United States of America

Overnight

A NOVEL BY

MATTHEW SMITH

M. EVANS
Lanham • New York • Boulder • Toronto • Plymouth, UK

To

G. W. V.

Overnight

I

IT TOOK PLACE AT 'CRAGIE,' OR NEAR 'CRAGIE,' IN LESS THAN twenty-four hours. It sprang from the experience, thought, emotion, habit and will of generations.

It began on a Saturday afternoon in the early fall of 1949.

Audrey Smyth and Reginald Laurens walked into the living room.

"There's no one here," said Audrey.

"That's good."

"You lied to me."

"Is that bad?" said Reggie. "I've got to hold my own."

"Well go right ahead. I certainly don't want to hold it."

Audrey snatched a cigarette from the table, used the heavy glass lighter. She lifted her shoulders and breasts, blew smoke into Reggie's face and gave him her profile. Reggie aimed a kick designed to miss. He almost landed.

"Now that was cute," said Audrey and flicked out a neat left jab which was six inches short. Reggie circled the giant divan which faced the fireplace and stood waiting for peace.

Although guests, they were at home here, Audrey Smyth and Reginald Laurens. They were twenty-five and twenty-seven and had been part of the place since they were born.

'Cragie' is, or was, a big farm estate on the sea near New London, Connecticut. It was owned by George Ridgley, middle-aged and decaying. Everything else was alive—the people, the house, the livestock, the land. The land rolled away to north and south and down toward the sea in fertile fields stoutly fenced in wire which followed the lines of the old stone walls and of bramble, locust and elm. During the summer, these fields were rich in wheat and oats, corn and buckwheat, timothy, clover and pasture-land. In barn-stall and pen, runway and pasture, were chickens, turkeys and pheasants, hogs, sheep and goats, prize cattle and blooded horses. The homespun farmers lived in three cozy cottages near the big, well stocked barns and five hundred yards from the main house.

There were three house guests—Reginald Laurens, Henry Curzen and Lesley Curzen. Henry was George Ridgley's friend and physician. Lesley Curzen, a startling beauty of twenty-six, was Henry's niece. Peter Drake, George's adopted son, twenty-nine, was away but due back that day. He was supposedly saying a delayed good-bye to the Army at Dix. Audrey Smyth had her own place, a great pile called 'Stoneleigh,' a few miles down the coast.

In the 'Cragie' library, Henry Curzen looked up startled from the pages of *Pelléas and Mélisande.* It had thus abruptly dawned on him that he was reading Peter and Lesley into the story. The thin black brows, such a marked contrast to the straight white hair, drew into a frown. Could there be some vague connection? Was this to be tabbed as warning foreknowledge? Nonsense. They were simply on his mind. He had no misleading gift of premonition. Where others were concerned, no matter how dear, his was a hands-off policy. He was of an intelligence far too pure to consciously make the mistake of planning. But he was human. And his heart carried an unacknowledged plan too strong for denial—a plan for the happiness of his very favorite child and woman, his Lesley, and the young man who was his very favorite male child, a love hidden from Henry because of his trained, thoughtful tolerance of all mankind—the young man Peter Drake.

Henry was as devoted to literature as to surgery. He went back to his book. He was almost finished. Lesley and Peter remained with him.

George and Lesley were following the crowd of spectators over the golf course. Her arm in his, Lesley was talking spiritedly but with no thought of what she was saying. Her mind was singing a happy song of love to Peter Drake.

"I don't know when I've ever enjoyed anything so much," she cried, tritely enough.

"Nor I," responded George feelingly. He locked his fingers in hers, squeezed her hand. His eyes shone. He straightened, put a little more life into his step. He was the great figure.

His palm was wet. Lesley was shocked involuntarily. She looked at him, looked away quickly. She could neither return nor destroy his heavy affection. But she would soon be free of that problem. She smiled, chatted on gayly. Her heart was away again, over the hills.

Cross-currents of excitement ran high at 'Cragie.' Each soul made frantic effort to hold to the course of his selection. But as they tried to guide on their stars, they all, by collusion, covered the tension with the human cloak of frivolity and outward calm, even to conscious thought. Yet behavior offers no strong security. Tradition can be torn away. A growing storm can test, then break, old lashings.

The 'Cragie' house was a big, T-shaped, quietly beautiful, early-American masterpiece. It faced the sea on a rocky but verdant rise of ground and was held bravely and softly by ancient oak, chestnut and evergreen. The living room was the magnet, the club-room. It was spacious and friendly and gave onto the informal garden which sloped away to an inlet beach. It was paneled and book-jammed and comfortable.

Audrey sat against the long console table backing the divan. Reggie walked to one of the big windows.

"I thought the whole damned Ridgley clan would be here," he said.

Audrey was angered and pleased. She had been avoiding Reggie for a month, except for a few hot lapses. He wanted to get her alone now to fight with her and to make love to her. That was all very well but she was busy.

"You can't call one man a clan."

"He's fifty-seven and he's single and respectable. And his name isn't Smyth."

"Or Curzen or Drake. But you're just one small, unhappy family."

"What about you?"

"I'm pure guest. I'm a pro. Got to be good at something."

"And since when have you been so damned happy?"

"I'm not unhappy."

"That's not my fault."

"Right."

Reggie had turned back. Now he turned away again. Audrey shot her cigarette into the fireplace, lighted another and tapped a foot. Reggie was in love. Audrey was not. Reggie knew that. Audrey did not. Reggie was wise there. Life was hell as it was. They were having an affair. But it was far from the affair others thought. It was a miserable game of touch and go which left Audrey content and Reggie nervous. And Reggie knew why. Audrey trafficked in carnal magnetism. She excited lust for fun and had a lot of fun. Sex was a healthy habit and taken in stride. Withal, she was an enchanting personality. And, physically, she was very desirable. She had black hair and white skin, chiselled features and a chiselled figure. She was slim, trim, sleek, chic, and sway-backed. Her exquisite young face with its clear stamp of sophistication and wantoness was exciting. Her body, so nicely, almost sharply, symmetrical, suggested seduction in its every line. At the moment, in her beige woolen suit, brown blouse and brown and white sport shoes, so smoothly designed and carried so well by their wearer, she made sex an undeniable factor in the great outdoors picture.

Reggie had been at 'Cragie' for a month. The previous month he had spent at Audrey's 'Stoneleigh.' Audrey had loved that month. She smiled. "And you're not a *pure* guest. But you're the perfect guest. I wish I could afford you."

"I'd make you a very special permanent rate."

"Thank you so much. First things first. I want more money—and I want a quick drink and I want to find George."

"I can get you the drink. The hell with the rest of the order." Reggie hopped to the small bar, a converted Sheraton cabinet, and mixed two heavy highballs.

Reggie had no money. Audrey was one of the richest girls in the United States. That was his Audrey, this love of his. Look at her. Her great-grandfather had had a Medicine Show. Later he had gone into the patent medicine business in Baltimore. Still later he had gone into everything. His original product was still an internationally advertised cure-all for babies. Audrey's father had been shy and retiring, affectionate and rather boyish. He had had the 'not belonging' complex. He was third generation 'new rich' and somewhat ashamed of his wealth but proud of and worshipful of his wife. She was from a fine old Virginia family which had been ecstatic over the alliance. And she was as charming as Audrey's father. They had been a very popular couple and had travelled a great deal.

In 1931, when Audrey was seven, they had been killed on a grade crossing in Florida. The car had stalled before an oncoming train. They had been paralyzed with fear. The scream of brakes and whistle had come in a dream. Then Audrey's father had leapt into action and torn her mother from the car—but too late. The locomotive was on them. It had been a Laurens car. It was murder, then. With the terrible logic of childhood, Audrey had reasoned that had her parents not known Reggie's father, they would not have owned one of his cars and would not have been killed. She had never said anything to Reggie about this. She had never been sufficiently angered by him. But she had never fully outgrown the vindictive notion and, at times, it made her want to hurt him. She did not know that he knew. Unlike her father, Audrey set great store by her money. She knew its value. She was no fool.

Reggie grunted to himself and handed Audrey her drink as he took a gulp of his own. "Solid," he said.

"Liquid. I want bigger stables." The jangle of heavy jewelry mingled with the clink of ice as she tilted her glass.

"If you could just get the forequarters, you could graft them onto most of your friends."

"But you don't understand, darling. I want stallions, not geldings." Audrey moved to the radio-phonograph set in the Duncan Phyfe chest and got dance music.

Reggie took another gulp and held his tongue. Bitchy or lovable, it was all the same. He was lost.

Audrey gave with design. Reggie was prodigal of his love. It was inherent with him. Even as a little boy, he had been brave and carefree and considerate—generous to a fault. The heartbreaking trials of childhood had been met in solitude. His parents had been gentle and understanding. His mother had been a Fitzgerald of Dublin. His father had been of that long Laurens line whose fortune was founded under Louis XV. Reggie's grandfather had built that fortune into small empire proportions with the Laurens motorcar. But with the birth of the big combines had come the death of the elder Laurens's wife, his own death and a sharp decline in the business he had built. Reggie's father had fought for years to save it but the Crash had finished him. He had salvaged what he could from the wreck. When Reggie was twenty, his mother had died of pneumonia. A year later his father had died. He had been very tired and had missed his wife terribly. Reggie had missed them both more than he could think, still did, always would. They had lost their big place on the water when Reggie was nine. But they had continued to come back every summer, living at the Club or renting one of the smaller cottages. And now Reggie was always welcome at the homes of his many friends for as long as he cared to stay and longer.

He had grown into a handsome young man with all his charming qualities nicely matured. He was dark, well made, had an easy grace and humorous dark brown eyes. In '42 he had gone into the Infantry. In '43 X-ray pictures showed spots on his lungs. He had managed to get a discharge. He had wished to make his own arrangements for the attempted cure. He had wanted to get better if he could. And he had. He had spent two years in Tucson, Arizona and had loved it. His personal cloud had in nowise dimmed the sunsets. In '45 he had come back East, completely healed.

Since his return, he had done nothing but rest, have fun and look around. He had a small income and no towering ambitions. He was in love with Audrey. That was ambition enough.

Audrey was soloing a rhumba which was a series of refined bumps and grinds.

"Must you do that?" asked Reggie.

"Certainly not. I'm a brilliant conversationalist."

"Bigger stables! Old George is no stallion. What's he—the fair haired stable boy?"

Audrey stopped dancing. "George Ridgley had just about reached the end of my patience."

"He's getting better. When a man gets better, he gets ideas."

"If Lesley Curzen gives them to him."

"He'd never have got better if she hadn't."

"Nuts. It was Henry who saved George and you know it."

They thought a moment. Henry Curzen, George Ridgley's oldest friend, was a noted surgeon and an advanced student of psychology. Lesley, as well as being beautiful, was cheerful and intelligent and was Henry's moral support and aide de camp. During a periodic illness ranging over the past few years, Henry had spent much of his time with George, and with Lesley's able assistance, had nursed him back from the grave. This time, they had been at 'Cragie' for almost a month with Henry making flying trips to New York for only those consultations and operations at which his presence was absolutely essential. Both Audrey and Reggie knew that Henry had more than a passing interest in psychiatry.

Reggie probed. "Think there's anything psychopathic in George's trouble—aside from his penchant for you?"

"Very funny."

"Screaming." Reggie snapped it out. Audrey had been leading George on for two years. He was sure of that. And she played a no-limit game. This had hurt Reggie deeply as did all her infidelities. He knew the attraction of an older man for a young woman—especially an older man of great means for a girl like Audrey. If she was letting George get away, there must be an alternate. There could be only one strong candidate for that post, the soon-to-return Peter Drake.

George's adopted son, Peter Drake, had been earmarked for the piano from birth. He had been studying in Italy when the war broke out. He had gone to England and joined up. He never knew why. He had survived Dunkirk and later had transferred to the American Forces. Convalescence in Europe had kept him after the war. Now he was back.

"If they haven't been shot away, Peter should make a racy stallion."

Audrey was startled but could not hide her excitement. "I hope he made the evening train. George and I are going to meet it."

"Funny kid—sticking out the whole show and hanging around for the epilogue. He's been point-heavy for years."

Through friends in the ETO, Reggie had learned that Peter had been hit badly several times. But Peter had never mentioned it in his letters and Reggie had said nothing to anyone. They were very close.

"You know Peter and 'duty,' " said Audrey. "And he was always afraid but never for himself."

"Then he'd better learn to be now—with you."

There was an angry glint in Audrey's smile. "How did you know, sweetie?"

Peter Drake was extremely rich as well as being heir apparent to the banking house of Ridgley.

"Intuition," said Reggie.

"I shouldn't wonder. You have a feline mind, darling." For all his marked masculinity, he must have. Else how could he know her most sacred secrets and plans? Damn him.

Audrey set down her glass and stepped close to him, fists clenched. "You're frail, but you're a wonderful lover, Reggie darling. There's just one thing. I wish you wouldn't sometimes take the attitude that you might be right. I heard of a province in France where the peasants have an ideal custom. As soon as they're married, a couple go to the cottage where they're to live and fight it out. I don't know whether it's fists, wrestling or rough and tumble. But the winner is head of the house from then on. And half the time, it's the woman. We're not getting married but we might as well be and I'd like to settle our differences some way here and now for good and all."

Reggie stood his ground watchfully, ready to move away with the punch. "You're giving George his last chance. Henry Curzen's in love with his work. I haven't any money. It must be Peter."

"Don't I think of anything but men?"

"Yes—marriage. Marriage and money and swank. But after his ten years in Europe, I don't think Peter will care to be part of a stable—even if he heads it."

"Why not? I admire courage and character. And I'm very fond of music." She relaxed her aggressive stance.

"And I always swore I'd fall in love with an honest woman."

"I'm far too honest—with you."

"Are you?" Reggie was trembling. He knew something must be done about that. He put down his glass and took her into his arms. He drew her close to him. Audrey's anger faded. She relaxed. This was more like it. Reggie held her amused gaze for a moment. Then he kissed her. Audrey's hands were high, her elbows resting on his arms. She let her hands drop and began to work them over his back. Reggie's right hand slid to her hips. Her body fitted into his nicely. She knew just how to move against him. The lips of her pouting mouth were soft and ripe. Her tongue was pointed and clean and red. Her level green eyes were open. Under their black lashes, they were usually calculating. Now they were alight with something special, a lovable quality in their depths. Audrey loved to make love. But, as a rule, she was objective about it. Even in bed when she was breathing gruntingly and making little whimpering noises, her eyes were wide in the semi-dark. She wanted to see if her vis-à-vis were really having such a stupendously wonderful time. Men were such fools, such delightful fools. It was a rich experience to do as one liked with them. And such fun and so absurdly easy—for her. Little wonder other women hated her so violently. She could mold any man who struck her fancy to please her fancy. But it was all different with Reggie somehow. She could almost lose herself in the sheer thrill of the thing. There was a gentle abandon in his caresses that was heaven. And she could never quite seem to do just as she liked with Reggie. He continued to be self-possessed at the most unexpected moments. Still, she was reasonably sure of him. And she must never lose him. That was definite. She allowed him to continue to kiss her now for quite two minutes. Then she slowly released herself.

Reggie was flushed, breathing hard and still trembling a little. His voice was a rough, halting whisper. "So you're far too honest with me, are you? Then tell me honestly how you feel about that."

"It's nice—but it won't do." Audrey produced compact and lipstick and began to adjust her makeup. She handed Reggie a cleaning tissue. He turned away to the angled mirror over the fireplace and went to work. She peered at him over her mirror, a mocking smile in her eyes. "Do you really care—or was that a trained squirrel?"

He caught her eye in the big mirror. "Wouldn't you rather have that than more money any day?"

"I'd rather have both."

Reggie crumpled the tissue and flung it into the fireplace. "I hope Lesley spikes your guns. That'd be sweet to see."

Audrey snapped her compact and returned it and lipstick to the handsome chaos of her alligator bag. Her eyes were flashing. "Lesley better be satisfied with George now that she's got him."

Reggie laughed, none too pleasantly. He began to feel better. He gave no sign of his hurt other than these occasional outbursts when the pain was too great. It was an old story. Audrey, Reggie, Lesley and Peter had grown up together, at least in the summers. And winter holidays had always found them together in New York. They had grown into four very good looking and charming adults and they had been four very handsome and personable children. But Audrey had had a little sadistic streak. When it threatened Peter, Lesley would always sense the danger and maneuver him into a position of safety. Audrey would then rush off home to stomp about and shed angry tears until some new and even more fiendish bit of juvenile torture would pop into her mind. She would then quickly recover and set about laying plans for its execution. Apart from this vicious streak, she had been a gay and imaginative little girl and Peter, Reggie and Lesley had adored her the greater part of the time. But they had learned to be wary. As they grew older, their relationships had remained more or less the same. Audrey liked them all, loved them in her way, but did not trust them. She trusted no one. Lesley Curzen was perhaps the only person she had reason to fear. Reggie knew that and, of course, Audrey knew it. Her anger was balm to Reggie at this point.

"And I think old George is a hell of a foster father," he said, "if he's ready to sacrifice his musical ward on the altar of consolation."

Audrey made the supreme effort. She restrained herself. Good God! She had passed Reggie on the road, out for a walk, and had stopped to pick him up. That had been a mistake. There was a time and a place fot every man. This was neither for Reggie. She snatched at her glass and took a long drink. "Will you find out where George is or shall I?" Her tone was imperious.

"I'll do it." He turned on his heel in disgust, walked to the hall door and pressed a wall button. He hated to see Audrey adopt the grand manner. It was so out of key. He came back below the divan. She was ignoring him. He decided to try it again. "I get it now—about Henry being here, I mean. George is definitely feeble minded, that is, he'll prove himself to be if he tosses Peter to the lioness just to save his own indelicate skin."

"You bastard!" said Audrey and hurled her glass at him. It missed and crashed into the great stone fireplace.

"That's a terse greeting," said Henry. He had just come into the room from the hall. Henry Curzen was fifty-eight. In appearance, he was grimly distinguished which belied his nature. Close inspection discovered in his eyes a vast gentleness which was the key to his spirit. He had neglected his work shamefully in helping George. His work was far more important than George Ridgley but that was not Henry's way of thinking. And he was enjoying this moment. "But a nice, clean shot, I'll admit."

Reggie really laughed now. Audrey, about to launch herself on him, was stopped in midair. She could say nothing. She could do nothing. She was furious. Henry frowned at Reggie, silenced him. Then he looked at Audrey. She looked at him, opened her mouth, then clamped it shut.

Henry's mouth twitched a little and finally, there was an answering twinkle in Audrey's eyes. Then they both laughed, laughed till the tears came. Henry's laugh was contagious and had a way of clearing the air. The tension was gone. Audrey stepped very close to Henry's side. She locked his right arm in both of hers and pressed it between her breasts so that his hand rested against her thighs. Reggie watched. An automatic gesture with Audrey. She was still laughing.

"Reggie needs to be psyched, Hank. And I know you've cured cases that were hopeless. It'd be a great act of mercy—for his friends."

Reggie grunted. "After you've done your good poorest, send the bill to Audrey and make it steep, make it vertical. There'd be nice-ironic justice in that."

"It'd be wasted on me," said Audrey, "even though you laughed till you kicked the padding out of your cell." She turned back to Henry. "What do you say?"

Henry brown-studied a moment—then, "But my analysis would be 'normal, down to earthy.'"

"Good God—not that!" wailed Reggie.

"He's earthy all right," agreed Audrey. "You can smell it where the varnish has cracked. But you're way off the beam on that normal thing."

"Verbal flight's not in my line," said Henry. "Let's say then, that he's normally abnormal."

Reggie chuckled. He lighted a cigarette, flicked it into

the fireplace and held onto the match. "I was until I was sold down to Audrey." He puffed at the match, blushed, threw it away and lighted another cigarette.

Audrey addressed herself to Henry. "Isn't an over-weening self-esteem a symptom of dementia praecox?"

"Don't try to knock down my ego," said Reggie. "You can't. It's a ghost. It's my guardian angel. Sometimes it gets fed up and leaves me on my own. But at other times it steps up without warning and lays all craft and opposition by the heels. I live for those latter, happier moments—and I live in them. I may not be living the full life at the moment but I'm still livin', honey chile."

"Verbose, aren't we?" said Audrey.

Reggie could hear her thinking. Thinking? Ordinarily, at a juncture such as this, she would have dropped onto the divan, displayed a lot of leg and inserted a cigarette in the long studded holder she used. But she was too restive for the allure act. And there was no reason to use it. Of course, Henry was cute. She liked his low clear voice. She liked the firm way he stood and the direct friendly way he looked at one. And he had money, oodles of money. She imagined it would take a bit of doing to get him to the point. But once there, she was sure he would make a strong lover despite his fifty-eight years. But she did not want Henry. She was prepared to want Peter Drake and she was going to use such means as were necessary to get him. She did not expect to have much trouble. And Audrey never did have much trouble. Glamour alone would probably turn the trick. And she did not have to concern herself with glamour. Not at any time. She spilled it about constantly. When not preoccupied, she liked to overplay it to watch the results.

At the moment, she was very much preoccupied. She loosed her hold on Henry. "Where's George?" she asked. She was all business.

"He and Lesley ran over to the Club to watch the finals."

"But Peter's coming home! We're meeting the evening train. I hope Lesley hasn't made him forget."

"Swell chance," said Henry. "It's all we've talked about since last night."

Peter had cabled a fortnight before that they could expect him. He had arrived from England the day before and gone directly to Fort Dix for separation processing. He had managed to get a call through in the evening. The conversation with George had been brief. Others were waiting. He had hoped to be able to get home the next day. He had no way of knowing definitely. Yes, he had been very happy to get back and he had been glad George was so pleased and glad to learn that Lesley, Henry and Reggie were still at 'Cragie.' He had sent his love. Later in the evening Reggie had relayed the news to Audrey. She had called George in the morning. The evening train seemed the most likely possibility. She had said she simply must go with him to meet it and, with no enthusiasm, he had said that that would be fine.

But George was unpredictable—an escaping male. He might pretend to forget or, on the excuse that it had got late, drive straight from the Club to the station. "I'd better whip over to the Club and find him anyway," she said.

"But they may have left by the time you get there," said Henry.

"Then I'll pass them on the road." She moved quickly to the garden door, turned in the doorway. "Coming, Reggie—or would you rather talk to Henry?"

"I'm coming but I'd rather talk to Henry."

She was gone. Reggie looked at Henry, then, with a shrug of resignation, followed her. By the time he reached the drive, which turned back on itself at this side of the house, she already had her red convertible headed toward the road with the motor racing. She barely gave him time to jump in beside her before she started. She tore down the drive and slammed on the brakes as she reached the road. After a quick look in both directions, she spurted off the gravel onto the macadam, righted the car and shot down the road in the direction of the Club.

"Take it easy, missy, or you'll kill us all." Reggie pretended to be gasping. "I mean you and me and the cop who's sure to follow us. We don't matter but he's got a job to do. He has to try to catch you, you know, and he's bound to break his neck, poor guy. Probably has a wife and kids, too," he sobbed. "Still, I can understand the mission is worth any sacrifice. See if you can't get the Star Spangled Banner on the radio."

"Go to hell," said Audrey.

Reggie was instantly sorry. He put his hand on her leg. She settled back in the seat.

II

HENRY CURZEN DID A QUAINT LITTLE JIG. THEN, MORE soberly, he cut the end off a cigar, stopped the music, and walked to the garden door. He wished them luck. He liked Audrey, as much for her faults as for her virtues. Henry liked women. And Reggie had always been one of his favorite persons. His mother and father had done a great job. They had married late in life, forty and fifty, and had had only two children, a little girl who had died at the age of three, and then Reggie. The Laurens men had always been free to do as they chose. Reggie's grandfather had wanted to be a great painter. When he had failed, he had come to America nursing a broken heart. America had not thought much of his paintings either. But his meticulous sketches of horses and carriages had excited much interest and brought many requests for special work. He had become a designer and maker of carriages. The most elegant equipages of the day had been the product of his pencil and his shops. A brilliant little French girl named Elise de Nemours had mended his broken heart and given him Reggie's father. In later years, he had made the natural switch to motorcars and handed the business over to Reggie's father. For over a decade Laurens Motors had led the field only to end in ultimate failure. The warlike technique of high pressure competition was beyond the scope of a Laurens.

Before entering the Army, Reggie had tentatively accepted several assignments in the hostile world of doers.

These sallies had ended amicably but quickly. Like his father and grandfather, he was made for the sweeter things of life. Business was for businessmen, politics for politicians. If he was to work, it must be with a free hand and simple honesty. His talks with Henry had shown a growing interest in philosophy tempered with a keen awareness of the sacred frauds and foibles of mankind. Henry had strongly encouraged him in this. It was all Reggie needed to complete his security for life. And one day he might add something of value to a quest that fostered compassion. This business with Audrey was a worry. That could blast much. Audrey was simply using him—or thought she was. But Reggie was not blind to shortcomings in others any more than to those in himself. He gave them no value in his dream or scheme of things but he knew the damage they could do. He was cool and skillful and alert. Henry could believe Reggie capable, quite without intent, of coming out of a dangerous involvement unscathed, yet having himself cut a deep impression smoothly and cleanly. Audrey might be toying with him but she might also suddenly find herself attached to her toy with the desperate affection of a child. Reggie was quite a toy.

Damn, a mosquito. It was too late in the season, too early in the evening. Still it was only one. And the light breeze was from the sea, not the land. Henry decided to light his cigar.

Peter Drake was coming home. Although he had been gone for eight years, Peter was still the heart of 'Cragie.' He had been a wonderful, most prepossessing child and he had grown into an exceptionally fine young man. And all that despite the fact that George, with an excess of zeal, had ever tried to dominate him. Peter was rather shy and quiet and utterly charming but he had not been born to be dominated. This homecoming was probably far from easy for him. Peter stacked up very well with Reggie in Henry's affections.

In fact, other than Lesley, Henry did not know which of his 'children' he loved most, Peter, Reggie or Audrey. Of course, Lesley was his very life. She was the child of his younger brother and a convent-bred Polish girl. Henry had been in the Medics and under fire in France all through World War I without getting a scratch. Lesley's father had been sent over just before the war ended and had been wounded the day he reached the Front Lines. He had never fully recovered. A little over three years after they had got back from France, he died. He never saw his daughter.

In 1925, Lesley's mother had run away, leaving her infant of two in the Curzen home. She had joined an older half-brother of Henry's, a very romantic type fellow who called himself a black sheep. The black sheep and Lesley's mother drifted about the resorts of the world and had never been back since. So far as Henry knew, they had never married. Lesley had become Henry's charge, a circumstance most happy for both of them. From the time she could speak, she had called him Hank and told him how much she loved him. They were great friends. She had been beautifully reared and reflected the essence of beauty in person and character. Her interest in his work was genuine and she had sufficient understanding of it to be of invaluable help. She was the bright particular light in the darkness of suffering in which he worked and the firmament of peace toward which he looked. Lesley. She was the one person of Henry's broad acquaintance who bespoke the joy of life. She was as dear to him as faith to the religious.

A discreet cough interrupted his meditation. Henry turned and looked into the battered face and kindly eyes of Fulton.

"Sorry to keep you waiting, sir. I was in the vegetable garden and just got back to the pantry and saw the register."

Fulton was an aged manservant and chief of staff at 'Cragie.' As a young man, with lovable yokel gullibility, he had allowed himself to be lured into the professional fight game. He had great strength and stamina and very little skill. For two years he had been a ring punching bag for bums on their way to the top. Then George's father had brought him to 'Cragie' as guard and bodyguard. Mrs. Williams, the housekeeper, had trained him with infinite patience. He was happy. He belonged in the country. And he had become a good butler.

"I didn't ring, Fulton. Must have been Miss Smyth or Mr. Laurens. They just left."

"Think I could overtake them, sir?"

"Not with anything short of jet propulsion."

"That's too bad." Fulton was upset. Henry gave him an encouraging smile. "About your things, Doctor. You and Miss Lesley still plan to leave tomorrow? Mr. George hoped you might change your mind, sir."

"No, we've really got to go this time, Fulton."

"We hate to lose you, sir. 'Cragie's' never the same without you and Miss Lesley. And now with Master Peter coming home, if you could just stay on, it would be perfect, sir." Fulton had nursed George's father through old age, had had to assume responsibility for George and later, largely, for Peter Drake. Of his three charges, he deemed Peter the most gracious, the best man. The kindred esteem he felt for Henry and Lesley was based on years of association.

Henry was touched by the old man's devotion. "Maybe we can make it again soon."

"Oh, I hope so, sir."

With a fair show of gusto, George Ridgley strode into the room from the hall. "Hello, hello, hello," he said and flopped onto the divan.

"George. You just missed Audrey. I thought you and Lesley were at the Club."

"We were. Deering was two up on Dorsay at the fifteenth. We had to leave then. Any news, Fulton?"

"I tried to reach you at the Club, sir. Master Peter called from New York."

"What did he say?"

"He had some matters to attend to in the City but expected he'd be on the evening train." Fulton's eyes sparkled. "If he couldn't make that, he was sure to be on the midnight."

"I should have been in town to meet him. That's your fault, Henry."

"Better not to overdo."

"Is there anything, Mr. George?"

"I don't think so, Fulton. Everything's ready?"

"Yes, sir."

"Good."

Fulton ducked his shaggy white head and withdrew.

George Ridgley sank back in the divan and stretched his legs. He was a big man. He had lost a lot of weight, his clothes hung on him loosely, but he was still a big man by any standard. His color was bad. He was sunburned but the skin in the new wrinkles, hollows and folds had an ashen quality. He was handsome in a rather worn way but looked more than his fifty-seven years. He thought he looked a young forty. A studied pose of granite strength had grown into a fairly convincing habit. One was to feel that here was a man who was invariably right and who would brook no interference. His large angular features and steel blue eyes under jutting brows lent support to the pose. In reality, he was a very frightened man—an ugly secret not to be admitted even to himself.

"Where's Lesley?" asked Henry.

"Went to her room. She'll be down in a minute."

"Audrey and Reggie went to the Club to look for you. They haven't been gone two minutes."

"Good. I'll be at the station before she can get back."

George appreciated the happy accident of having missed her. The drive forked as it came up the hill. He had taken the branch which led past the other side of the house. He had dropped Lesley and driven on to the long garage which occupied a mere niche in the barns. He had taken a quick, satisfying look around, had switched to a larger car and driven back to the house. He must have been in the garage when Audrey drove off.

"Why are you suddenly so rude to Audrey?" asked Henry.

"She bores me."

"That's a damned shame."

"These things happen, you know." George was complacent.

"Joe College," said Henry.

"What do you mean?"

"It's time you stopped hurting people needlessly—or otherwise."

"Don't be silly. She loves it." George was the perennial adolescent. He believed the flat statements he heard and read about women. He understood women. He would never know that the men who said they knew nothing about them were the only ones who understood women.

"Audrey likes being hurt as much as you do."

"Then why is she so persistent?"

"Why don't you ask me 'why is a woman'?"

"Well I've got more important things to do than to keep a promiscuous glamour gal in a happy frame of mind—if any."

"What could be more important, for instance—directing the destiny of the universe?"

The color crept up George's neck. "I don't give a damn about the universe. That's your baby." He checked himself. The color faded. "Don't fight with me, Hank. I'm in a very peaceful mood and very happy. And reason enough. It's a great day in my life."

Henry nodded. "There'll never be a greater."

"Oh, I don't just mean because Peter's coming home or because I'm better. There's still another reason that tops them all."

"What's that?"

George paused. "I don't know just how you're going to take it." The color was back.

Henry looked at him. "I'd better sit down," he said and slid into one of the armchairs which flanked the divan. "All right. Let's have it."

"I've"—George swallowed—"I've fallen in love."

"I beg your pardon?"

"I know it isn't possible but I have."

George had not been what he called in love for nearly thirty years. Then it had been Katherine Cosgrove Drake, Peter's mother. When she died, such capacity as he had for loving died with her. Henry had given up hoping that time would heal the wound. George kept it open.

Henry studied him. "You're on the level about this?"

"If you have any doubts, just take my pulse and temp. And you'd better check your own before you hear the rest."

"There's more?"

"There's usually a lady."

"Of course. Stupid of me." Henry waited.

"It's—" George's voice cracked. He cleared his throat. Good Lord, behaving like a schoolboy. Why should he be afraid of Henry? He made another effort and this time bleated it out. "It's Lesley."

The cigar was crushed in Henry's fingers. It began to burn his hand. He looked down, saw what had happened and flung it away from him. He jumped up and stamped out the burning shreds. George was grinning foolishly.

"That's not funny, George."

The grin disappeared. "It wasn't intended for laughs." It was a noble sentiment. It ranked with the best his life had expressed.

"You have a Russian sense of humor—as light as death." Henry was still suffering the brain-shudder of a George-Lesley picture.

"You don't believe me?" George sounded like a hurt, spoiled child.

"Just how revolting can one man be?"

"That's a hell of a thing to say to your best friend!"

"What's that got to do with it?"

"Everything!"

Henry stopped. He was shocked beyond words. He did not doubt that George believed himself sincere in this gruesome bit of whimsy. But how to fight it? His thought refused to crystallize. The murkiness of emotion. Some way to shrug it off. He forced himself to look at George, to see him, the George of the moment. His big face was purple. His eyes were flashing. He was highly indignant. An impish caricature of outraged omnipotence. Henry's face relaxed. He began to chuckle, he laughed. He dropped back into the chair and laughed till his sides ached. That was better. George had slowly joined in half-heartedly and was now grinning again uncertainly. Henry wiped his eyes. He was all right again. Good old sense of the ridiculous.

"If not my best friend, certainly my oldest. Do you realize, Georgie, that we'll soon be old men and that Lesley is still a child?"

"She's twenty-six."

"But, good God, twenty-six is a child to you and me."

"Speak for yourself. I'm not your age, Hank, and I'm not your type. I'm a much younger man in every way."

"That's a matter of opinion," said Henry gravely. He was just two months older than George.

"What do I do with my spare time—what are my outside interests? They're all active and athletic. What do you do with yours? You haven't any."

"Is playing golf being athletic?"

"Certainly, if you play the hard-driving game I do. And what about my swimming and the rowing machine?"

"All very praiseworthy. But you're still middle aged plus."

"A man's as old as he thinks. What about your own zany arguments? 'There's neither time nor space. There's only now. And an instant of pure love, could it be realized, would be the eternal now.' Do you think age makes any difference?"

"Yes, if it's fundamental!" Lesley was adult in mind and young in spirit. George was old in spirit and had the mind of a boy. Design was inscrutable, could not be ignored. Henry felt a little groggy. George could not digest the philosophy with which he tried to nourish him. And each belch was another breath on the mirror of Henry's mind. He must clear it somehow. He went on. "And you might be one of the family. That makes the whole idea about as attractive as incest."

"That's a pretty thought." George was angry again. "Why weren't you equally concerned about Audrey, then? She's only twenty-five and she's like family, too."

"That's different," snapped Henry.

"Right. I'm not in love with Audrey."

George was in love with no one. His love was a mania—a mad determination to have the objects of his affection as he would have them. He forbade them to be otherwise, while knowing in his heart of hearts that he was wrong. He was not in love with Lesley, had not been in love with Katherine. Lesley was not what he thought nor had Katherine been what he thought. Henry was troubled. George was arrogant but he was a dear fellow for all his blundering idealism. He was worth saving. Henry had always felt that. But George's perversity seemed to pyramid instead of decrease. It was very discouraging. Still, there must be some way to meet this new ogre of inanity.

Henry sighed and cocked an eyebrow. "How does Lesley feel about all this?"

"I don't know. I haven't asked her."

"What?"

"Oh, I'm sure she knows but I haven't told her, in so many words."

"But you're going to tell her?"

"Tonight. I propose to propose tonight." George was being debonair, a hangover from the day of the epigram and airy persiflage.

Tonight. They were not to get away unmolested. "If you're asking me to sanction the thing, I can't."

"Let's be really old fashioned. What sort of dowry can she offer?"

"A dowry. In his most receptive moments, George could never appreciate the least part of the real dowry Lesley would bring to a marriage. Henry smiled grimly. "What do you think she'll say?"

"Yes."

"And if she doesn't?"

"She will." There was a sudden anger in George's eyes.

"You think she's in love with you?"

"Enough to want to marry me. That's all I care about." His passionate devotion would create anything lacking, destroy anything undesirable.

Henry knew he must jolt this giant pygmy back into some semblance of balance. "I've never told you much about your trouble. Would you like to hear about it?"

George was instantly frightented and suspicious. "If you think I should."

"I think you should." Henry lighted a fresh cigar. George reached for a cigarette, forgot about it. Henry leaned forward. "It was septicemia, strep, internally produced. Not bad but it almost killed you. Next time it will. Arterial complications and brain tumor. Cerebral hemorrhage or increasing pressure; a constant danger. That's it plus chronic."

"Sounds great." George was pale under the sunburn.

"You should avoid even a ripple on your bile. Same goes for your spleen. No emotional orgies, no feeding of neuroses, no functional fluctuations affecting your heart, circulation and nervous system, no suppressed hysteria and sudden rages. You're well now. If you want to stay well, you've got to strike a calm level and maintain it. That's going to be hard work. But from here on in, it's up to you." Henry mistrusted quick decisions. But George had brought his directed imagination to a high point of excitement. Lesley could not possibly care for the old goat—any more than as she might be fond of a grumpy uncle. When he learned that, he would have to be protected by a greater concern. Shock, unrelieved by selfish concentration, would be disastrous.

George moistened his lips. "Why have you decided to tell me all this?"

"You force me to. I've preached at you for years and there's nothing I detest more. But you'd have none of it." Henry had believed that if George could learn a little peace, discover a little joy in living, the ills which menaced him would decrease proportionably in virulence.

"Escapist theories leave me cold, Hank."

"Intelligent compromise isn't escapist bunk, George."

"When I go soft and mellow, I'll know I'm through."

"Joe College."

"I wish you'd drop that damn Joe College line."

"Always the strong man no matter how painful."

"For a strong man, I seem to be shot through with a hell of a lot of weakness."

"You'd think yourself in good company. Check your symptoms with those of the other iron men. You've got a lot in common."

"There's some comfort in that."

"Little enough. And talking of preaching, you've heard the pulpit call hatred and jealousy cankers of the soul. I'm no authority on soul. But medical science has learned that the more venomous passions, if sustained, can and do fertilize malignancy."

At school, George had decided that Henry was the only boy who understood him. He had felt that the others respected his name and money but, aside from that, looked on him with ill-concealed contempt, even laughed at him. This had been true in part. But George had been no exception. No one had escaped the withering critiques these lads had formulated from out of their belligerent bewilderment. Youth exploring puberty is apt to be cruel. But George had taken it to heart. The seeds of bitterness thus sown and nurtured through the ensuing years had burst into life when Peter's mother died and had since grown into a rotting jungle of self-righteously camouflaged aversion and fury. This was his secret garden. If he disappeared into it once more, became deeply enmeshed in its treacherous tendrils, he would be lowering on himself and his life a curtain of hopeless pain.

"Which is to say cancer," continued Henry. "Is that clear and simple enough?"

Cancer. Cancer of the brain! Panic was surging through George but he fought it off savagely. He must hear it all. There was a mesmeric lure in the terror of it. "In other words, if I'm not a good boy, I'll die early and miserably. Is that it?"

"Death isn't the worst thing that could happen to you," said Henry.

"And what is this fate worse than death? I'm unmarried—but I'm not fitted by Nature to bear a child."

George had guts. Misery and fear were deep in his eyes. Yet could he attempt a lame joke. Henry felt a great sense of pity for him. But he had to see this thing through. He rose and stood before the fireplace. He looked down at George, then spoke. "You could lose your mind," he said quietly.

George drew in his breath sharply. He stared at Henry but ceased to see him. He could see only the spectre of insanity—the one deep secret dread of his life. He had always known it was there, ceaselessly stalking him. In his blacker moods, it had been burningly clear. But he had always escaped. Now it was horribly close and he could do nothing. He wanted to cry out but no sound would come. He was bound and naked. There was no help from anywhere. And he could neither remember nor reach for the weapons he had prepared. With a malevolent leer it crouched, ready to spring. He closed his eyes, strained at his bonds. There were hot, blinding flashes.

He turned his head aside, tears of anguish streaming down his cheeks. His whole body was covered with sweat. And then, abruptly, it was over. The nightmare passed. Slowly he opened his eyes. With a rattling rush he released his breath. He sank back against the divan. He breathed rapidly through his mouth. He stopped to swallow, then continued. At last, he stopped again, swallowed again and shook his head to clear it. The room spun. He waited for it to stop. He belabored his reason, his senses, until they fell into line with actualities. He wiped his face with his hands. Shakily, but with jaw set, he got to his feet, steadied himself against the divan. He could see Henry again. His voice came. "You couldn't be mistaken?"

"No."

Incisive, factual. Henry was hammering at him in a way he understood, not mucking about with all that intangible claptrap. This carried conviction. But it must not be allowed to stand as Henry had set it up. It formed an invincible block to ultimate vindication. The demon of madness was the sole enemy which could defeat purpose. Henry could be exaggerating the whole thing because of Lesley.

"How long have you known all this, Hank?"

"For a good many years."

"Then what I just told you couldn't have made you overstate the case?"

"Hardly." Lesley was his dearest friend, his niece and his

child. His love for her was unbounded. She meant more to him than anything in this world or beyond—meant more than his profession. But concern for her had not influenced him in this. It had been concern for George. "I was speaking purely as your physician," he said.

Henry did not lie. George tapped his reserves. He could take it. His voice was hollow but steady. "Then I'm through after all."

"No one is ever through."

George snorted through his teeth. Then, suddenly, life flowed back into him, light to his eyes. If this thing were hopeless, Henry would never have told him about it. He had been blind not to see that! "By God, you're right. You say all I need is to find pleasure in living. If I marry Lesley that should be easy."

Henry stared at him, shook his head and grunted helplessly. "And if you don't?" he asked.

"I will."

"Of course Lesley will have nothing to say about it."

"I've told you how I'm sure she feels."

"That's marvelous. Lesley's got to be in love with you because *you've* decided you're in love with her. And that minor miracle is only one item. Peter's got to come out of the war a great musician because *you've* plotted his life for him. And Audrey isn't going to get hurt by your switch in affections because *you* aren't. Add—the Democrats ruin the country and the Republicans need sounder leadership—*yours*. We're going to have world-wide depression again because banking isn't under *your* sole supervision. And we're going to have to go to war with Russia because there's no other way to stop those damned maniacs."

"Right all the way. A perfect score." George reseated himself on the divan. "Congratulations, old cock."

"Your recuperative powers are amazing. One more futile

warning—obstinacy is the most treacherous crutch you can use."

"Abstract Pollyanna theories would be a safer one, I suppose?" He was tough. He was a realist. He would stand or fall on that basis. A sudden thought struck him forcibly. "Hank—about what you said—if it should happen, if I were to go crazy—would I know it?"

"That's hard to say."

"Well—would I have sane moments—moments when I could grasp what was told me?"

"That's almost certain. Why?"

"Just this. If I should go overboard and not know it, I want you to promise to tell me."

"And I must also promise to see that you're at no point deprived of your little jewelled snuffbox."

"Exactly."

George carried on his person at all times two small capsules which compounded a deadly drug. He had explained to Henry that these were protection against an utterly hopeless situation which would never arise. They enabled him to rush in without being a fool. He was a fatalist with a final trick up his sleeve.

"In my book," said Henry, "no one is incurable until he's been dead for a half hour. That's how far removed I am from being a murderer."

"And I don't want to be the victim of humanitarian principles. If I choose to take my own life, that's my business. It's an extremely personal matter and concerns no one else. You've given me the setup. You'll either promise to tell me or I'll play it safe and wash out at the first hint of failure." A moment ago, he had been unable to think of his one sure out. That must never happen again.

"Trying to bully me, George, is just plain silly."

"All right. If you persist in this lousy attitude, you know

what'll happen. That makes it not only murder but premeditated. And we've been friends for half a century. I'd do as much for you and more."

George could even admit his age to gain a point. Why did humor always temper tragedy? There was a shadow of a smile on Henry's lips. "There are stronger loyalties than human ties, for me at any rate."

"Don't be so damned smug." He would have to get at Henry on his own ground. "You're a hell of a long way from being infallible. You admit that. What do you think Mother would tell you to do? You don't have to think. You know."

Ellen Lowel Ridgley, George's mother, had been a rarely lovely spirit. Henry had always looked upon her with awe and a very, very deep sense of gratitude. At school, where Henry and George had met as youngsters, their fellow tykes had considered Henry a stout chap and George a bore. Henry, already kind and sympathetic, had seen in George much unborn nobility and a need for friendship. A holiday visit with the Ridgleys had clinched the friendship. Ellen Ridgley had become Henry's second mother and had remained so until she died. He had adored his own mother but had never got to know her. She had been something of a sensation—a famous beauty, a delightful creature, a social lioness and hostess extraordinary. She had lead a consistently colorful and happy life and had died in the South of France at the age of sixty-eight with a popular young baron at her bedside.

Henry's father had been a great surgeon with a constitution equal to the rigors of his calling. He had rarely been home day or night. He had been twenty-two years older than his wife and had had three mistresses whom he had seen as rarely as he had his family. He had ignored symptoms of cancer and had died under the knife and his own directions at the age of seventy-nine. Henry had been a thoughtful and affectionate little boy and Ellen Ridgley had met a sore need. He had lived in the glowing mystic wonder of her infinite sweetness. Ellen had watched over her son, George, with growing misgivings and had gradually come to rely on Henry to soothe his hurts, to protect and help him.

When Henry returned from France at the end of 1919, he had found George in a desperate state. Peter's mother was in the hospital. Later, in 1920, she had died bearing him and George had believed himself responsible. He had been an Under Secretary of the Treasury and it had been only the insistent urgency of this assignment coupled with routine banking duties which had saved him from cracking altogether. For tedious months, Henry and Ellen had worked hard and carefully in their unspoken conspiracy to bring him back to normal. They had partially succeeded. And then Ellen had died, right there in the living room. Hers had been a curious, unknown ailment, a steady lessening of energy until her final quiet sleep in the Chippendale rocker drawn close to the fire. Henry's silent grief was unending. For years, he had searched for a quality. He had had many charming, very charming, love affairs. It was absurd that he could not even remember all of them now. They had been so important, were among the most precious moments of his life. But he had never married. It was his private belief that the quality he sought did not exist. If it had not even existed in Ellen, it hardly mattered. It was something beyond analysis. . . .

He was planning to marry now. Zara Moore, glamorous portrait painter *enceinte,* had herself suggested this concession to custom. She had pointed out that the child might develop into a famous surgeon instead of a talented painter and should therefore be legitimate. Henry had thanked her. The matter was settled. As soon as they both had time, they would get around to it. Zara resembled Ellen in no least way, which was perhaps a good thing. It would be nicer for Zara. Nothing to live up to. Not that Zara would give a damn one way or the other. But Zara was no help here. Ellen was.

Ellen had had a swift sure way of solving problems—kindness and a modicum of pressure. Henry had used the pressure. Yet he hesitated. There is no more rigid code than that of the world of medicine. Henry never deviated from its tenets more than he felt obliged to.

But this was a unique case. Most cases were. If he gave his promise, George might, just might, wing his way to complete health. If he refused, George might, probably would, bow out at the first sign of danger. Henry knew what Ellen would say. He often acted on what she would say. Why not now? He had opened the way for all this. It was up to him to keep it clear. "Yes, I know what she'd tell me to do," he said.

"Well?"

"O.K." George was neither dull nor scrupulous. He knew he held the place of a favorite brother. But this was not born of felicity grown out of a life in common. Henry loved him because he was Ellen's son. But Henry could never understand how George had contrived to have so little of her in his makeup.

"Spoken like a gent," said George. "That's all I need. Now I can go ahead with a sure hand."

"Now you can marry Lesley," said Henry dryly.

"Right. You act as though it were the end of everything when it's really the beginning—for me. And I don't imagine Lesley's love life has been so dreamy up to now that she'll think me exactly a dud."

"More boys have threatened violence over Lesley than have turned to look at other girls."

"Those were boys. A man is something else again."

"God's gift to women. George Ridgley, the great lover. The ebb tide threat to impotence, the dashing conqueror of senility. Hysterics to the bobby soxers."

"Of course it's perfectly all right for you to hurl yourself after exotic babes."

"Zara Moore is not a babe."

"But she's about fifteen years closer to it than you are, laddie, and looks more like thirty."

"That's just her good fortune—and mine."

"Well good fortune can bless other beds than yours. Luckily it isn't your province to dictate its visitations."

"Subtlety of expression always defeats me."

"Elegance dates a man. If it suits you, stick to it. It doesn't suit me."

Henry threw up his hands. "Vanity has always made a strong bid for inclusion in the fatal list. Is it really such an incomparably comfortable feeling to be absolutely sure of oneself?"

"Not bad," said George. "And your sarcasm is wasted. I'm feeling much too good to resent it." It was George's one unacknowledged and burning ambition to prove to himself that he was sure of himself. This should do it. This was the one time in his life that he must win unconditionally.

Lesley walked into the room.

III

GEORGE GOT TO HIS FEET AS QUICKLY AS HE COULD.

"For Heaven's sake, George, do stay put," said Lesley. "Never stand when you can sit, never sit when you can lie. Have you forgotten?"

"No," said George meekly and sat down.

"Are we ready?" asked Lesley.

George started up again, glanced at his watch, at the grandfather clock in the corner and at the grandmother clock visible through the hall door, then sank back onto the divan. His heart was pounding. "We've still plenty of time," he said.

"I could do with a drink," said Lesley and walked to the bar. "Anybody else?" She glanced at George, looked enquiringly at Henry.

"It's okay for George," said Henry, "but make it light. I'll mix my own." He joined Lesley at the bar.

The clink of ice, the gurgle of whiskey, the fizz of soda. Lesley could hear George breathing, could hear the clock ticking, could hear the slow breeze through the trees. Berta, the parlormaid, came in, switched on the lamps, emptied the ashtrays, removed the used glasses and went quietly away again. Lesley handed George his drink.

"Thank you," said George. His eyes followed her every move.

Lesley smiled and went back to the bar to mix her own drink. She had instantly sensed the air of constraint. Hank was ill at ease. George looked as though he needed a drink.

He had probably been telling Hank that he was in love with her. Too bad of him to do that. He was not in love with her. Infatuated perhaps, but that was all. She had seen it happening and had tried to stop it while still being nice to him. That just did not work. She could honestly say she had not wanted it to happen. It was none of her doing. She had been solicitous, true, but not more so than with anyone else and she had been trying to help Hank. She was very fond of George at his best, always had been. But it was a strange and not really pleasant sensation to have a man of his type and age, and an invalid to boot, dilating his nostrils over her. A nurse—at least the average nurse—would probably know what to do, and do it. She was not a nurse.

She chuckled softly, took her drink and moved to the garden door. She just must stop taking everything so seriously.

The tang of the sea blended with the sweet zest of the fields and of the flowers and the trees, the plants, the earth and the grass. The sea, the sky and the long vague clouds were a thousand shades of pink and blue, of green and gray. Peter was coming back to a pleasant house. Peter was coming home. He would soon be there, actually walking about, cocking his head, looking, listening or just standing with that faint smile on his lips and a far away look in his eyes. All the hurt would begin to heal. The joy of remembrance made real.

Lights winked faintly over the water. Peter knew and loved every bit of it, much as a lover must carry his mistress through all of living. It was a dream of a house. The rooms were huge, low-ceilinged, peaceful and gay. Patchwork quilts and gingham, linen, lace and silk. William Speakman long-case clocks. A secure, vibrant silence. The smell of old wood and oil, of rag rugs, of leather, tobacco and lavender water, of scrubbing and wall paper, old books and paintings and good food and drink. Eighteenth century broadloom rugs too. The floors were pegged, the ceilings were beamed, the beds were four posters and the baths were ultra modern.

It was Peter's house. George simply lived there. There was a bubbling feeling low in her throat. Perhaps Peter would laugh and his eyes would dance. The furniture was sweet, early-American and Victorian, Georgian colonial and Empire, Edwardian and conservative modern. And out of it all, not discord but harmony and comfort. The knotty pine paneling was like satin, the quaint fireplaces companionable, the sampler screens, bright, slight minions. The sparkling silver and glass, the polished brass, the glowing pewter, the soft, black lustre of iron. Peter loved all these things. Lesley loved them, too. Was there ever a time when Peter had not tied in with all that she loved? In all of art and charm and joy and loveliness, in eagerness and laughter and tears. She did not see him in the paintings and books, she did not hear him in the music or the mystery of the night, she did not walk at his side through the lanes and the city streets, but he was always there. Not just a part of it. Rather was it a part of him.

There was greatness in Peter and he was beautiful. All right—he was not an Adonis—but he was beautiful. She could feel him close to her now. He must really be near this time. And he was going to be all right. Lesley laughed silently, joyously. She always had to laugh when she was happy. God was in His Heaven. All was right with the World.

She remembered her heavy companions and turned.

"Why so solemn?" she asked. George and Henry were startled out of their respective sombre reveries. She strode over to the fireplace and stood with her back to it. She seemed about to take off. There was nothing earthbound about the girl. "Fulton tells me Peter's really on his way."

"He'll be on the train we're meeting," said George.

"It's nice you can be so definite," said Henry.

"I think I know Peter," retorted George. "Allow me to know a few things, please."

"I can't stop you."

"Peter's conservative, dependable and considerate. Training tells."

"Dear God, I hope he's happy," said Lesley softly.

"I hope so, too," said George. "I know I am."

Henry shook the ice in his glass and went back for a refill.

"I wish we didn't have to go," said Lesley. She had to say something.

"Then why not stay?" said George hopefully.

"Hank can't neglect his practice any longer."

"Why should he worry about a handful of hypochondriacs?"

"How I love to hear the business man talk about the professional man," croaked Henry.

"I'm not a business man. I'm a banker."

"I apologize. I'll close out my account Monday morning."

George was a banker and a good one. Henry was right. There was much that was solid and worthwhile about him. The banking tradition had been a fine one in the Ridgley family since Revolutionary times. In the fabulous twenties, many of George's acquaintances of the banking and financial world had come to him with sure-fire schemes, ready to let him in on them. They had meant well. But George's answer had invariably been the same—"Sounds great, Bill (or Joe or Charlie or whatever). You'll undoubtedly make a killing out of it. But I don't think it's good banking." When the Crash came in '29, the house of Ridgley was strong and solvent. In that year and for some years following, it was able to save many another house and thus, figuratively and often literally, to save the lives of thousands of depositors little and big. For that alone, George could be forgiven much.

"You know Hank's work is terribly important," said Lesley. "If you don't, you should, after all he's done for you."

"You don't know half of it," said George with a significant glance at Henry's back.

"I'm sure I don't." She would not give George the gambit. "No one will ever know all the good he's done. People who devote their lives to helping others should hold high place among the immortals." Lesley launched herself into a simple eulogy fired with enthusiasm and deep affection.

Drink in hand, Henry returned to his armchair. He watched Lesley as she talked. He could not find it in his heart to blame George. Any man who looked on her and failed to conceive a mad passion for her must be glandless, idiot, eunuch or pervert, poor devil.

She was a handsome girl, tall, straight and strong, perfectly made. She was wearing rust red sport suit and shoes. The jacket made her shoulders look broad and square. Her shoulders really were broad and square, yet softly feminine. Her tapering waist was slim, her hips, narrow but firmly rounded. And best of all, perhaps, her legs. They were exquisitely, vitally shaped and extremely long, especially from knee to trim, sturdy ankle. And the leg-line flowed without break into the winged footline over the narrow heels, triumphal arches and high insteps. But her arms were really as warmly, maddeningly divine as her legs. A man could but breathlessly long to feel them about him and to know the touch of the capable, lovely hands with their long, tapering fingers. Her black angora sweater revealed breasts that were full and high and lifted. Lesley was really incredibly beautiful. Her skin was a clear, light, golden brown. Her thick, wavy hair was red-blonde and fell to her shoulders. Her hazel eyes, under their heavy lashes were really a mischievous, smoldering, deep dark brown. They were unusually wide-set and slanted provocatively upward under the arching brows of her low, wide forehead. Hers was indeed the face of a poet's angel. The cheekbones were noticeable and moderately high, the cheeks, slightly hollowed, the pretty, friendly nose, with its faintly flaring nostrils, tilted ever so little, the mouth was full-lipped and generous, the even white teeth looked as though they could bite, tentatively, enquiringly, passionately, as well as flash into a smile, the jaw line was firm and clear, clean-cut without over-prominence—the whole mounted on the soft lines of a full-throated neck. There was all of life in the girl and a gallant charm. Her vibrant health and uncontrollable happiness lifted her fellows and swept them along with her. And Henry knew, as George could not, that her beauty was complete. Her every quality was replete with beauty. Her character was beautiful. She was beautiful in her heart—beautiful spiritually, mentally, morally, and emotionally.

Lesley would be a great woman. She already was a great woman. When excited or in repose, her body would always follow her thought. Her movements and attitudes were naturally graceful and sensuous. Her spirit was naturally graceful and sensuous. She had a way of looking directly into the eyes of the person she addressed—a trick which often came dangerously close to increasing Henry's practice in cases of heart trouble. Her voice was arresting, hypnotic—alive, pleasantly cultured, deep and vaguely husky.

"So if Hank's work isn't of first importance," concluded Lesley, "then I don't know what is."

George was obviously enchanted. He opened his mouth, closed it, then opened it again to speak. "It must be. But there's something even more important at the moment, to me at any rate, and that is to find some way of keeping you here. Maybe I could enjoy a relapse."

"Don't talk that way. You know what Goethe said, "Be careful what you wish for because you might get it."

Aside from world news and financial reports, George read Ed Sullivan, Westbrook Pegler and the farm journals. The farm journals were so that he could pretend an intelligent interest in farming, especially with Peter, who had a natural love of the soil and all of life. Pegler he thought would make a good President and he felt Sullivan kept him young. He had nodded over Goethe once but that had been thirty-five years agone.

"You're quite a disciple of Hank's, aren't you?"

"I'm not nearly bright enough for that."

"Who is? He makes it all so damned complicated. My own ideas are much simpler."

"Go ahead," said Henry. "Recite the neurotic credo. We've never heard it."

"Lesley likes my philosophy."

"Your what?"

"My approach to life."

"Your reproach, you mean—and even Lesley couldn't like it."

"I think I like you best when you're happy," said Lesley.

"That would be when he's talking about himself," said Henry, "so you must like him most of the time after all."

"He goes on about Peter a lot, too, Hank, and he always lights up when he does that." She looked at George affectionately. "You'll be happy to have him back, won't you?"

"Very," said George. His feeling for Peter, which he adjudged to be love, was a sort of fierce pride which he took in the boy. George had always made a great show of being home-loving. Actually, he was not. His desire was to conquer. It was essential to the maintenance of his morale. And this could not be done at home.

'Cragie' and the attractive Edwardian town house on Fifth Avenue in New York had seen but little of him through the years. He had been abroad a great deal and a goodly portion of his time at home had been devoted to work and to business, political and social functions. He and Peter had been in daily communication by one means or another during Peter's early years but were not really intimately acquainted. George did not realize this. It had not been necessary to conquer Peter, who was unconquerable, because the lad's dreams had been in accord with George's plans for him. And he had been obedient, amenable and had his mother's gentle, fiery spirit.

"He was a musician before he went to Italy. Now after all he's been through, he must be a great one."

"And God help him if he isn't," said Henry.

"God help him if he is," said Lesley.

"Both remarks are over my head."

"I just meant that any artist needs God's help."

"And I," said Henry, "just meant that wars don't make artists but destroy them and poor Peter may have to try to make you understand that on top of all the hell he's already suffered."

"But I feel George is right, Hank, in a way. If Peter isn't a great musician now, I know he will be some day."

"What makes you so sure?"

"It's just one of those things you know."

"That's good enough," said Henry.

"Peter was always an artist in his heart, even as a little boy. And I always knew he'd be great."

"And are you equally sure he wouldn't have chosen some other field if his tender guardian had allowed him any choice?"

"He'd have chosen music. He loves it. He really does."

"I like *your* ideas, too," said George.

"How can you say that?" asked Lesley. "You've never heard them."

"No. Never formally, I guess, at that," admitted George. "Well I like what comes out of them. And if you don't mind, I'd like to hear them."

"You'd only laugh," objected Lesley. "And you *wouldn't* like them."

"But you say it does me good to laugh. And anyway, I could never laugh at you."

"Well, to begin with, I believe in God," said Lesley simply.

"I don't think that's particularly funny," said George. "What kind of god?"

"A God of beauty. His cathedral is the universe, the world the cathedral garden, and divine service or prayer the good our lives attest."

"A bit of a heretic, aren't you?"

"I don't see any quarrel with the fundamentals of religion," countered Henry.

"If a Communist tried to be a communist today, he'd be rated a traitor by the Party, wouldn't he?" asked George.

"Lesley isn't trying to sell her ideas to a church."

"I wouldn't sell them for anything, darling. But George said he'd like to hear them."

"He did and he would," said George. "Your ideas are a form of faith, Lesley. And I suppose faith is always taken simply on faith. Or are there ever outside ideas to support it?"

"I think so. I think science supports it. So does Hank."

"Forget Hank. Tell me about science."

"Science says now that the universe is held in consciousness, or force that takes its form in consciousness. The poets and philosophers have been saying that for centuries. Everything is as we see it. If we're unaware of it, it doesn't exist. And I believe that if we look with understanding, look for the beauty in everything, we usually find it. It's a hard job but it's worth it. Everyone wants to really live, everyone wants to lead a gracious and happy life. Everyone wants an understanding hearts. I'm not very good at it, but I try to believe in good and the power of good. And I do believe that good is of God and the only real power, the only real part of consciousness, and that if we try to work with it and for it, it will work with us and for us. So you see, in a way, science and philosophy do support my belief in God—and certainly art does. How's that?"

"Wonderful," said George abstractedly, delightedly.

"You're wasting your time, Lesley," said Henry. "I've been

at him for years and now when he knows why he should listen, it still doesn't mean a thing."

"I'm listening," said George. "You try it for a while. But tell me, Lesley—perhaps I shouldn't ask, but I'd like to know—have you ever proved it?"

"Yes. Perhaps not in anything you'd consider important. But Peter and I used to make it work. And if I ever do have to face anything really big, I think I'll try to be loyal to it, to the idea, I mean."

"I'm sure you will." George loved to hear Lesley talk.

"Mind you, I don't deny the ignorant, the stupid, the crass, the vulgar, the brutal, the cruel, I don't underrate the terrible blackness of pain and poverty, or of misery, heartbreak and despair. And I think we should always do all we can without question to relieve suffering the way Hank does. But I don't think the sordid and dreadful aspects of life have any real power, only the ghastly power we're misguided enough to give them. They can be defeated and they die. They're not immortal like the good and the beautiful. They don't tie in with the infinite and eternal."

"But there are so many problems as you go through the years, Lesley, problems where you can't count on any nice balance to help you, problems such as those that spring from love and hate, for instance."

"But I don't think you can hate if you know how to love. And if you know how to love, there can be no problem there. I'm not sure I know how but I hope I'll learn because I feel there's more of a beauty in love than in anything else, the kind of beauty that'll overcome anything ugly if you'll let it."

"I guess I don't know how to love. And anyway, Lesley, supposing you're right in all this, then—what is good and what is evil, what is beauty and what's ugliness? Which is which? Who's to say? Who's to sit in judgment?"

"There's no answer to that of course. But I don't trust intellectual arguments. They have no heart. They're fascinating as hell but they're bad friends. All I know is something always tells me what's right. It's almost like a clear silent voice inside. It may not be what I want to hear, often it isn't, but if I'll listen and obey it, there's always a right result sooner or later. Haven't you ever found it that way, too?"

"No, I can't say I have—but then, you see, I've never tried it."

"Don't disturb his misery, Lesley," said Henry. "He'd be lost without it."

George chose to ignore Henry. "Lesley, do you know what you are?"

"I've got a rough idea," said Lesley.

"You're a pagan, a hedonist and an elemental Christian."

"I'm a hedonist all right if hedonists are those guys who like to live well." She dipped into her drink.

"They are. And you're pure woman. You're all a woman should be and never is. If you're not the perfect woman, you're the perfect counterfeit."

"Well! Thank you, sir. I want to be all you say but I fear me so far it's just counterfeit, sir."

"I can bear it. In fact, I think the counterfeit of perfection is the most we can ever hope for."

"But if perfection couldn't be, where would we get the idea in the first place?"

"We get lots of ideas that are quite impossible, don't we?"

"I hope not—at least not the good ones. If I thought things like love and friendship couldn't be, couldn't be true and unselfish, crystal pure, then I'd feel that all beauty, art, the whole business, was just the most terrible hoax and I think I'd want to quit."

"But you wouldn't. I didn't quit and I never knew why either—until now."

"You didn't quit because you never got started," said Henry. "And you'd better get started now if you're going to meet that train."

"You're being awfully mean to George, Hank."

"It's a form of affection and George has a nature that demands affection."

George had jumped to his feet and again glanced at his watch. "We have a few minutes grace but we will have to start soon," he said. "And it's not really necessary, but if you don't mind, I would like to check everything with Fulton just once more. I won't be a minute." Peter's clothes and car must be in readiness, his favorite dishes served perfectly at dinner, his gifts laid out on his bed, his room, otherwise, just as he left it. George could be very thoughtful.

"Scoot," said Lesley.

George started, turned back. He had heard enough of what Lesley had said to realize that Henry's training and influence were deeply entrenched in her mind and character. If he got her, he would be marrying Henry too, and a Henry he could not deride until he was able to lead her away from such weakening and rather dangerous twaddle. But he was so mad about the girl that he could stand even the noble shadow of Henry for a while. George did not know that Lesley's lovely nature had influenced Henry's opinions, tremendously. And George decided that Henry's philosophy, while obviously wrong, might not really be so bad if the many happy hours he had spent in Lesley's company—the only really happy hours of his entire life—were in any sense due to it.

"One more question on ideas," said George, "and the last. What are your ideas about men? What kind of men do you like?"

"I like kind men. I like them all."

"No, but seriously, you must have some preference. Do

you like them thin or fat, tall or short, strong or weak, intelligent or stupid, old or young—what?"

"Yes," said Lesley.

"Oh, now please."

George was going to get down to cases despite all her dodging about. Lesley sighed within herself. "I like them gentle, so I must like them strong and intelligent, and they can all be that. No, I honestly don't know. But I don't think shapes and sizes mean so very much. And I don't think age matters, do you?"

"I do not," said George.

"I mean age as measured by years. Some older men have such a good hold on what Hank calls the joy of life that they're more exciting than the young Greek gods. And some young men have a natural understanding that makes them as sweet and lovable as the gentle men who are much older."

"I see," George said.

"Peter was like a little boy in lots of ways, right up to the time he went abroad. But he always had that nice quality you find in older men, too."

"You're pretty well sold on Peter, aren't you?"

"Except for Hank, he was the best friend I'll ever have."

"When you were little, I always had a funny feeling that you and Peter were one and the same child," said George musingly.

"That's the nicest thing you've ever said to me," cried Lesley.

"But tell me, Lesley," George went on, "how do you catalogue me? Do you consider me young or old, or both?"

"Well—" Lesley felt she must tread carefully, "when I don't think of you as a sort of uncle whom I don't know very well, I suppose I think of you as young, that is, when you're happy. When you're boasting about Peter, for instance, you're quite a young uncle."

"Thank you, Lesley." George gave Henry a quick glance

of triumph, then with a pathetic spring to his step, went into the hall and off toward the rear of the house.

Henry walked to the garden door and stood looking out over the darkening sea. Lesley finished her drink, put down her glass, went and stood beside him.

"Wonderful, isn't it?" she said.

"It is that," said Henry.

"What's the matter, darling?"

Henry looked into the devastating mystery of her eyes. His own were troubled. "Lesley, are you in love with George?"

"Of course not, darling."

Henry gave a sigh of relief. "I didn't think you could be," he said. Her cordiality and graciousness had been no more than she would show any of his friends. And she had been sweet to George and even dared ridicule of her convictions, not because she cared for him but simply through an unthinking desire to help him.

Henry could have sworn that if Lesley were in love with anyone, it was Peter. And after a separation of ten years—but that was another problem. The immediate problem of George remained. He was glad he had told him all that he had.

Lesley's brows drew together in a frown of concern as she watched him. She loved this uncle-father of hers and knew his every mood. "Why do you ask me that, Hank?"

"Because he thinks you are."

"George thinks I'm in love with him?" she asked incredulously. "He couldn't."

"But he does. You see, he's convinced that he's in love with you."

"I don't believe it."

"Neither do I. But he believes it. You knew of course?"

"He's got a crush, Hank. No more than that. And he took me by surprise. You must realize it's the last thing I'd expect—and why. He's like your not too nice brother."

"I know. It must be distasteful to you. I'm sorry."

"Don't be. It isn't. I really like him when he's human. That may not be often, but he's a patient and a friend of yours."

"That's very sweet of you. What worries me is what we're going to do about him."

"We're going to do whatever you think best."

"George is a wishful thinker number one. When he's thwarted, he works himself into a suppressed species of violent fury that's the deadliest sort of poison."

In a non-technical way, Lesley was quite conversant with George's case. She had not wanted to be a doctor. There was only one doctor anyway and that was her Hank. And Henry had never allowed her to become involved in the dogma and doggerel of the physician. But he often consulted her simply, as he would another specialist.

"And just at this point, anything like that would finish him off, wouldn't it?" she asked.

"If it didn't, he'd polish himself off. And I'd have to help him indirectly. He got me to promise that."

"That was a rather filthy trick. I suppose he beat you over the head with Ellen?"

"No matter." Henry's tolerance was well nigh unlimited. "The thing is that this is the biggest emotional hurdle he's set up for himself in thirty years—this and his determination to have Peter justify his mother's death. He believed he was in love with Katherine Drake, too. But you know the story."

"Yes," said Lesley.

George fancied himself a man of the world and irresistible. In point of fact, he was inexperienced and maladroit. And his naïveté was not attractive. His bedroom manners were atrocious. The few affairs he (and he only) had enjoyed, had been invariably quick round-trips. And he had always given the woman a great deal of money or a very expensive present as though he were paying blackmail. By far the most elaborate of the half dozen custom built domestic and foreign rockets in Audrey's garage was a gift from George. His jousts with Audrey, the most recent of his drab and spotty career, had been to satisfy himself that he was still virile. The thought of satisfying Audrey in any way whatsoever had never entered his head.

All this weedy growth had stemmed from his youth. He had been an absurdly pompous young man, fearful of placing himself in an embarrassing position. He had been vain, proud, self-conscious and too easily offended. He had got nowhere with girls. His good looks had not been enough. The only women who had tolerated him had been those who were thinking in terms of the altar, position and life security. He had been aware of this without fully accepting it. He had torn at one spastic and shocked her almost to the point of cure. He had been very frightened about that afterward and had turned to being devoutly romantic. As month followed month and year followed year, he had burningly longed for the great love.

In the spring of 1919, when he was twenty-seven and already a national Napoleon of finance, he had met Katherine Cosgrove Drake. The Peter Cosgroves, a simple, timid, elderly couple who lived very much unto themselves in a big house on Murray Hill in New York, had been of those Cosgroves who were the leading manufacturers of high explosives in the world. They had been childless until late middle life and then the miracle of Katherine had happened. She had had a clucking, blissfully happy rearing at their hands and had developed into an ethereal young woman with a flower-like beauty and a temperament of amazing fire for a personality so delicate. She had been passionately fond of music and had shown marked talent in composition and rendition. She had played the piano, harp and violin. But the piano had been her first love.

She had married Pierce Drake, a young cleric of unusual

promise who sang well. She had been a virgin. There was a village of Cragie, no longer to be found on any map, a mile and a quarter inland from the Ridgley 'Cragie.' At that time, with its sawmill, tannery and foundry going full blast, it was a flourishing little hamlet. It had a picturesque, interdenominational chapel, a gift from the Ridgleys. Drake had been appointed rector. He had brought his bride to live in the tiny rectory. Within a year, he had gone from ascetic to religious fanatic to wild-eyed celibate with peridocal fallings from grace which had very nearly killed both his wife and himself.

When Katherine met George, she had been confused, hurt and desperately lonely. She had not felt she could turn to her parents. She had turned to George. In him, she had made herself see her saviour-knight and to a degree, she had been right. George had fallen madly in love—for him—and knight-like had ravished and then championed her. But all had not gone well. George had demanded that she divorce Drake and marry him. Katherine had begged for time. George had tried to cover his fury with exaggerated tenderness but his raging impatience had fired his passion to the white heat of mania. Katherine had had to face unbridled ardor and endless tirades from both her husband and George. They had brought her to the verge of nervous collapse. And then it had become obvious that she was going to have a child.

George had become even more vehement in his insistence on divorce and marriage and Drake had lost such shreds of sanity as remained to him. Katherine had had to be removed from both of them.

Drake had taken to brooding and roaming the countryside and praying aloud almost incessantly. He had been a weird, a gaunt and frightening figure. Finally he had disappeared entirely and later had been found drowned in an old stone quarry in a treacherous bit of woodland five miles back from the village. Katherine had been in the hospital and carefully guarded from the outside world but somehow the news had leaked through to her and, in giving birth to Peter, she had died. It was then, for a long time, that it had been thought that George would die, too, or take his own life. But that had not been George's way.

With the distraction of his private and governmental work and with the help his mother and Henry had given him, he had at last settled down to a sort of grim business of seeing it through. Before her death, Katherine had stipulated that George be made the guardian of her child. She had felt that her dear parents could not live very long. And she had been right. Within a few months, they had both died brokenhearted and bewildered. George had then legally adopted Peter.

Yes, Lesley knew the story. Almost everyone knew the story but Peter.

"George has always believed himself to be Peter's father," said Henry.

"But he isn't, of course?" said Lesley.

"No. Katherine confided in me a good deal. Being a doctor, I was allowed to call on her. We got on well together. After that, I visited her frequently. She knew what George thought. Just before she died, she told me she had decided to let it go at that. It meant so much to him. She was wise in that, perhaps."

"Perhaps. She must have known he'd guard her child carefully. She seemed to know she was going to die."

"Yes, but the bad part is that George blames himself, and of course Peter too, for her death. He loved her as best he knew how, and as best he knows how, he has tried to atone for his crime. A dreadful idea. And he's determined that she shall live, go in living in Peter and through Peter. He's never been really relaxed and happy except for that one brief period when he first knew Katherine. And now he thinks he's going to be with you."

"And what do we do?" asked Lesley.

"I just want you to let him down as gently as possible. And I know you will."

"Of course, darling."

"But without any least sacrifice to yourself. You must promise me that."

A car swung into the turn of the drive and skidded to a stop on the gravel. Heavy doors slammed.

"That'll be Audrey back," said Henry. "She made a quick trip. You promise me, Lesley?"

"Let me do the worrying for both of us, darling."

George was back. "Let's go, Lesley. You're all set?"

"Yes." Lesley moved toward George.

"Lesley—" Henry started to speak.

"Hank," said George, interrupting, "if Audrey comes back, be a dear chap and try to get rid of her."

"I will not," said Henry.

There was the sound of another motor near the house.

"There's a car now," said George excitedly. "Come on, Lesley!"

Audrey walked rapidly into the room from the garden. George winced. Reggie appeared.

"George darling, where have you been?!" said Audrey. "I've been everywhere looking for you."

"I'm tired of having my life risked because of you," said Reggie to George.

"I'm sorry, Audrey. I can't talk now." George felt trapped. "I have to dash but I'll be back later, less than an hour."

"But what about Peter?" We were going to meet him!"

"We were? But I've asked Lesley now and with all the luggage, there won't be room for more than one. I'm sorry."

"Then why couldn't Reggie follow in my car? On the way back, one of us could ride with him."

"Don't be silly," said George with mounting irritation. "I

mean, it'd be a fleeting greeting at best. Why not stay here with Hank? He'll be all alone."

"On no," objected Audrey. "It'll be such fun for Peter to have a delegation meet him."

"Peter hates fuss. You know that," snapped George.

"Then why is Lesley going?"

"That's right," said Lesley. "We'll all stay here and wait for you."

"No, please!" said George too forcibly. He was seething inwardly. "I want you there with me. I really do." It would be so right to have Lesley beside him as he met Peter.

"All right," said Lesley quietly.

"Well—you'd better get started or you'll be late," said Henry in an effort to save what was left of the situation.

"No," said George perversely. "Fulton will watch it for me."

"Then couldn't we have a drink meanwhile," suggested Reggie, "to Peter, and Audrey, and the Bill of Rights?"

"I should think you'd be willing to stay here and drink your head off," barked George, "while Lesley and I go to the station."

"I would," replied Reggie.

"Now really, it isn't worth all this, George," interposed Henry. "It's your party and Peter's. Why not follow Lesley's suggestion and go alone?"

"I tell you I won't!" George was livid and getting louder. "Good God, what is this? Am I a child suddenly? I won't have my life ordered. I never have and I don't intend to start now. You may not think it important but it is to me—damned important! And I—"

George swayed, his knees buckled a little. He grasped the edge of the console table and bent over it in pain, his elbows pressed into his sides. There was a sharp, penetrating ache at the base of his skull. He felt nauseated. Everything went black for the fraction of a second but he hung on. Henry and Lesley were instantly at his side. After a moment, he straightened a little, pushed himself erect with his fingertips. In a dazed way, he gazed about him, wiped his face and neck with trembling hands.

"Easy does it," said Henry.

George attempted a smile. "Damned foolishness," he muttered.

"What is it?" whispered Audrey.

"What's the matter, George?" asked Reggie.

"Better now?" enquired Lesley solicitously.

"Yes, thanks," said George gratefully.

"A little too much excitement today," said Henry. "Better rest awhile, George."

"No, I'm all right now, thanks," George assured him. "I'm sorry I got so excited over such a trifle. I—it was very stupid. Please forgive me."

Everyone spoke at once as nice persons will in a group when embarrassed. George felt he must redeem himself in Lesley's eyes. He spoke over the babble.

"About that drink," he shouted and got their attention. "We'll all have one and then we'll all go to the station. But make it snappy."

This announcement was met with huzzahs and hosannas and a wild rush and clatter. Audrey started the radio-phonograph again. Reggie and Lesley poured drinks and sang with the music. George and Henry watched. Audrey swung away from the machine, stopped abruptly and stood staring. The others noticed and turned to look. And there, suddenly, was Peter.

There stood Peter Drake with Fulton beside him and Mickey and Mike whimpering and whining and trying to climb around his neck. It was a moment of stunned silence.

Mickey and Mike were two old Irish setters with the manners of puppies. They had been in and out of the house and up and down the road all day. No one seems to know how much dogs know. The chances are they know nothing. But Mickey and Mike had seemed to know that day that Peter was coming home.

Peter dropped his arm from around Fulton's shoulders, pushed the dogs down and stood looking at the speechless group.

"Well, hello," he said.

IV

PANDEMONIUM!

In less than thirty seconds, Peter's back and sides were sore, his ears were ringing, his hands ached and bore tooth-marks, his hair and clothes were rumpled and his face and collar were covered with lipstick. He broke away, dashed to the fireplace, grabbed the poker and stood at bay. The others stopped, hesitating, exhausted, gasping, laughing breathlessly. The dogs sat back on their haunches, eyes brightly expectant, tongues lolling.

Peter was over six feet tall. He was too thin but he was wiry and his posture was good and easy. He had light brown curly hair, gray eyes and a Byronic cast of feature. There was poetry about him, the suggestion of an eager seeking after beauty, an urgent love of charm, a constant readiness to scale the heights, a keenly sure awareness, an ever loyal watchfulness, a ceaseless willingness to aid his fellows, a happy, tireless strength which must unfailingly defeat despair. He was highly strung, sensitive and nervous but smoothly controlled. He loved to laugh and he loved uninhibited expressions of affection such as that just accorded him. He felt strangely happy.

Slowly, keeping a cautious lookout, he relaxed, gingerly tested his injuries, adjusted his jacket and tie, and returned the poker to its stand. Then he straightened up and smiled warily.

"Well—hello," he said.

George came forward, put his hands on Peter's shoulders and looked at him for a long moment. "It's good to see you, Peter," he said.

Peter grinned. "Good to see you, George." He looked past George at the others. "Good to see all of you."

Audrey laughed shoutingly. "Look at you!" she gurgled.

Peter turned and examined himself in the big mirror. "My God," he exclaimed, "peace paint." He took out his handkerchief.

"No, no, let me," cried Audrey. She dug out tissues and a tiny jar of cold cream. Then she and Lesley began to repair the damage.

"Makes me feel like a horse," said Peter.

"No, no, NO! You don't know what you're saying," yipped Reggie. Audrey caught him neatly in the eye with a grease-laden tissue.

"Nothing to be done with the collar, I'm afraid," this from Lesley.

"And I just bought this shirt," wailed Peter. It was an off-white sport shirt. "They're harder to get than Scotch in England."

"Where's your uniform?" asked Reggie.

"The Smithsonian Institute wanted it." He was clad in a suit of soft gray tweed.

"You're a louse," said Audrey. "How did you get here?"

"Flew."

"How?" asked George.

"In my last saloon when it looked as though I were going to miss my train, a genial character informed me that small ships could be chartered for taxi hauls at a nominal price and on short notice. So I called the airport, everything was arranged in nothing flat, and here I am."

"Another minute and you'd have missed us," said George.

"Was I wrong? I can go back and start all over again."

"Indeed not," said George. But he was mildly disturbed

by this new recklessness. "As a rule, I hate surprises but this is the one big exception."

"There," said Lesley. She stepped back and drew Audrey with her. Together they scrutinized the result of their labor.

"Not bad," said Audrey.

"Looks a little healthy but otherwise quite civilized," commented Lesley.

"I thought we were about to have a drink," suggested Peter.

"You'll want to pour your own, of course," said Reggie.

"That I will," agreed Peter.

They all converged noisily upon the bar. Fulton retired jerkily, dragging the dogs. Lesley wanted to pour her own drink, too. She needed a stiff one. Her heart was doing such fantastic flips.

Peter did look so very sweet. There was a new firmness to his mouth and chin. But they were still gentle, too, like his warm, inpetuous eyes. He was the cleanest looking man in the world. And in all the flurry of excitement she had yet been aware that his dear lips were still the softest she had ever known. He might not be pretty but he was damned invitingly attractive, deeply, disturbingly appealing. And there he was, close to her. She gave him a cigarette, took one herself. His hand trembled as he lighted hers. Lesley looked up. Their eyes met. She saw the loneliness, the fire, the weariness and hope, the tender, passionate desire. Her sweet lips parted but she ceased to breathe. Peter almost dared believe that he found sympathtic answer in the deeply burning luster of her lovely mystic eyes. For an infinite instant of unrecorded time, their kindred spirits blended into one eternal flame. And then they were back. With a wispy, admonishing smile, Lesley gently pushed his hand and lighter toward his own cigarette. He started as out of a dream. They both laughed a little, like children. The others had their drinks. Lesley added to the one she already had partially ready. Peter took about four ounces of Scotch and a little water. Henry handed George a very long and very pale highball. George examined it critically.

"Think I can take it?" he asked.

"That's your second in a quarter of an hour and I shouldn't have let you have the first," said Henry.

"Were you very ill, George?" enquired Peter.

"Hank says so. But I'm not now and I'm going to have a drink with you." He drank off some of his highball, added whiskey and stirred it.

"Don't let him do it, Hank, if he shouldn't."

"You can't forbid a problem child anything. And it won't hurt him as much as the petulance that'd follow if he didn't get it."

"Has he been at bat often?" asked Peter.

"Five times in the last two years," replied Henry. "But he's managed to squeeze out a weak single each time up."

Even though it showed genuine concern, George disliked any discussion which made him seem less than perfect, especially before Lesley. He shut off the radio-phonograph. "And what about you, Peter?" he enquired gruffly. "Have you been well?"

"Very," lied Peter, "and consistently."

"Nothing more serious with the rest of us than hangovers, in case you'd like to know," volunteered Reggie. "Not that they're to be passed over lightly."

"It's so absurd that Man should concoct something to make him feel so heavenly only to make him feel so awful afterward," said Audrey.

"Now let's not get profound about the thing," pleaded Reggie. "It was just a comment."

"But I think Audrey's got something," declared Peter. "What's this marijuana I've read so much about? They say the band boys go to town on it."

"It leads to drinking coffee," said Lesley.

"And you're not that kind of musician," added Reggie. "If you got hot on the platform, Carnegie Hall would collapse."

"Besides which it's an aphrodisiac and insane-making and who needs that?" said Audrey. "And it smells awful and goes on smelling for months like scandal."

"But it doesn't leave a hangover," said Henry, "and we haven't been able to establish that it's habit-forming or injurious—yet."

"Well, what are we waiting for?" asked Peter.

"It's possible to drink like a gentleman," replied Henry.

"Which leaves our original problem, like all our other problems, unsolved."

"Which leaves the poetry of incentive unvulgarized."

"Which leaves me holding the bag for speaking out of turn," concluded Reggie.

They drifted over to the divan and armchairs and chatted gaily on like carefree trolls. Peter was led into talking a little of his experiences abroad and gave the reason for prolonged delay in his return as "just one of those things." He averted further questioning by sincere interest in all that had happened to the others during his absence. But frequently, he would catch himself looking at Lesley, thinking of her to the exclusion of all else, and would have to pull himself up sharply. She was so breath-takingly beautiful, such a divinely lovely, heart-rendingly warm and joyous revelation. He remembered that she had ever been that to him. The inspiration for God walked the Earth in Lesley. Peter had always loved her with a deep immeasurable love. And he loved her now, fully, reverentially, passionately. But she had always been his adorable sweet sister, his brave and understanding mother, his truest, dearest, ever friend. When the inevitable time had come that he needed her as wife and mistress, too, he had not been able to reconcile his longing with their old feeling of oneness.

That had been the beginning of an intimate estrangement.

It had carried through several years. But just before he left for Italy, he had begun to kiss her in a new way. She had sweetly, shyly, ardently implored him to take her then. But he would not. He had been ten thousand times a fool, the only fool, not to try to win and hold her to himself. But always to his crying need there came the same sure answer—he was not worthy and could never hope to be. And no romantic nonsense that. He knew her too well. Yet what one knows another? And no man knows himself. She had been with him constantly but in the recent years of disillusionment and shock and near-despair, the vision of her had been blurred as had all loveliness and life and goodly meaning. Again now he was seeing her for the first time. And he was raptly conscious of every least detail.

The throbbing warmth within him was a strongly happy, fearful reawakening. He realized the shaking of his body and downed a big gulp of his drink.

He tried to listen to what was being said. There was talk of war again. When Peter's return was imminent, there had been lengthy discussion of the proper behavior. Should they or should they not mention the war?

"For God's sake," Reggie had finally exploded, provoked by Audrey, "just don't be conscious. Don't avoid the subject but don't ride it either." They were doing well. They touched upon it only lightly as they normally would. The war was already being forgotten. The conversation flowed through innocent, pleasant channels. Peter felt relaxed except for his thudding heart. But George was impatient for reassurance on the score of Peter's work. No one could garrote a bit of charming chit-chat so speedily and deftly as George.

"Have you been practicing at least a few hours every day, Peter?" he asked. "I mean, of course, since the cessation of hostilities?"

"That would have been a little difficult, George," said Peter tolerantly.

"I should think you could have found some way if you'd been anxious enough."

There was an awkward pause followed by a little movement amongst the others. Lesley stood up and set her drink aside.

"No kick to that," she said. "I want a cocktail but I have to go make myself pretty first."

"We're not dressing?" ejaculated Peter as the others also rose. "I don't think I'll be able to."

"I'll help you," said Audrey.

"That'll be lovely. But what I meant was that my dinner jacket probably won't fit."

"Why not wear your uniform?" suggested George.

"I'll starve first."

"Will you be at the Club later?" asked Audrey.

"But aren't you coming to dinner?" cried Peter.

"No. I haven't been asked. Isn't that pathetic?"

"Oh but you've got to be here—mustn't she, George?"

"Why of course, Audrey. I thought I had asked you," said George lamely.

"All right. I'd love it." She moved to the garden door. "Save me a cocktail," she begged and was on her way. She had a new wine colored gown that was the sexiest bit of chic she had ever owned. She was going to enjoy this dinner party no end. To hell with George and his juvenile rudeness.

Lesley and Henry walked into the hall with Reggie tagging along. "Be seeing you," he called over his shoulder.

"Right," said Peter.

'Check your watches . . . Any questions? . . . Move out!' Just like that. There was no way to stop them. Peter knew that they were leaving him there with George through a misguided effort to be considerate. He would have much preferred to have them stay. Of course they would have been embarrassed by George's rooting about his privacy. But he would not have minded in the least. He needed them. Peter rather dreaded this interview with George, for 'interview' it was bound to be. He was very fond of George and grateful to him for many things. But George's parental attitude and unfailing efforts to promote what he believed were his best interests had ever seemed to Peter far too intense and had always made him quite uncomfortable. Had this not been so, his filial feeling would have been much stronger. Peter eyed his drink, stepped to the bar and sweetened it.

"You're not doing too much of that, I hope?" said George.

"I may have been just lately," replied Peter. "I had to do something."

"Going back to the old routine after all the excitement was very boring, I suppose," opined George. He must make Peter feel that he took a tolerant and understanding view of things.

"The whole business was rather dreary," said Peter. Peter was taciturn even with himself. There were those things which bore no thinking or talking about. Gauche, cringing, grinning spectacle cleaving into mental imagery. Forgotten only in the beatitude of relaxation. Springing back with the first fling of tension.

"Did you see much combat?"

"A bit—here and there."

"Was it all pretty awful, what you saw?"

"Ghastly."

Peter was frowning at his drink. He had hated the Army, hated the war, hated the entire fulsome swamp. But in time, the hatred had sunk into a dull all-pervading, never-ending ache. He had been a good soldier. He had never bitched. He had talked but little and after the first few weeks, he had ceased to listen other than to commands. The few sympathetic ears he had later found had come as a surprise. Military life had toughened his body and in combat he found that it had toughened his mind and his spirit. He had a reputation for being a hard man and dependable—and a wild man on leave. A good soldier. Privately, Peter laughed derisively about that. A lousy machine that was no part of the lonely man who took care of it and ran it. He had been commissioned in the field. Shortly before the war ended, he had been a lieutenant commanding a regiment and had been hit for the third time. Now a captain, it was understood that before his terminal leave ended he would be made a full colonel. He cared nothing about that.

He had served under a pouter-pigeon named Flea and decided that all regimental commanders were dangerous idiots. His decorations were numerous and he viewed them as tragi-farcical. He had accepted them to avoid fuss. Once the whole thing was over, he had set about trying to recover himself. That had been a laborious and depressing task and only vaguely successful. But he had had time, blessed time.

He had been in such bad shape that he had been hospitalized in England.

Later, by request, he was returned to duty with the occupational forces. But too soon. Twenty months of strain in heart-rending chaos and he was back in the same hospital.

As he convalesced, for the second time, he had managed to arrange matters so that he could stay on until he was entirely well. He wanted to get out quickly when he got back.

Coming over on the transport, he had realized that he was still not prepared for his return. But he had given up worrying about it. His mind had been so filled with a million haunting, flashing thoughts that he had been unable to think clearly. It was all a dream, startlingly clear in spots, hazy for the most part. It had been that way for days and weeks and months—years now. He had seen so much of violent death, of blood and bones, of screaming misery and vicious arrogance. And it was still going on. Pollution in high places, widespread abuse of petty authority, plots and conspiracies threatening the life of the world. Self, self, self. Self satisfaction, self aggrandizement, self preservation. An insane struggle for power and continued existence with no point, no objective, no thought.

Stories had seeped through of cannibalism in the ravaged areas. Ugly tales of old folk hurried to their graves, of babies stillborn without reason. There had been speculation as to how a human carcass should be cleaned. Probably the degenerates who ate them didn't bother to clean them. Had Peter not already known the limits of horror, he would have lashed out madly at such sacrilege. But he had seen brutality and cruelty far beyond the nightmares of the damned. And murder for food was possibly less to be condemned than murder for gain. The latter had been, at the very least, the unwilling avocation of everyone involved in the filthy mass hypnotism.

He had seen men gouge, kick and trample the faces and helpless bodies of those they had fatally wounded, he had seen men cohabit with women who were dying or just dead at their hands, he had seen a woman drink the blood of a man whose throat she had cut and spew it out into his face, he had seen all the basest behavior of which the human animal is capable, time and time and time again.

On rare occasions, he had seen nobility and self sacrifice which his mind and heart almost dared not believe. He had fought his way through it all, fighting not so much as a soldier as fighting off the unthinkable horror. He had fought to save his balance, fought for the day when he could again believe beauty inviolate no matter how flagrantly evil and ugliness gave him the lie. When, when, when? He had come a long way—but when?

"Well, you can forget all that now," intoned George, "and begin to think about your work."

Peter looked up from his drink. The frown slackened. "I'll be a happy man if you're right," he said sardonically.

"Of course I'm right. It was an unpleasant experience for all of us. But there's nothing to be gained by brooding over it. The thing is to forget it and forge ahead. War is simply one of the necessary evils in this stupid world of ours."

"If I thought that, I'd die of a broken heart. Maybe I have anyway and don't know it."

"Oh come now, Peter. You're too sensitive. There are certain modes of living that have to be protected."

"And what about the men who were killed?" asked Peter angrily. "What about the men who were maimed, butchered, crippled? What about the men who were hurt, broken, ruined for life? What happens to them? Who's going to . . . ? Oh, the hell with it," he ended quietly.

"I know. It's tragic. But at least, we're through with it all now."

"Is that the general feeling over here?"

"Naturally."

"Short of a miracle, we won't be through with it for years. And short of a miracle, there won't be anything left to live for when we are. That's the part no one seems to get, even over there. But it's no good talking about it. My fault."

"I don't mind talking about it and neither should you." George was a touch pompous. "When you've got a problem to face, face it. No sense trying to dodge it. You don't win that way."

"You don't win. Those who have had to face this one can tell you that. And they had to face it in a damned ugly way."

"And why not? It was their duty. I was in Government service in the first World War. I wasn't in the trenches but I'd have been glad to be if I hadn't been more valuable elsewhere."

"Yes, I know." The fact remained that George had not been in the trenches. Why did these men always have to apologize? Why did they have to be arrogantly sure that one heard of their staggering contribution to the war effort—whatever that was? If the damned fools had any sense they would have kept clear of it entirely. But no one had any sense. He had none himself but it might help some if others had. "And I'm sure you worked hard during this one, too."

"When I was able—putting over Bond Drives and conferring with the Treasury. But I wrote you about all that."

"Yes."

"Have you been able to get at a piano at all lately?"

"There was a piano of sorts where I was recently quartered. I used to play at playing that occasionally." Sporadic efforts launched in that direction in Germany had all foundered shortly before the collapse which had sent him back to the hospital in England. His second recuperation had been slower, softer. There had been a studio upright in the hospital. One day Peter had given in to a tenth-way urge to sit down to it. He had run his fingers over the keys. He had improvised a little. Then he had played several light things out of the past. The tone had been bloody awful and his fingers stiff as splints. But it had been fun in a rather bitter sort of way. He had gone on playing for a quarter of an hour, skirting the classics but flirting with them. There had begun to be a subdued glow in the darkness of his heart. But it had been almost completely extinguished when he had begun to try to draw real music from the earnest, pathetic little instrument. And his hands had refused to obey his feeling commands. He had banged out a crashing discord and stood up. It was then that he had discovered his audience—a dozen men in pajamas and robes. They had made him sit down again and play and play until time for chow. That had been the beginning. The piano had had wheels at one end and handles at the other. Every day after that, it had been shunted from ward to ward while Peter played, mostly requests covering a field of staggering diversity. He had felt that his touch was little short of abominable, his technique technical, his expression cramped, his playing uncomfortably close to unmusical—but if the poor bastards got anything out of it, he would gladly play till his hands fell off. Their delight had been undeniable, their craving for more inexhaustible, their grateful applause, long, loud, enthusiastic and sincere.

Peter had been as happy as it was possible for him to be, God bless them. He had begun to visit a local conservatory of music frequently in the evenings. He had found a concert grand there with a lovely quality. Often he would woo the flame of genius far into the night. There had been occasional great moments but he had been unable to sustain them. He had quickly regained his old proficiency and improved upon it to the maximum point attainable—and retainable with diligent practice. But skill was one thing, inspired interpretation quite another. He had played a great deal for the men coming over on the transport. It had been top flight playing from the standpoint of expertness and exactitude but rarely had it been more than that. He knew that after a month of steady practice, he could play on any concert platform in the country and get away with it. But one thing Peter would not be was pseudo—not even a shade pseudo. He could not expect George to understand that. But, at least, he must be made to understand that his dream was unlikely to be realized for some time if ever.

"Were your quarters pleasant in England?"

"Overcrowded but bright. And the service was excellent, every attention. And the food was much better and much more of it than the civilian gets."

"You don't look it but I'm glad to hear it. Your piano here is in perfect tune. It's been kept that way. You'll play for us later of course?"

"You won't like it."

"How do you know?"

"I won't like it."

"But if the piano you had was bad, you couldn't tell. You were good enough to be playing concerts on the Continent before you went into the service. How were they, by the way?"

"They were very minor and they were a long time ago."

"You're too modest. And I'm sure your art has matured since then just as you have."

"A man must be given a chance to practice his art, particularly the musician. I've been able to play a few good instruments and the truth of that has been brought home to me. And I'm sorry as hell to do it but now I'm bringing it home to you."

"But your musicianship's good, isn't it?"

"No. It's too erratic. I'm too erratic. Which is to say, I'm a flop. It's a lousy admission to have to make but you say it's best to face things and there it is."

"Peter, you're doing a lot of wild talking and I don't like it." Anger was mounting in George but he suppressed it. "You're not a flop and you're not going to be."

"Surely you don't think I want to be? I've been doing my damnedest, as a matter of fact—if anything, trying too hard. It's been like butting my head against a stone wall. But I've gone on until I thought my head would come off."

Peter could use the old-fashioned phrase with feeling. He had seen a red-bearded major trying to get information from a man suspected of espionage. They had been in a spring house. The major had grasped the man by the tunic and shaken him back and forth with each answer he gave so that with every shake the poor devil's head had crashed back against the rough stone of the wall. The man had at last collapsed and the major had let him drop in disgust. Peter remembered the matted, pulpy mass of hair and blood. "I want you to understand that because I know all it means to you."

"Never mind me," snapped George. "What about your mother and your own pride? You've got to succeed. Your whole life has been planned to give what it takes. You can't suddenly go weak-kneed about it now. You've got to see it through and it's got to be all we expected."

"I'm not quitting, George," said Peter quietly. "I think I have at least enough guts to go on trying. But that's what it takes—guts. The work isn't what it should be and there's no use lying about it to you or to myself either."

"But why isn't it what it should be? That's your fault, isn't it?"

"Not entirely. The work's no good because it can't be any good without inspiration. And I haven't known the least inspiration in any way for a long, long time—and God knows that isn't because I haven't wanted it."

"Then work harder. If you work hard enough, you'll find the inspiration." George spoke with the blind conviction of the insensitive. "You can't win anything without a fight. No man ever lived who didn't have his battles. And it may seem hell to fight but it's nothing to the hell you'll know if you don't."

"It seems it's nothing but hell no matter what you do. And I don't think you can get inspiration by fighting for it. It's because of fighting, because of the whole stinking, horrible mess, that I feel so all gone inside. At least that's what finished the job."

"And who's responsible for the mess? The world's always been in a mess and always will be. It has nothing to do with you."

"I can't help feeling that it has. If the men who are doing the kind of work I'm trying to do, the honest men in all fields of creative work, can't bring enough beauty into the world to put it right, or at least to help a lot, then they're selling their souls for a fake and what's called their inspiration isn't worth a damn."

"Don't talk like a fool, Peter. You've got sense enough to know that crusaders and reformers are never appreciated by anyone but themselves. You can't change the world. But you can do what's expected of you. Music was your mother's life. She'd want it to be your life as well. Everything's been done to make that possible and now it's up to you."

"Yes, I know." Peter thought it best to ease away from the subject. He had said enough. And the old familiar intensity was more marked than ever. "You see, all my faith has been shot from under me. If I can just find something, anything, I can believe in, I'll be all right."

"Then find it." George was quivering inwardly. He could not seem to force a definite commitment from Peter. But he would get one before he was through. George would accept no facts contrary to his desires. He decided how things should be and then decided that was how they were. As a result, he was always facing frustration. But he would not accept frustration either. He fought even the suggestion of it ceaselessly. And it must be said for him that almost always he seemed to fight with amazing success. In truth, he had never won once in his life. But George would not allow himself to be burdened with the truth. Peter's career was one of the very few things around which he fondly fancied he had built the major portion of his life's endeavor. It could not develop other than as he knew it must develop. He went on. "Everything else is coming right at last. It's been years but it's been worth it. And this has got to come right, too. There can't be any doubt and there's no alternative. Do you understand, Peter?"

"Yes, of course, George. It may take a little time but let's not worry about it, shall we?" Peter was irritated and unhappy but he spoke placatingly. George was getting him down, saying all the wrong, expected, run-of-the-mill things, making demands before he had a chance to take off his coat. If only people would leave him alone. But he had known they would not, known particularly that George would not, could not.

In town that day, he had felt a kind of freedom, not thrilling, just pleasantly detached. He could feel his way about absently, alertly, aimlessly, carefully, as he chose. He was beholden to no one. A free, long-lost, independent spirit seeking a restful, cheering haven. He had hoped that, in a different way, the feeling might carry over into 'Cragie.' But it had been a faint hope, no hope at all really. As the day wore on and the time drew near when he must make the final quick move which would take him home, his footsteps had begun to drag more and more, all his movements had been drugged into slow motion. He had drunk slowly, spoken with a sigh in his throat, smiled listlessly. Then the moment when that unreasoning self-discipline, vitally stimulated by clear visions of Lesley, had snapped him into action.

And here he was. But it had been a day. He had really done absolutely nothing. A glorious, uneventful, portentous day.

V

PETER HAD CLEARED AT FORT DIX EARLY THAT SATURDAY morning, taxied to Trenton, and caught a train to New York. He arrived at Pennsylvania Station, took a cab to Grand Central Terminal, checked his gear, stepped into a phone booth and called his tailor. Earl Benham was delighted to hear from him, very happy to know that he was all right. He was sincerely upset about not being able to take care of Peter instantly and perfectly. But his hands were tied. Fittings alone would take about six weeks and he had no suitable materials.

"Now that I like," said Peter, "that adjective 'suitable.' "

"I've been associating with Alec Clark," said Earl. "But really, Peter, you know the place is yours. It's just that I'd rather not make you anything out of the stuff I've got on hand. I know you're anxious to get out of uniform. Why not try some ready-mades until I can find something really special for you?"

"Will I be able to find fitting garments in these Machine Age trappings?"

"Not altogether fitting for your kingly person even after alterations. But you'll be surprised how good they'll look if you have any luck."

As Peter left Grand Central, he noted the ever-fascinating, slanting rays of sunlight, the abstracted commuters pouring out of the gates, the expressionless gatemen and information clerks, the redcaps with toothy smiles or sulking. He mounted the west steps, paused on the gallery to watch the scene for a moment and walked out into Vanderbilt Avenue, ducking through the cabs at the covered entrance. The streaming motor traffic, the hurrying pedestrians, the raucous voices, the highlights and shadows of the big buildings, the terrifying clatter and indifference—all so familiar, changeless. There had never been a war. In the narrow canyons of the 40's and 50's and on Fifth and Madison Avenues were many good men's shops. Peter stepped out, escaped death by a hair and was roundly cursed by three drivers. However, he had learned courage and carried on as though he were not really frightened. He felt a sudden exhilaration and laughed at the wild absurdity. Abercrombie and Fitch, Brooks, Tripler's, Finchley's, Broadstreet's Saks, De Pinna's, all the stores, were properly deprecating about their stock and the quality of the materials and workmanship. War-time sales talk—like the prices! But Peter managed to outfit himself completely. He wanted one suit to be got ready that morning.

"But utterly impossible, my dear captain," cried the elegant salesman, moving his midriff as though he felt the urge to go or vice versa. "It's so maddeningly ridiculous. We're working under the most frightful handicap. Even if I were to watch over it myself, personally, every moment I could spare, it would still be a week before the spoiled brutes would have it ready for you. And then we'd have to trust in the Lord."

Peter resisted an impulse to pinch the temperamental cheek and said, "Just wrap it up. I'll alter it myself."

Suit, shirts, ties, shoes, underwear, socks and handkerchiefs under his arm, Peter wandered westward. On 44th, just off Sixth, now the Avenue of the Americas, he found a genial little tailor. The suit was already chalk-marked.

"Shuwar, I fix for you. Two hours mebbe." He studied Peter. "Mebbe von."

Peter went out whistling.

He wandered up Broadway. There were the usual derelicts, jumpy and wild-eyed from dope or weak, mean and demoralized by liquor. Too early for the daily load. One man was ranting and screaming about veterans, one bedraggled harridan was cursing God and everyone who passed. Both were ignored. There were quite a number of well-groomed, carefully, if colorfully, dressed, men and women, many of them with curiously likeable expressions and personalities. They were no doubt actors, musicians, entertainers. Some were frowningly worried, an occasional one obviously haunted by fear. There was much misery in New York but Peter felt close to these people, wished he could do something for them. Some of them nodded, gave him the ghost of a smile. Peter was pleased and rather proud. There was something—they recognized a colleague despite the uniform. He was one of them. The thought warmed him. But he still had a long way to go before he could take his right place among them again. How long, Oh Lord?

A pretty girl. Peter never failed to gain life at the sight of a pretty girl. There were a lot of very pretty girls, tripping, striding, slouching, strutting along, models, chorus girls, career girls, made up to look like prize bedfellows. An optical illusion but stimulating. Peter did not miss one. And he spoke to them, almost audibly. Like all the sane, lonely in multitudes, he had developed the saving, bemusing habit of talking to himself. There was no one else to listen. "Very nice!" he would say. And then, "Relax, darling. I don't want you."

But he knew they had to walk with downcast eyes or looking straight ahead, with all the would-be wolves on the street, looking important, lounging along or loafing at the curb, anything from bald and prosperous shopkeepers, bookmakers, pimps and gangsters to brilliantined, zoot-suited youths with pimples and bad teeth. Peter checked the male parade for a moment—theatrical agents, and managers, stagehands, song peddlers, money lenders, fighters and wrestlers, jockeys, salesmen killing the morning, clerks, business men, ballplayers, professional hard guys, professional Jews, professional Irishmen, professional Englishmen, professional Americans, professional Reds, professional men, promoters, gamblers, racketeers, union bosses, clergymen, politicians, sheep—it was endless.

He noted the older women. They could be housewives from Brooklyn, the Bronx or Jersey, or determined petty executives from the cramped hosiery, hat and shoe stores which were fronts for manufacturing houses. The younger, less attractive, women might well be the strained secretarial brains of the successful flotsam and jetsam of the bleary office buildings. He decided to stick with the pretty girls. The noise of a pneumatic drill on street repair made him jump, sent him hurrying on.

A cool-looking bar drew him in. He had several beers and listened to the harrowing experiences of a jovial drunk. Here was an adventure in normal living, the system which took on cognizance of the ferocity of fear. His eyes found the clock with a start. He decided his suit must be ready.

As he walked back down Broadway, he again amused himself by noticing the passersby. The universe centered about the life of each one. They did not even know that he existed. But then, he had never heard of them either. The situation could be multiplied millions upon millions of times. The tense struggle led backward into nowhere.

Glancing into shops and restaurants, he saw employees, grumblingly weary of life and their imagined knowledge of human nature, treating customers as though they were doing them an ill-deserved favor. Extraordinary. Surely these people could not really like being pushed around? There were a lot of other pretty girls now. But these were of a different type. They wore erotic makeups and looked as though they could take care of themselves under any circumstances, were unlikely to be hurt by anything. The professional hard guys were more numerous.

The whole atmosphere was rude, crude, cheap, surly, grasping and stubbornly vicious. It was rather depressing and the blare from the record shops and penny arcades was getting on his nerves. Peter's normal gait was rapid and now he increased it. He had to do some fancy open field running. The usual throngs of out-of-towners dragged gawking along, stopped to look at the cheap displays and garish advertisements, listened to pitchmen, slowed the general current of this midway to a crawl. He was glad to turn into 44th Street, choked as it was with busses and prostitutes and wistful members of The Lambs.

The tailor was ready for him. Peter stepped into the semi-curtained, drab little booth at the rear of the shop and in a matter of minutes was the complete civilian—sartorially. He studied himself in the cracked mirror, breathed deeply of the musty air and laughed. Very odd and very nice and very relaxing and very welcome indeed.

"How you like, Kepten?"

"Wonderful," said Peter.

The tailor put his uniform into the suit box, folding it carefully. "My boy's a kepten, too, heen Intelligence," he said proudly. "He's wit da Chif of Steff."

"Wonderful," said Peter again. "He's doing very well. A Lawyer?"

"Head of 'is cless."

This happy little man, struggling through the years, had put a son through law school and the boy had turned out to be all that he longed for. Peter put a hand on his shoulder. "You're a very lucky man," he said. Neither spoke for a moment. "Now—how much do I owe you?"

"Aw," the little fellow shrugged. "Two dollars."

Peter made him take five. "Send him something," he said. "I'm wishing you luck, kepten—lots of luck."

"And I'm wishing you luck, sir." They shook hands warmly.

Peter swung eastward, stepping along lightly, a half-song in his heart. He went back to Grand Central and checked the box. He was hungry. It was time for lunch. He got into a cab and told the driver to take him to the St. Regis. The driver wanted to talk. Peter wanted to look. The driver talked. Peter m'med and yesed and looked. Everything on Madison Avenue was most attractive and clean. The shops were as tempting as a cocktail. The men were very well dressed. And the women!—they had astounding chic, they were meticulously groomed, they were fascinatingly lovely, many of them surpassing beauties. You could have Paris and the Riviera. These women were the smartest in the world. Peter had to hold on. These hackmen were the best drivers in the world but they had a lot of cowboy in them. This one should have been a barber anyway.

The St. Regis was brightly busy. Peter had to wait for a table in the newly situated King Cole Room but once seated he was waited on instantly. Unlike the West Side, the East Side seemed to like its job. He ordered and sat back. He had been hearing numberless foreign accents. Oh for the life of a refugee. The painting over the bar had been cleaned and retouched. It was old—had once been in the late famous Knickerbocker Bar. He thought they had got King Cole's collar a shade too white. But it was a long time since he had been intimate with white collars. There were several familiar faces in the room but no one seemed to recognize him. Ten years had no doubt changed him more than he realized. He had a dry martini, shrimp cocktail, jellied consomme, lamb chops, broccoli, candied sweets, green salad, strawberry shortcake and a pot of coffee. He felt warmed and dallied over his coffee and cigarette. It was pleasant to do just as he liked, to eat what he felt like eating. If he chose, he could order it all over again. He decided to do just that and enjoyed it tremendously. Then he had a brandy and signed the check. The captain came over and chatted effusively. He complimented Peter on his clothes. Peter went into the Men's Room to have another look and then went out and stepped over to Fifth Avenue.

It was all very cheerful. He liked Bonwit Teller's windows and Tiffany's new home was good modern, imposing and sedate. The Squibb Building had a scrubbed look. The Savoy Plaza and the Sherry Netherland had a playful aspect, the 'big-top' canopy of the Pierre was festive and he was conscious of the charm of the Metropolitan and Knickerbocker Clubs. Central Park looked inviting, the nursemaids immaculate, the children strong, healthy and happy. Peter knew he was marking time but there was more than one train to New London and he was not going to be pinned down by the conventional musts, not yet anyway. The more outrageous his detachment, the smoother his condition. Not a very satisfactory treatment but the best he knew at the moment.

He walked on into the upper 60's and looked at the big Edwardian, Ridgley town house. It was closed except for the basement entrance. Carter would be down there smoking his pipe and reading the paper. He would have liked to go in and look around but then he would have to admit that he had been roaming the city. He walked on and turned into East 79th Street. The Curzen house was open but of course Lesley and Hank were not at home. He visualized the interior of their peaceful cool-looking home and felt an overwhelming longing to be in there with Lesley. He must have stood and thought about her almost a half hour. Why should he be doing that when he could be with her at 'Cragie'? He loved Lesley and he loved 'Cragie.' Why all this stalling about? What was he afraid of? He knew. He was a damned fool to allow such nonsense to spoil anything so perfect. But he was very sensitive to the moods and demands of others. If his reception should be as he feared it would be, it would spoil it all. He had best forget it and enjoy himself.

He walked back and into the Park, walked around the reservoir. He thought of all the telephone calls he should make and decided not to make them. They had waited for years. They could wait a little longer.

He returned to Fifth Avenue and walked back and forth through the 70's and 60's between Fifth and Lexington. Peter liked to walk and today it calmed him. There were many changes but most of the places he loved were much as he had last seen them. He was grateful for that in a city where physical change was constant.

When he got to 59th Street, he went into the Plaza. It had had things done to it but all the old charm was there. He went into the modernly enlarged Oak Bar and had a Scotch. Not necessary to order a double here. Wow!

He interrupted his drink to call 'Cragie.' George was out but he had a nice chat with Fulton. That was good. He returned to his table. He wished it were night and that the Hartmans were playing the Persian Room. They were the sort of tonic he needed. In hospital, and he had had several sieges there now wisely dimmed in memory, he had read Benchley, Lardner, and the two mad Smiths, Throne and H. Allen. He had read only a little at a time. He had known their crazy, wonderful stuff could not last forever and he had saved them. And they had saved him. There was something very reassuring, restful and delightful about the Oak Bar. He regretted leaving it but he wanted to see a little more.

As he started downtown, the gowns in Bergdorf Goodman's and the Delman shoes ticked his heart, brought Lesley sharply to mind again. If he had any sure hold on what he believed to be reality, it was Lesley. But he dared not think it was much of a personal hold. That would be dangerous. The Tailored Woman was still one of the handsomest stores ever conceived. The objects of art and the paintings displayed by the Peikin Galleries were as exquisite and striking as ever. The Gotham seemed to be enjoying a good phase. The University Club, the older members framed in its windows, was its sumptuous self. St. Thomas's was dignified, elegant and impersonal. All the shops were fascinating but Peter crossed and lingered longest over Georg Jensen's windows. If he went in he would end by buying almost everything. And he could not trust himself to visit Scribner's or Brentano's or to go down to 43rd and look into Schirmer's Music Store. He was really having fun now. St. Patrick's had had its beautiful face lifted after nearly a century. Rockefeller Center was cold, spectacular, for out-of-town consumption. Peter walked to Madison Avenue between the Cathedral and the handsome windows of Saks Fifth Avenue.

He crossed Madison and went into Weston Court, justly famed bar of the New Weston Hotel. A little later, they would be standing three to six deep but now he was able to get a foot on the rail. They had Bell's Scotch, twenty years old, and served the biggest drink in New York. Peter was just starting his first highball when he was pounced upon by Kenneth Casey, broker and unpublicized playboy. Ken was one of Peter's favorites. He was big, gentle, personable and liked fun, especially on week-ends. The ensuing greeting was little short of boisterous. The language was lusty but inoffensive. It was evident that both men were laughing at the words and phrases. Peter wanted to order a drink but Ken already had one.

"And when did you return to all this savagery, Peter?"

"I haven't returned formally. I haven't been home yet."

"Damned if that isn't typical. You haven't changed a bit."

Peter objected. "I hoped I'd improved beyond recognition."

"I recognized you. And I'm feeling no pain," said Ken. "Anyway, we don't want you to change."

"Thank you, sir—but that's a questionable compliment. I heard of an Englishman in this country telling an Irishman, 'I was born an Englishman, I've lived an Englishman and I'll die an Englishman.' And the Irishman said, 'Good Lord, man—you mean to say you've got no ambition at all?' "

No one changed basically. George would not have changed.

They talked sports, social life, food, drink, everything but war, work and intimate relationships. Peter wanted to know about '21,' Sardi's, the Colony. Did they still get glamour for lunch? He had noticed the Stork as he passed 53rd. Was it still the nicest of the night-clubs? Did Ken get to the Monte Carlo, El Morocco and Copacabana? What of the harum-scarum spots on 52nd? Peter recalled happy visits to the Ritz Carlton, Weylin, Barberry Room and 'East Side Tony's' Trouville.

"Just about now we'd see some very choice material," said Ken. "Let's go."

"No, I've got to head for Grand Central." Peter was tempted. He liked to play, too. He had slept around a great deal on his various leaves and when he could get away from the hospital. He had formed no tender attachments but that had seemed accident. However, in the past few months, with Lesley an unacknowledged but ever nearer possibility, his interest in other women had become more and more passive. It might be a wild, good thing to make a night of it, to blot out the problems which weighed on his mind and which would be strongly accentuated when George behaved according to form. But then that would mean he would not see Lesley for another day either. It was Lesley who got him. He had felt a nervous drowsiness overtaking him. He wanted to speak softly, slowly, smile lazily, stretch his muscles and let them relax. Now he snapped to action. "I want to do the Game Cock and the Biltmore and sniff the excitement in the Commodore Bar. If I'm going to miss my train, I'm going to miss it in the orthodox way."

It was then that a very British Captain Sanders, talking to (AP) Whittaker and his pipe, turned and told Peter about the planes. It seemed a great idea. Peter thanked him and made the call. There was another drink. Ken accompanied him to Grand Central and then on to the airport. They arranged to meet the following Wednesday, same time, same spot. He was on his way. As Peter flew over the country he loved, his spirits rose and fell with the little Cessna as he thought of Lesley or did not think of Lesley.

VI

IT HAD REALLY BEEN GREAT FUN, AS HE LOOKED BACK ON IT, fun under a sort of threat. And now he had faced the threat. And it was just as he had feared. The thing which he feared had come upon him. And it was not over, might never be over, unless he simply broke it, which he hesitated to do. With Peter, fear was knowledge, knowledge of his fellows, frequently depressing knowledge. It shackled him. And these shackles were the very blocks to achievement which must be shaken off before freedom of expression in reality could be made possible. The old vicious circle which Peter still believed could be squared without resorting to the human sledge. Such method must leave the job forever incomplete. George was still at him.

"Have you done any composing?" he asked.

"Yes and no, George. A few mad bits have rattled around my brain. But they can't be finished because they can't be started."

"That's a vague answer. You're being evasive, Peter. You sound neurotic. I hope you haven't fallen into the lazy habit of self-pity."

"I hope I haven't." This was as difficult as dealing with an idiot child. Peter had heard and remembered, countless phrases. But they were a jumbled mass, lacked form as yet. Counterpoint took no cognizance of rotting flesh and speechless agony. They were not the stuff of which music was made. "If I sound vague, it's simply the accident of my condition."

"Well, you'll be all right now. If I seem a little hard on you, Peter, it's only because I know what's best. I try to treat you as I would my son—if I had one."

"I know, George. And I'd like to be able to show my gratitude by behaving as a dutiful son would and should. It's just that—well, I don't want you to expect too much—not at first anyway."

"I'm sure you exaggerate the whole thing—over-anxiety probably. I'll expect your work to be all that it should be and I know I won't be disappointed."

What was the use? "If you'll excuse me now, George, I'd like to look about a bit before I change."

"Of course. But don't be too long. Would you like me to show you around?"

"No, I'd rather be alone, thanks—discover things for myself." He hated to be abrupt but he had to be free of George at once.

"As you like," said George. He was offended by this callous treatment after all the plans he had made. He should be given the privilege of conducting everything. "I'd better start to dress now anyway. Dinner will be at half past eight."

"See you at dinner, then," said Peter and walked out into the garden.

George watched him go, moved to the bar, angrily tossed off a straight drink, coughed sputteringly and went upstairs to his room.

Peter walked around until he thought George would have gone and then started back toward the house. When he reached it, he walked slowly back and forth for a while. The spaced flagstone path which ran across the front of the house had once been a driveway. During his long illness, which had really been nothing but age, George's father had had it removed. He wanted no vehicles obstructing his view of the sea. A capital idea. Peter paused, looked and listened. The garden, the inlet beach and the sea, the fields, the trees and the barns and snug cottages were most picturesque and peaceful in the dying glow. The house, touched artistically with ivy and with the red of the bricks showing through the white paint here and there, was really beautiful, alive, quiet, softly lighted—faint, welcome sounds of preparation from the kitchen, water running into a tub somewhere. The birds were at their evening prayers. The vital hush of good was over everything. For a moment, Peter felt deeply, fully happy. He wished for Lesley. Life suddenly had promise when he thought of her. If life could be as of that instant, then would life be real, then would the brassy mirage of ugliness be washed into oblivion. Peter was breathing freely and deeply as he stepped back into the living room. Lesley was there. He stopped and stood looking at her unbelievingly.

"I came down to see you," she said. She wore a magnificent blue-gray housecoat and matching spike-heeled mules. Her rich, red-blonde hair caught the lights, her beautiful, warm, womanly face wore an expression of loving concern and expectancy.

"That's wonderful of you," whispered Peter.

Lesley sat on the divan, took two cigarettes, and held one out to Peter. Peter crossed to her, took both cigarettes, stooped, kneeling on the divan, kissed her hair, her cheek, lighted the cigarettes and put one between her lips.

"George came up and banged his door but I didn't hear you," she said. "I was afraid that maybe he had been giving you a rough time of it."

"Thank God for you, Lesley." Peter sat beside her. "I'm going to need you badly—especially these next few days."

"Hank and I are leaving in the morning."

"No!"

"We have to. Hank has to get back to work. And there's a very special reason why I have to go, too." The situation with George was impossible. "I have no choice."

"I see," said Peter. He was instantly, completely deflated.

There was a sharp sickness in the pit of his stomach. No balancing realization flashed across his consciousness. It never occured to him that this sickness and his immediate acceptance of defeat were but part of another sickness which was still with him. Lesley was in love with someone else. A great spirit and intensely passionate nature such as hers would demand affection, command the best of love, devotion, adoration, loyalty and respect, even willing slavery and certainly all-consuming desire. Scores of men must be in love with her and she must have found in one or more, sufficient sweetness, understanding and sensitivity as well as boundless ardor to warrant her response. He was out of the picture. Of course, she remained his friend, his best, his only, ever friend. He could not doubt that she loved him. She loved everyone but she loved him more than most. And he had always known that she could never be in love with him, could never, in her greater way, feel about him as he felt about her. Peter was an idealist. To him, Lesley was the divine perfection of all that he lived for. In himself, he discovered little but imperfection. If she had once thought that she wanted him, thus to express their complete oneness, it had simply been a manifestation of her tender graciousness. The all-pervading restlessness which had possessed him was back, stronger than ever, and he was too tired, too entirely confused, to fight it. But he tried to cover it with a smile.

"That's a bit of a blow, darling," he said.

"I'm sorry, Peter."

"I shouldn't have come back, Lesley—not yet anyway." He was surprised by a flicker of pain in her eyes and added quickly. "If you hadn't been here I shouldn't have come." What could he say to her? First George. And now Lesley, his one link to reality, all but gone. But was she? She was still there. She still understood. Deep in his heart and the sure recesses of his mind he had seen that the rest could not be. It was hard to be sane, keep his vision clear, feeling as he did. "I had hoped it might be all right somehow. But I was wrong."

"It's got to be all right," said Lesley passionately.

"No, honey." God bless her. "It's the old story of asking too much and refusing to believe that it is too much."

"It isn't too much ever, no matter what. You deserve the loveliest of everything. You're the sort of a man who makes it possible. It's yours and you must have it all always. And nothing must be allowed to hurt it or keep it from you, or to hurt you."

Peter's heart began to lighten. He tugged at his rooted loneliness and it began to give a little. "You're wonderful, Lesley—wonderful as ever."

"I'm not wonderful at all. But you are. What's the trouble, Peter?"

What *was* the trouble? "The work for one thing. It's no good. And George is no help whatever. I tried to make him understand. It's no use and I can't blame him. I don't fully understand it myself."

"But are you sure—about the work, I mean?"

"Yes. It's adroit enough but it's mechanical. It has no life. And I'm not able to imbue it with more than a breath here and there. Such spirit as I have left soon won't be fertile enough to achieve even that. Everything's been pure crawling hell for so long, Lesley. And now this, as a sort of permanent hell. But I suppose that's what hell is—permanent defeat. And it creeps into every department of life. Don't think I'm moaning the blues. But I'd give my soul to snap out of it. I've got no soul in it. It'll just about kill George, too, I imagine."

Lesley smiled but there was a tightness around her heart. Peter was suffering and, instinctively, she was suffering with him, suffering deeply. "But the work isn't for George, or for you, either, is it?"

"No. But I have to answer to him. And to myself, too."

"Why? What's there to answer for? All you can do is do your best. And that you always do. And if there isn't much more beauty in your best at its worst than you have any idea of, then there isn't any real beauty at all and you have nothing to worry about."

"You haven't heard me play."

"I've heard you talk. You can't ever have really questioned your talent, Peter? You know you're good. You have a great gift and it's been given you in trust. It's not for you or for George. It's for me and thousands of others. You know all that and I think you know that's really all that matters. You're doing your best by that gift as you always have. It can't be taken from you. If it seems to be partially lost, that's only temporary. It's just an unhappy delusion, real enough while it lasts but it can't last long, I'm sure, because you're always very close to reality, Peter, and in reality it hasn't been lost at all."

He gazed at her with intent admiration. Strong stirrings of gratitude brought a mist to his eyes. "I feel close to reality now, with you," he said. "But it's the first time I've felt close to it in a good many years. If faith is tested endlessly, it gets dimmed. And I was always ridden by doubts. You know that."

"Why didn't you write me about things, Peter darling? Of course I knew you wouldn't."

"I didn't want to burden you with my silly troubles."

"That's not fair."

"You know I'm no letter writer."

"Your letters were wonderful. But they got fewer and fewer and then—"

"Petered out altogether. That'd be a good title for the whole picture—'Peter peters out.'"

"Oh, Peter—please."

He was being stupid and clumsy, feigning a lightness he was far from feeling. Pretense with Lesley could be nothing but offense. "There were long periods when I couldn't write at all and I got out of the way of it. Then when I could, my spirits would be dragging so, I couldn't finish. I'm sorry, Lesley darlin'. But I thought of you a lot—whenever I was allowed to think."

When Peter had gone to England to join up, he had deliberately started to space his letters at ever greater intervals and finally had stopped writing entirely. Up to that time, he had written Lesley at least twice a week. He had believed that if Lesley were accustomed to hearing from him regularly and suddenly did not hear, she would be wild with worry; if she did not expect to hear from him, the worry would still be there but would be dulled by custom. He had meant well. Had he known his silence was a pyramiding form of torture for her, he would have written every day.

"You were wounded, weren't you?"

"How did you know?"

"I didn't. But I felt that you were."

"Three times. But not very seriously." It had been serious enough. Just how Peter had kept off the 'critical list' was one of the myriad military mysteries which would now never be solved. "As a matter of fact, this past year in England was a sort of recuperative stay. It was spent in the hospital."

"Darling, how dreadful."

"Not at all, Lesley. It was quite nice. And I was up and about. It was more a sort of rest than anything else and was granted me as a favor."

Lesley knew he was minimizing the whole business. She longed to take him into her arms. "If you'd just let me know, I'd have come over to be with you," she said.

Peter's shoulders jerked involuntarily. He was deeply touched and excited. For the past year and more, he had been thinking of Lesley in terms of worldly wisdom won the hard way. When he had left her, she had been a child, relatively. She would now be a woman. He, too, would have changed, changed into manhood, changed greatly, beyond recall. What he had grown into had always been there but she had never seen it. He could not hope to find the old relationship even remotely the same. Worldly wisdom might be all right for some. It was not for him. If Lesley would have traveled to England to be with him, she must love him more than he would have believed possible, could not be wholly in love with anyone else. That there was someone else, he did not doubt. But he was not lost. He must hold the same place in her heart that he had when he left, change or no change. The thought was thrilling, overwhelming. He took her hand, kissed it.

"You're a darling," he said.

"I've missed you so terribly, Peter, been desperately worried about you. I don't suppose you'll tell me about things now either?"

He could never tell that which did not bear thinking about—even to Lesley, especially to Lesley. "I don't think they're things to be talked about, honey. They're just ghosts that haunt me when I try to look up. Maybe they'll let me go someday."

"I'm not afraid of ghosts." Lesley was familiar with the wide-spread epidemic of shock suffered by the troops. If this was so common to unimaginative men, then was it miraculous that Peter had come through it all without losing his mind. She knew that the best way to lay ghosts was to bring them into the light. But she also knew that this would take time, could be done only little by little, as, in a relaxed moment, they had a drink together, or as he wakened beside her in the night. "Maybe you'll tell me something about them in the things you compose," she said.

"If I ever compose. What I've got so far doesn't say anything. And the worst of it is it doesn't seem to matter. For eight years, without the least break, I had it thrown into my teeth that depravity ruled the world. And what I saw began to seem just a grotesque exaggeration of a constant condition. The kind of thing we believed in is eclipsed by unrelenting tragedy of that sort." An unwonted fire crept into Peter's eyes. "We're all degenerate, fantastic freaks and homicidal maniacs—potentially, at least. I can't get free of the ghosts, Lesley. You're a great white flame. All the rest of it's black, blackness filled with hideous shapes. I had hoped to recapture the old faith and hope. Everyone and everything conspire to prevent that. They won't leave me alone. And I can't think they ever will. One of my friends had half his side torn away and crawled around saying, 'Leave me alone, just leave me alone' over and over again until the blood poured out of his mouth and his face plowed into the dirt. That was his dying wish and I think I know what he meant. And it was things like that that made me act without thinking. I'd see someone hurt beside me and I'd see red."

Peter had heard teeth, bones and cartilage crunch under the butt of his rifle, heard it clearly in the midst of all the uproar. He had heard his hard driven bayonet go squishing into guts and come sucking out of gaping wounds. Time and again he had seen flesh spatter under the impact of a round from his carbine at short range. He had seen a half dozen men blasted out of a crater by one grenade. He had seen tongues bitten off, eyes knocked out of their sockets. He had seen men standing without faces just before they crumpled. He had seen screaming madness and mangled agony and left it and gone on.

"I'm not trying to excuse anything I did. I can't." He had been a wild, savage automaton with no spark of soul in him. "It may not have been quite so degraded as some of what I saw around me. But what of that? There's no pardon in heaven or hell for any of it. And there's even less excuse for me than for the others. They might have believed in what they were doing. I did not. If I could be that false, you must see that I can't believe in myself now—or ever again." The fire died away.

Lesley had heard all that Peter had left unsaid each time he paused. She was quaking inwardly, was unable to speak. She drew in her stomach and breathed deeply through her nose. She felt she must rally quickly. And she did. "But you still believe in the work," she said tremulously.

"Why do you say that?"

"You wouldn't be worried about it if you didn't."

Peter looked at her alertly. "That sounds true enough," he said hopefully.

"You're just terribly unhappy about it because you're not satisfied with it, or with yourself." She was getting control of herself. "That's because you're an artist, Peter."

"If I'm an artist, I should have proved it by this time." The morose note again.

"You have. You just can't see it yet. So much has happened to obscure it." Peter was adult, kind, intelligent, yet temperamental beyond belief. But she knew why. "Some artists develop very slowly. I'm sure all the best ones must. And you could never be anything but the best. You've done all the groundwork, all the hard part that gets no recognition to encourage it. And the other thing, if you just go on, I'm sure one day it will suddenly be there. And then you'll build and build and build. You'll do great work, Peter. You'll create the most beautiful musical cathedrals in the world. I know you will."

Her enthusiasm was not to be denied, was brightly refreshing. Peter laughed delightedly. "I love you, Lesley." Then his eyes clouded. "But even if—suppose all you say is true. What does it matter? With all the brutality in the world—if you could have seen, if you could see the aftermath—it makes you wonder if it's worth it, if anything's worthwhile."

"I know. It's awful—awful. There's no understanding

it. But then, we're so close to it. And there's so much we don't understand, isn't there? And there is the other thing, the thing that made you love music in the first place. If we're just true to that sort of thing in us, live for that, I'm sure a lot of good must come of it in the long run, don't you think?"

"Maybe," said Peter. He was vaguely aware that they were a long way from point to point logic. But he believed that such understanding as could be cozened to their hearts was not to be gleaned from hopeless complexity with mathematical precision. "It once seemed to."

"It's just got to. The bad part's got you down. It'd get any feeling person down. But it can't keep you there. You're a superlatively fine person, Peter. That means that the strain of it all has been infinitely greater for you than for the average from scratch. The power of beauty and simplicity, greatness, that we believed in is what kept me going through it all and it must be what kept you going, too, even if you didn't know it. It was hard for me to go on believing. I knew we weren't told the truth. And I always fear what I don't know more than the worst that I do know. I could guess a little. And it had me half crazy. It was like a fiendish, senseless puzzle of filthy, terrifying ugliness. And you were hopelessly involved in it. And I couldn't reach out and save you. I wasn't so far wrong. But you're back, thank God. The fact that you held on through it all proves our belief, clinches my faith forever. Surely you must see that, Peter. And one day you'll come back stronger than ever, I know. I wish I could help."

You're helping right now."

"Not as I want to. But I do believe in you, Peter. And I want you to believe in yourself—please, in every way. God knows you should. And as for the work—just go on being good to your good gift. Think what it means. No, you don't even have to think about it. Just take care of it. Take care of your art, Peter dear, and your art will take care of you. I'm sure of it. I'm sure."

Lesley's housecoat was of a heavy silk brocade and buttoned down the front. She wore nothing under it and as she would lean forward in her earnestness, it would break into generous diamond-shaped openings in the most amazing places. She would not have worn it thus with anyone else. Peter got to his feet, stood looking down at her. Behind the sad intensity of his eyes was a friendly chuckle at his expense. He might still be a sick man but emotionally, he was nothing short of robust.

There was a tremor in his voice which he could not control. "Lesley—would it disturb you very much if your old playmate should go in for worshiping you?"

Lesley rose and looked into his eyes. "Anything, everything would be perfect if only he'd be himself."

"In spite of the special reason you have for going back to town?" Again he tried to be light. He dared not ask her outright if she had a lover.

"Oh that," she scoffed. "You mustn't worry about that. It's just something I have to worry about."

She stepped very close to him. His arms were around her. He kissed her. Her response was instantaneous and complete. He was thrilled past all bearing. He drew her into him until she gasped into his mouth. Then he released her a little. They were both breathing hard and stood thus, more gently locked, until they became quieter. At last, Lesley spoke.

"It's good you're back, Peter."

"It's very good," he whispered. His head was spinning. He had to steady himself. He was dazed and quakingly happy.

She tucked his right arm around her waist, slid her left around his, and they walked from the room into the hall.

VII

THREE FOURTHS OF THE WAY UP THE GRACEFUL, CURVING stairway was a landing with a doorway which led to the second floor of the rear wing. Lesley stopped there, kissed Peter again, but lightly, and went on up the stair. Peter watched her until she disappeared toward her room, then turned and went through the doorway. Mrs. Williams's little apartment was at the base of the T. Peter walked down the hallway. Her sitting room door was open. The tiny table lamp was lighted but she sat by the window gazing over the valley at the fading light behind the hills. Peter crossed the room and stood near her. She looked up.

"God bless me!" she said.

Peter stooped and kissed her, then knelt beside her chair, his arm around her. There were tears and twinkles. They shared many terrible, wonderful secrets, these two. As well as housekeeper, Mrs. Williams was Peter's 'nanny.'

"You're back," she said.

"I'm back."

"I've been waiting for you."

"I got here as soon as I could."

"They told me you were downstairs. I meant to be down there to meet you."

"It's better this way."

As Peter entered the house, the whole staff had appeared from nowhere. Fulton had been at the door of his cab and in the hall had been Mrs. Dugan, the best cook in Connecticut, Berta, the parlormaid, Mary and Margaret, upstairs maids, and Annie the kitchenmaid with talents as a cook second only to those of Mrs. Dugan. Peter had put his arms around each one. They were very dear and faithful and were weeping as women will. There was no Mr. Dugan and no Mr. Williams and the maids, now well along, had remained single. A little like a nunnery, thought Peter, with Fulton as the grand old priest living nearby. Fulton's quarters were directly under those of Mrs. Williams, adjoined the staff dining hall and the back stair and commanded a view of the rear entrance. He was able to keep a constant, protective eye on his little flock. Their honest, affectionate reception had meant much to Peter. He was anxious to see the farmers and their families, too. They would be planning a formal call at noon the next day. But he longed to know the rich contentment he always felt with them in their own environment. He would get over to see them after dinner. He hoped it would all be as before.

"You're thin, Peter," said Mrs. Williams.

"A little."

"We'll have to fatten you up."

Peter laughed. She smoothed his hair.

"Did you miss me?" she asked.

"There's no way to tell you," said Peter.

"I missed you."

"Thanks for everything."

"Did it all reach you?"

"Most of it. Was I ever popular? And you helped me—helped me through lots of rough spots."

"That's good."

No one knew how old Mrs. Williams was. Certainly she was eighty, probably ninety, and had worked hard all her life. Peter knew she had prayed steadily for him. Whenever opportunity offered throughout the day, she had knelt and asked God to protect him. It was very difficult for her to get back to her feet but that never mattered. Often she had lost herself in those prayers for such a long time that she had had to call one of the maids, whose rooms were all near hers, to help her up. But she still looked wonderful. Her cheeks were firm and her eyes bright behind steel-rimmed spectacles. And she was as immaculate as ever. Her smooth white hair was done in a bun, her brown, bony hands were well cared for, her slight figure was covered in pleated black satin with a touch of white lace. Her meals were served to her in her sitting room by Fulton. But she managed one complete tour of the house every day.

"Are they keeping you busy?" asked Peter.

"A little here and a little there. I'm getting old, Peter."

"You'll never get old."

"Oh I don't mean I creak. It's just that I've slowed down. And I really don't mind, Peter. In fact, I rather like it."

"That's good."

"And I don't always remember things too well. But that's a blessing sometimes. The past is very clear, though, and seems like yesterday."

Night was coming on apace. Mrs. Williams talked about the house and the personalities who had peopled it, about the land and the sea and what they had seen together, about Peter's childhood and his mystical mother. There was a mesmeric something about it all and Peter dreamily dreaded the moment when the spell must be broken. . . .

Lesley sang in her bath. Her rich contralto was thundering harmony against the tiles, her interrupting bursts of laughter, music from the hills. She stepped out, snapped a great Turkish towel from the rack, caught sight of herself in the full-length mirror and stopped. Not bad, not bad at all. Her lithe, glistening body was magnificently beautiful. She began to dry herself. The long, smooth muscles rippled under the perfect contours as she moved. An exhilarating spectacle, that.

Desire began to grow within her, a strong desire for Peter. She stood with legs straight, heels together. She noted with satisfaction that she could have held a coin between her thighs and calves. She lifted herself onto her toes and looked, with pardonable pleasure, at the eager calf muscles and soaring insteps. She wished Peter could see her now. Once, when she was thirteen and Peter sixteen, they had roamed the fields and woods and had stopped in the grassy shade of the hillside and taken off their clothes. They had been naively curious and Peter had been thrilled by the sight of her. Would he be thrilled now? She could not but believe that he would. How wonderful if he would come to her at this moment. Low within her, she felt an intoxicating, quivering yearning. She rubbed her legs together, moved her hips, ran her hands over her body. Her breasts were taut, sensitive. It would be Heaven to feel Peter against her, to feel his strong, firm, loving hands on her, to have him crush her to him as he had, to know the sweet, intense mystery of his lips and eyes, to feel him within her. She did not believe, even at that moment, that this was the answer to everything. But she felt that much which burdened him could be forgotten in her arms. She would forget all else. Perhaps he would, too. She would do everything to make him forget. Oh, dear God, how she loved him, how passionately, completely she wanted him. She was breathing quickly. She laughed a little, softly, and began to dress.

As she sat on the bed and drew on her dark, sheer stockings, she raised each long leg high to appraise it and ran her hands over it to straighten the seam. She imagined what it would be like to raise her legs thus in pure animal ecstasy with Peter. When, when, when, if ever? He had said that he loved her but he had said it lightly. He had hinted at more when he had spoken of worshiping her. But he had made no declaration of the grand passion. She could not doubt that he had found her attractive. When she returned his kiss, that had been obvious. And she could be almost certain that it was much more than that. She had seen and felt much more. She thought she had found a deep, burning passion within him which made 'the grand passion' but tepid stuff. And she was madly happy. But she must be careful. What she found might just possibly be her overwhelming desire to have it so. She had always loved Peter so desperately. She did not know when she had not adored him in her heart. And she had always known she could never really love anyone else. He had never actually taken her but she had become what might be called a demi-virgin with him. It had been her first intimacy, the only time she had given of herself unreservedly. She was his, had been his, in their constant companionship, for years. Peter was her first lover, could be her only ever lover. Other men had seemed to sense this. She was not for a lonely man except that lonely man be Peter.

There was enough of the masculine in her to make her despise deceit. She was always careful not to mislead. Had she known that many of the men who courted her had enough of the feminine in them to make them naturally deceitful in a rather fetid and self-satisfied way, she would not have been so concerned. But then, neither would she have been interested. Her popularity was exceptional and many a good man loved her while knowing full well that his suit was hopeless of complete fulfilment. And reason enough. She was utterly charming, genuinely appreciative and quickly understanding. She was gay, unspoiled and gracious. She was simple, direct and honest. And she was sanely enthusiastic and quite uncluttered by complexes and similar nonsensical addenda. She was the most refreshing companion in the world. A woman to be loved, regardless. She touched herself intimately with perfume. Perhaps one day Peter would bathe her and anoint her and kneel beside her. Peter with his dear boyishness and savage passion. That would be very sweet indeed. She knew he was sick, sick with the heavy vapor of horror which engulfed his thought. But she dared not dwell on it or she would become so stricken as to be quite useless to him. If he would just love her. But he must have known many beautiful and sophisticated women in Europe, been loved by them. She might not have enough to give him. Lesley was aware of her beauty, of many of her divine qualities, but there was a very real humility about her.

She got into a black petticoat and black strapless 'bra.' She was going to wear a black strapless gown which was richly simple. And black satin evening shoes with spikes of moderately dizzy height. Peter had always liked her in black. She would wear her hair up. She would give those European women a run for their money. There was a tap at the door and Mary and Margaret, the upstairs maids, came in. They always behaved as though they were her personal maids. While they helped her dress and did her hair, there was a great deal of hushed excitement and complimentary talk about Peter and, of course, about Lesley. They thought Peter quite the handsomest and finest man who ever lived. They could not say enough about him. Lesley was blissfully content. Mary and Margaret thought she was perfectly beautiful. Mary and Margaret were right. . . .

George knocked about his room for a while, anger about the definite fighting the numbness of his brain, and then the drink calmed him. Peter had not been away for the weekend. It had been a matter of eight years. He must expect him to be changed. He had become a man and he had been through a war. Peter had always been obedient and respectful. But now he had become accustomed to being obeyed and respected as well. He had held a place in the world of men, an important place. There was a certain period of 'readjustment' to be gone through, George understood. He gave himself a mental pat on the back. A drink always had a salutary effect, made him more reasonable. Hank might not think he could be human. Hank was wrong. But any change in Peter affecting his work, or general attitude, should be for the better. Their brief talk had been very unsatisfactory. There was certainly nothing to be gained by encouraging laziness, indifference or moodiness. George felt he could be patient about other things, if need be, but there was an urgency about the realization of perfection in Peter's work which could not be denied. It should be great as of this moment. He had waited such a long time—ever since Katherine's death. He could not allow anything to delay the fullest atonement possible. It would be a glorious day when the cruel injustice of her death should be avenged, when she would live again through Peter's work. And that day must be today, not tomorrow. It had waited too long. George threw his clothes into a chair as he undressed instead of hanging them up with care, then sat on them as he took off his shoes and socks. Revolutionary behavior. He would not have Fulton about. He hated to have anyone help him.

His bath was drawn but the temperature was no longer just right. He had to adjust it. That was annoying. He bumped an elbow on the washstand, stubbed a toe against the tub and, jerking upward in pain, struck his head against the towel rack. God damn it. Bruises always stayed with him for weeks. As he examined his injuries in the mirror, he noticed that the flesh on his chest was flabby, that there were long wrinkles below it from stooping. He drew himself up and pulled in his stomach. He had been letting himself go. Now that he was better, he would take care of all that quickly. He still could not believe that he was really better but he should be able to dispel his fear by a lot of sensible and manly activity. Then he really would be better. He found ordinary things such as this taking of a bath, something of an effort. That was no good. He had to drag himself out of bed in the morning. He had to force himself to eat and exercise and keep his interest alive. At night, he wanted to go to bed without brushing his teeth. That could not go on—and, of course, would not.

He turned his thought to Lesley. In that department, at least, all was as it should be. She was a wonderful girl and she got him as excited as a boy. As he dried himself, however, he felt no great stirrings within him. Of course, there were times when even the thought of Lesley failed to excite him. That was a matter of grave concern to him. A man could not hold a woman unless he was virile, especially a young woman. But his occasional periods of impotence must be due to his illness. They could not be because of his age. At fifty-seven, he was still relatively young, had taken good care of himself, and had known very few women. It would be a horribly embarrassing experience if he should fail her on their wedding night. But that would never happen. It had happened once or twice with others. But this would be different. It was all in the mind. Worrying only made it worse. He shuddered. Perhaps he was catching cold.

His clothes were laid out perfectly. He could find no fault with them. This was to be the greatest evening of his life. He would declare himself to Lesley and take her into his arms. Peter would play as it had been given to few to be able to play. He dressed with care. It was irritatingly tedious but it was worth it. The lowering cloud of Henry's warning kept threatening to extinguish the brightness of everything. A cocktail would pick him up. . . .

Yvonne and Celeste were being blasted by their mistress. They were doing her hair and her nails very expertly but could not be meticulous enough to please her this evening. However, they had learned to take these word-lashings complacently. Audrey, always flamboyantly generous, was particularly so after one of her outbursts. If the evening went well, they could expect handsome reward. And Audrey's special occasions always went well. And she always fussed over them but not like this. This must be a very special night. She was really on the war path. Well, that was good. It was hard to take but would be well worth it.

Audrey examined herself critically in her dressing table mirror. Where her filmy negilgee fell away from, or otherwise revealed, her slim person, she had to admit there was little left to be desired. And that was an apt way to describe it. What was there was certainly most desirable. She studied her face. She had done a facile job on her makeup—only a few more touches. Her soft, pouting mouth looked moist and warm, her great green eyes, dreamy and lustful, her skin was creamy white, her black hair, piled on top of her head, was shining midnight blue. She thought about Peter. He looked a little tired and embittered. What he needed was a woman. The woman he needed was herself. If he had had more than his share of women, that had no bearing on the matter. He needed a woman who knew how to make love to him artistically, a woman who would make love for hours on end with only a little time out now and then for rest and a cigarette. It might prove tiring in a damned pleasant fashion, perhaps even tiresome if important things needed attention, but before very long, Peter would find himself wanting her all the time. Any man who was conscious of her wanted her and she would make Peter constantly aware of her. And he really should make a terrific lover with his shyness and his burning intensity.

As far as George was concerned, again to hell with him. Peter could give her all that George could and love and youth as well. Their combined wealth would make her one of the great women of the world. In a way, George would be easier to handle. He was rather stupid and unusually gullible. Flattery could get anything from him. And she would still be young when he was gone. But he was such a bore, so vain and pompous and stuffy. No, Peter was her meat. And one day he would inherit the Ridgley fortune. Even if the going got very rough, she could hang on that long. His career would be something of a problem but it would keep him pretty well occupied. She could see more of Reggie and others. And Peter would be too busy to seriously oppose any ideas she had regarding a yacht and planes, new homes, travel and entertainment. Her clothes and jewelry even now were the envy of royalty. But she would outdo herself. And if Peter should drop his career, she would coax him into absorbing interest in all the more worthwhile sides of graceful living. There would be no stables in the world to compare with those which she would build.

Audrey felt waves of happiness rising into her throat. Yvonne and Celeste got her into her wine-colored gown, adjusted it, not a simple operation. It was cut low in front and back. It really was sensational, a designer's dream and provocative. Provocative? It was on fire. And the matching shoes were glowing embers, the startling, few jewels, sudden sparks. She whirled about before the mirror. It seemed that with the slightest movement the breasts must be exposed, that a flip of the skirt would reveal the smoothest thighs and hips in Christendom—and the lines were truly magnificent. She was a perfect study of lush chic. Audrey smiled on Yvonne and Celeste, patted them affectionately. She was ready to leave. She would drive herself and kidnap Peter before the evening was over. . . .

When Henry went to Lesley's room, she was downstairs with Peter. He had not got her promise to remember to think of herself in this business with George. Of course she had known he would be around and that was why she was out. She had never changed so quickly before. He went back to his own room and completed his toilet rapidly. George could certainly louse things up. He could throw sharp hazard into what should have been the happiest of festive nights. Peter's return was occasion for rejoicing, not alarm. George should wear a muzzle. Any man who was sure he was right was a constant menace. Not that George was sure. None of these tin supermen was ever sure. It was in their stubborn determination to be shown sure that the danger lay. They were social blights. If Lesley had to let George know where he stood, if Peter was even temporarily alienated from music and quiet submission, there would be hell to pay. The whole evening could be the biggest bust of its kind that Henry had ever had to endure. He nicked his chin with the razor, used the styptic pencil. When Lesley saw that, she would know he was still upset. Too bad. He must get her promise before George could get at her. George with all his goodness and perverse stupidity. His unconcern over personal sanctity as displayed in his treatment of Audrey, for example, was deplorable. Audrey needed no champion. She was case hardened and knew her way about. And she might be angered by shabby treatment and, if chance offered, vengeful, but she would never carry the memory of it or be hurt by it. But Audrey was complete female and should be handled guardedly but lovingly. George's insensitivity about Reggie might be partially excusable. Reggie was so adroitly poised that even Audrey herself might not know how completely he was in love with her. Hard to believe but possible. Be that as it might, their intimacy had been evident and only an egoistic dolt could take it as entirely casual. And George's almost immediate stand with Peter had been selfishly callous and shockingly bad taste. God alone knew the hurtful repercussions which could result from such blind, gratuitous cruelty. Henry could only fearfully surmise what they might be. But he did not know the time and tireless care which the healing of new wounds over old demanded. He wished devoutly that Peter had been coming home to Lesley and to no one else. No situation ever seemed altogether sane, happy, or even decently protected. Intelligence found small place in the daily pattern.

He finished dressing, took a telephoned report from the Curzen Hospital in New York, called Zara Moore in East-hampton, dashed off several notes and read Epicurus until he could no longer delay his appearance downstairs. . . .

Reggie, his nocturnal grooming almost complete, was musing on the inevitability of heart-break and the gradual death of the spirit, when there was a knock on his door. There was not the least chance that it would be Audrey.

"Come in," he called.

The door opened. It was Peter.

"How nearly ready are you?" he asked.

"Just a little more spit."

"Then come over and keep me human while I dress."

"Gladly," said Reggie.

Peter turned away and encountered Fulton in the hall. The rough parchment of the square, uneven face lighted in a smile of rare affection.

"Are you ready to change now, sir?" he asked.

"Bless you, Fulton, but I can manage very nicely, I'm sure. Well, perhaps not nicely, I'd need you for that, but I haven't had anyone help me dress for—you'll have to start to train me all over again and very, very slowly. But not tonight. I know you must have your hands more than full downstairs."

"Oh, that's all arranged, sir."

"Then if you would do something for me, steal a few minutes to relax. And while you're doing that, if it isn't asking too much, break out a bottle of the best you have in stock and take a wee sip to my dearest wish."

"Drink to you, Master Peter? With all my heart. I have to step in to see Master Reggie for just a minute." They were still children to Fulton. "But then I shall go directly to the pantry and lift my glass and my eyes to you and to your good wish. And I'll be happier than happy as I do so, because I know your wish will be granted you, just as all our wishes for you have been granted us."

The unquestioning faith behind this pronouncement made Peter happy, too.

"Thank you, Fulton."

The old man bowed and left him.

VIII

PETER WENT ON TO HIS ROOM. AT THE DOOR, HE HESITATED for a moment, pushed down a world of conflicting emotions and went in. It was almost exactly as he had last seen it and scarcely remembered it. In the closets hung all the clothes he had sent home from England at the outset of the War. And a number of gifts were laid out on his bed. Otherwise, the staff had seen to it that it was just as he had left it.

He kicked off his shoes and walked about on the soft rag rugs and polished floor. Hot damn. It was a big corner room. Through the north windows, Peter could see the lights of the farm cottages, through the east he could see and feel the sea. Rich in antiquity, the furnishings were of the best and most comfortable. Those blessed traditions of a bygone era, the cabinet maker's art and sense of peaceful ease, were in everything. But for the touches of modernity in clothes, electricity and bath, Peter could have been certain that he must have come by stage. The ornaments and clock, the fireplace, the paintings, the general decor, supported the illusion. A room in which to read Dickens. Peter glanced at the huge Empire desk raked across the corner of the room between the windows. Inspection brought remembrance. His books and papers, his pencils and pens, his calendar and desk clock, his sheet music, date book, music manuscript paper, ah yes, and those other modern bridges, his telephone and typewriter, all were in place. And he knew this would hold true with everything in the room. If he needed anything, he would know just where to look for it and could be sure it would be there. It was sweet of them to have gone to all that trouble.

He turned to the high, wide, old four poster with its lacy canopy. There was an order for a car, there was an order for a concert grand, and there were generous orders on the leading music stores and men's furnishing stores in New York, all from George.

There were a dozen monogrammed white shirts and a yellow gold wrist watch equipped to do everything but talk, from Lesley. She must have made the shirts. There was a sensational, compact recording machine from Henry. There was an exquisite, profusely illustrated edition of Boccaccio's "Decameron" and an elaborately handsome music case from Audrey. There were a half dozen conservatively striking Charvet ties from Reggie. There were four suits of heavy black silk pajamas from Mrs. Williams and the staff. There was a case of Grant's Scotch from the farmers. Again was Peter deeply touched and delighted.

Most of the gifts represented careful thought, hours of effort and boundless generosity. How determined these dear persons had been that his homecoming should be an extraordinarily happy one. How much love was here. Fulton had unpacked his gear. There was little enough. But the pictures of his mother and Lesley, in the tooled leather folding frame, were in their place on his chest of drawers. They were among the few treasures he had stored in London and been lucky enough to recover. He carried a smaller stained photograph of Lesley in his wallet. He had tried to talk to it during recess from grim experience. It had not been easy. Their understanding had seemed hopelessly remote from the roaring breath of circumstance. He spoke to the larger picture now and felt warm, right response.

He whipped off his clothes happily and bathed and shaved in eight minutes flat. He came out of the bathroom tingling.

Reggie had come in and Peter had shouted his thanks to him from the shower. As Peter dressed they rattled on about matters of no consequence. Reggie was a good Joe.

Peter put on one of the shirts. The collar was soft, wide-slotted and rolled. It would fit any masculine neck comfortably. Lesley should open a shop. "Feels marvelous," he said.

"They're beautiful," said Reggie. A pity Lesley could not be there to see the obvious satisfaction Peter derived from her exquisite, painstaking handiwork, see his eyes shining. Such were the little, big things Peter needed. Reggie hoped Audrey would have no luck with Peter. It was dangerous for Reggie to admit her to himself—and he was on to her.

The trousers of Peter's dinner clothes fitted perfectly, were even a little loose around the waist. And he could still tie a bow. Amazing.

He tried the shoes, did a few dance steps. They were going to be all right. The jacket felt tight across the shoulders and chest. But it would get by. He checked accessories.

"What have you been doing, Reggie?"

"Eating, sleeping, drinking and—"

"Never mind."

"Having fun," said Reggie with great hauteur.

"The fully rounded life."

"And it's refreshing to have someone ask me what I've been doing instead of asking what I'm going to do. That's a very favorite question. 'Well'—they don't add a 'little man'—'well, and what do you plan to do now that you're out of the service?' It never occurs to the clucks that you might just want to get drunk for a while and not make any plans at all. I've got an answer for them though. You better think of one, too."

"What's yours?" Handkerchiefs, breast and hip pockets. Cigarette case, breast pocket.

"I'm writing a play," said Reggie. "Everyone writes a play, so that's a very acceptable answer."

Wallet, papers, fountain pen, inside breast pockets. Lighter, watch pocket. Change, match pocket. "But don't they ask you about it?"

"Oh, I've got a plot. Would you like to hear it?"

"Is it long?"

"No."

"I'd like to hear it." Lesley's wrist watch. Keys, left trousers pocket. No dog tags, no jug, no orders, no contraceptives, no money concealed on his person. He was back in the old routine.

"It's romantic drama. Naturally, I wouldn't fool with anything less poetic." Reggie spoke with modest pride. "It's about the royal family of a small but happy kingdom. It starts with the young King and Queen. They're very happily married. They don't know one another very well and they're extremely polite and considerate. He has a mistress. She has a lover. The mistress gets in trouble. The King asks the Queen to go into confinement with the mistress, accept the child as her own. She agrees. It's a boy. Then the Queen gets in trouble. She asks the King to return the favor, to let her have the child and accept it as his. He agrees. It's a girl. Eighteen years elapse. Now comes the sweet part. The kids fall in love. But thinking they're brother and sister, and having been nicely brought up, they can't do anything about it. Life is painfully beautiful. Now—complications. The King falls for the Princess. The Queen falls for the Prince. The King tells the Queen. She says if he tips his hand to the girl, she'll tell the boy the truth, too. He says she wouldn't dare, threatens her. Their first quarrel. Quite a scene. Thinking he's safe, the King hints the truth to the Princess, makes a polite pass. The Queen keeps her word. Over the horrified protestations of the King, she spills the beans to both kids, hoping to ensnare the Prince. A hell of a scene. And then the climax. The kids rush into one another's arms. Emotional chaos. Their Majesties are very wroth indeed. They want to kill the kids and one another and themselves. Unbearable tension. But finally, before tragedy can stalk through their lives, all is forgiven in a burst of noblesse oblige. The kids are shipped off to South America incognito to live happily ever after. Then the King turns to the Queen and looks at her as though he were seeing her for the first time. He takes a drink and looks again. The old girl sees what's up and starts to preen herself. Things are tough. We're at the final curtain. The King chucks the Queen under the second chin and asks her jocularly if she doesn't think it's about time they had a legitimate heir to the throne. She pretends to mull this over and then says coyly that she thinks it's a hell of a swell idea. How do you like it?"

"Very affecting," said Peter. "Have you got a producer?"

Reggie was getting the kind of laughs from Peter that were good to hear. "They're all after it," he said, "but I don't think one of them has sufficient delicacy of feeling to present it tastefully. Nevertheless, I've lined up a tentative cast—all Alec Clark's suggestions—Sally Forth, a strident ingenue, for the girl; Well Call, a pretty, personality juvenile, for the boy; Hank O'Hare, an Irish comedian, for the King's jester and confessor; Helen Highwater, a big-busted character woman, as a lady-in-waiting and confidante; Haidee Haye, a brittle gush and acid English leading woman, as the Queen and Noah Vail, an elegant blueshirt leading man, as the King. Great, huh?"

Peter gave way to a mighty groan, the punster's greatest applause, and made a lunge for Reggie. But Reggie, having studied Alec Clark's technique, had the door open and darted into the hall.

They walked down the hallway laughing. Peter thought

how chimerical it all seemed. It had been 'up one moment and down the next' from the time he had stepped off the transport. This moment was definitely 'up.' Lesley's door was open, her room empty. She must already be having a cocktail. Peter's step lightened and quickened with his heart.

IX

THE COCKTAIL CHATTER AND THE COCKTAILS HAD ZIP, TANG and kick.

Peter, accompanied by Reggie, stopped on his way downstairs to thank Mrs. Williams and then invaded the pantry and kitchen to thank Fulton and the rest of the staff before joining his good friends in the living room.

He at once expressed his thanks to them. And Peter could pack such feeling into a simple "thank you" as to make the one thanked hug him to his or her heart. That set the bright spirit of the gathering to fairly spinning. There were several exuberant rounds.

They moved on to the dining room. It adjoined the living room, was baronial, a banquet hall, but curiously intimate. The sideboard with its row of giant silver tureens, their covers suspended from the ceiling by chains and pulleys, was comforting to look upon. Peter sniffed the sweet aroma and thought of Locke-Ober in Boston. He and Lesley. He was happy. He was home. He glanced at the drop-lighted portraits which lined the oak-panelled walls, the Ridgley crest inset above the fireplace, the fireplace with spit, grill and Dutch oven which were actually used in cold or raw weather, the heavy, high-backed armchairs which were luxurious relaxation. The company settled into their places.

The dinner was a gourmet-gourmand dream. One lived well at 'Cragie.' The slight condescension in George's manner, designed to convey the impression of admirable restraint and boredom with the trivial, gave way to smiling pride as he witnessed the obvious success of his party. By common, unspoken consent, the others were determined to make it just such a success. Relaxed gaiety and charm held throughout the meal.

"Life begins at 'Cragie,' " was Reggie's comment.

George bowed, a little uncertain of Reggie's meaning.

The long Georgian table was candle-lighted and eyes, teeth, jewels, glasses, silver and plate danced and sparkled under the liquid flames. The velvet woodwork glowed and mellowed and cloth and clothes were regally, somberly joyous. Faces were uniformly beautiful, even those of the Ridgley ancestors in stern oil, and the food was simmering splendor.

"It's too perfect," said Lesley softly.

Peter looked at her. "It is."

Assisted by Berta, Mary and Margaret, Fulton served 'old style' with deft, bright smoothness. The platters, both steaming and cold, were staggering but each item was delectable, succulent. And the subtly persuasive wines of rare vintage were delicious. There were oysters, clams and crabmeat, Sherry, onion soup and chicken and clam broths, grave, pompano, English sole and terrapin, Burgundy, pheasant, turkey, grouse and canvasback duck, Champagne, tenderloin steak, broiled chops, bacon, and baked ham, baked corn on the cob, mushrooms, six green vegetables, maplenut covered mashed sweet potatoes, gravies and hot and cold sauces, creamery butter, hot rolls and date and nut bread, chutney, cream cheese, stewed fruits and preserves, sherbets, Stout, Swiss, German, Dutch, English and American cheeses, pâté de foie gras and caviar, Chablis and lobster salad, hot spiced apple pie, French ice cream, fudge cake and fruit and nuts, all, all and more, testing the strength of the mammoth and stout old board.

Peter felt he must taste everything. This colossus was made

up of his favorite dishes miraculously prepared and blended by that saint of the larder, Mrs. Dugan, and her worthy disciple, Annie. If he failed at any point, someone would be hurt. And worried. Even Mrs. Williams would know. But with Lesley seated across from him on George's left and Audrey, scarcely less tempting, to his right, he found concentration and appreciation extremely difficult and the hope of easy digestion highly improbable. Lesley's young breasts, partially concealed in black and accentuated by shadows, rose and fell with the slow, full rhythm of a sea swell. And her eyes were so lovingly upon him that he could almost feel the long lashes brush his cheek. He struggled manfully.

Audrey recrossed her lush legs and swung the knees toward Peter. As she leaned over the left arm of her chair, it seemed certain the wine gown must slip away from her lovely body.

"Peter darling," she cried. "You're not doing this feast justice—or yourself either."

Peter gazed on her with admiration. "I'll gladly fight for it as long as I live," he said, "but I've long since ceased to look for justice in myself or in others, at home or abroad."

"What a cynical remark."

"Not cynical, sad—sad and unbecoming. Just the reverse of your gown."

"Oh, you like it?" Audrey was really pleased.

"Very much," said Peter and meant it.

"Tell me more."

"And what happens to the feast?"

"All right. But eat something this time."

Peter returned to his dinner and to Lesley. Of the others, only George was unaware of the electrical attraction. His thought was on this night of triumph now so well begun. Audrey worked on Peter unscrupulously with every chance he would give her. And her social grace was such that she gave no sign of her fury, other than an occasional fleeting shadow in her eyes which none but Reggie could recognize. Reggie sat across from her, amused and pleased and mildly alarmed. Henry, at the foot of the table studied George, facing him across the dancing distance, and quickly realized there could be no immediate cause for apprehension. All went well for a time.

The meal over, all cross fire conversation was interrupted and the gracious hand of pleasantry received a sharp crack across the knuckles. George pulled himself out of overstuffed lethargy.

"Coffee will be served in the music room," he announced.

Momentarily banished, the brave spirit of politeness was again present in muted form as the party obediently arose from the happy hour.

The music room was across the hall from the dining room. It should have been attractive. Instead it had a rigid look. Peter had been gone from it too long. The concert grand piano was open. Violin and cello rested on and against small oval-backed satin and gilded chairs. Gilded music stands were set before them. Tall stand lamps flanked formally placed chairs and side tables. More gilt. The walls were of wood a quarter of the way up from the heavily carpeted floor. Above the wood, painted pale green, came charming cut-out wallpaper of trees and fields on a cream plaster wall. A crystal chandelier hung from a ginger bread ceiling. A cold room. When it had been Peter's workshop, the decor had been far simpler. And with the drapes thrown back, the even north light pouring through the windows and a clear view of sun-splashed fields and the farm cottages beyond, it had been warm, alive.

As Peter entered this former sanctuary, he felt a distinct chill. As the company reassembled there, it was evident that the strain was to be generally felt. Peter was frankly nervous. George strode to the chair which he considered his. The others stood about awkwardly. Peter looked around, patted the piano for comfort.

"Very pretty, George," he said. "Reminds me of private concerts I played years ago in Europe."

"Glad you like it, Peter."

Peter had not said that he liked it. The party found places and settled down. Fulton came in with coffee, liqueurs and port, served everyone and left the tray on a coffee table within easy reach of most. There was a little murmured conversation, then silence.

Peter forced a grin. "Seems a rather solemn occasion," he said. " 'The doomed man was reported to have enjoyed his last meal—and cigarette.' " He tamped out his cigarette.

Audrey and Reggie laughed a little at this. George snorted. Henry smiled sympathetically. Lesley was momentarily unhappy.

Peter moved around to the keyboard, seated himself before it, adjusted the bench, ran his fingers over the keys. The The tone was good. But he had no stomach for this.

"Well, here goes," he said. "God help you"—and then to himself—"and me, too, please."

And He did. When Peter started to play, his nervousness was dissipated in inquiry. Music was his real mistress and he would know why there was no answer to his pleading. He made love now for no one's benefit but that mistress. Only George's presence made it awkward. But even that could not stay his desire. It was good love making. But it lacked heart. He tried Bach, Beethoven, Brahms, Chopin, even some of his own earlier work. Still no reply. All but George must see how broken-hearted he was by his failure. Lesley would understand completely. Without embarrassment, he went on trying—and without anger. It was excellent playing. But that was all. He labored to give it life. It was a labor of love but futile for the most part. The only anger and embarrassment were felt by George and they were devastating enough but of trifling character in face of the greater mood. The others were happy to be able to applaud his efforts with some sincerity and to listen with more than moderate enjoyment. And among the liqueurs was Napoleon brandy eighty years old when it had been bottled forty-three years before. It could not fail to drive tenseness from all nerves and warm the coldly formal atmosphere of this little-used French Victorian chamber. Anxiety apart, it all became increasingly pleasant—for everyone but George, almost forgotten by everyone but himself. George became increasingly restive. Peter went on playing.

An hour later, Audrey and Reggie were playing backgammon. They were seated at a Dutch chess table before one of the east windows in the living room. The music formed a semi-remote background. Reggie was winning. Audrey was in a foul mood. She slammed out the dice and made a bad move.

"Isn't Peter ever going to stop?" she queried irritably.

"He plays very nicely I think," said Reggie blandly. He threw two sixes and made the most of them.

Audrey shook the dice violently. "And 'very nicely' lets him out. I bet George is raging." She smiled and became less violent.

"That ought to please you," said Reggie dryly.

"It does. A real set-back might do him some good, make him a little more human." She threw a seven.

"Too bad you can't have one, too, then," said Reggie as Audrey decided on another poor move.

"You're the last person in the world who should accuse me of not being human."

"You have your moments. But this isn't one of them." Two sixes again. He moved expertly to his best advantage.

"No?" Audrey snatched up the cup, held it in clenched

fist. "I hope you don't think I play this stupid game with you because I like it."

Reggie was imperturbable as he finished his move. "It isn't the game that's stupid. It can be played intelligently. Double."

"Then how is it you always win?" She set the cup down with a bang. "It must be because I let you."

"So your little losses have begun to get you again?"

"Little losses?" stormed Audrey. "My little losses have kept you in cigarettes and platinum for a good many years."

"And that remark is in the very best taste."

"So is your arrogance." She became coldly furious. "Don't be an ingrate, Reggie. It's the most tactful way I could think of to repay you for being nice when I wanted you to be. I expect you to have some pride, you see."

"Then don't expect me to be the dog around the house, too." He bit off his anger. "Your preoccupation with money is very depressing, my dear. I think it's probably the most vulgar note in your character—and God knows you're no symphony."

"What a son-of-a-bitch you can be when you want to."

"I just warned you not to take that view, to quit trying to kick me about imbecile-fashion as an outlet for your pique. I'm not the one who's killed your chances with Peter. It's Lesley who's done that."

She was too angry to dissemble further. "You're terribly clever, aren't you?"

"No. If I were, I'd be in Tibet." He moved away and took up his favorite stand before the fireplace.

Audrey got up from her place at the table, talked at him through her teeth. "If I want Peter I'll get him. And Lesley won't stop me if George learns what she's doing."

"That's another thing I like about you, Audrey. You always play fair."

She folded her arms, gave him an icy smile. "When I go after something I want, I'm not playing."

He looked at her for a time in a perplexed and rather hopeless way. "You seemed to want me last night. And several other nights. You were just playing then, weren't you?" He spoke quietly.

Audrey softened instantly. "You know I wasn't." There was an unaccustomed tenderness in her eyes as she looked at him. "And you know I loved you." She turned away and looked out at the winking lights across the water. Last night *had* been fun.

She had had Reggie over for dinner. It had been a pleasant dinner and a good dinner. Afterward, they had slowly sipped several B-and-B's and talked. Reggie had been very amusing and a little courtly. She had been quite excited when he had given her the news of Peter's impending arrival. A few mental gyrations, and she had made her plans. She had then relaxed happily and decided to settle into complete enjoyment of her evening with Reggie—perhaps the last for a long time to come. Later, they had gone upstairs and to bed as though it were the most natural thing in the world, which no doubt it was. She had wanted to rid her palate of the heavy taste of George. And she had.

Reggie had been wonderful. His touch was dynamite. And she loved to run her hands over his bronzed young body, so lean and sensitive and alert. What was it about Reggie that no other man could give her? Perhaps they were 'perfectly matched physically.' She had read how unique that was and how essential to a happy marriage. But she gave such statements little credence or importance. She cared nothing for the dogma of science in the sexual field or any other. Science was a bore and highly fallible. The same applied to scientists unless they were sweet looking which they almost never were. She was a woman of action. Trial and error with individual persons and problems, that was the way. No need to go about dreaming and brooding and looking worried and wise. No need to think at all until you ran into a nasty, serious snag. Time enough then to stew over things and put them right. Or, what was usually better, throw them out and forget them. Was she hitting a snag now?

She hated to lose money—even to Reggie. It was a bad omen that she should have lost tonight when she was particularly anxious to win. Was she in for a run of bad luck? Was everything going to go wrong? She tried to pooh-pooh the idea but it persisted. She was not superstitious. But she had the careful gambler's awareness of, and respect for, the law of average, percentages. Things had been going too well. She felt Reggie behind her and her spine tingled. She turned and faced him. He was very close to her. She was almost overwhelmed by an instant urge to make him take her again then and there. But she fought it down. She knew she must resist even the suggestion of any such feeling. There was important work to be done. She forced herself to return to the subject of their debate.

"But I'm not fool enough to try to make a life of that kind of love." The hard glint was back in her eyes.

Reggie felt as though cold fingers had whipped across his mouth. "And what do you think a life with Peter Drake would be?"

"A life I understand." She sat back against the edge of the table. "The general feel of it would be right. And I'd have all I want." She picked up a brandy and soda which she had been drinking, looked up at him over the rim of the glass.

"You'd do a lot better to hang onto me. I'm the only man I know with enough patience to beat you into some semblance of womanhood."

She lowered her glass. "I don't seem to have done anything to your self-confidence."

"Nor, by some miracle, to my self-respect," said Reggie hotly, "in spite of your charming hint of charity. You see, I happen to know you don't know the meaning of charity—or love—or anything else if it comes to that."

She clucked her tongue. She was in the saddle. "There are times, Reggie, when one would never suspect that you find me awe-inspiring."

"I don't. I find what I feel for you awe-inspiring. And I damned well resent being thrown into constant panic, too."

She stood, questioned him eagerly. "Why the panic?"

"You wouldn't understand," said Reggie and turned away again in disgust.

George came into the room from the hall, glum anger clouding his big features. He went straight to the cabinet bar and helped himself to a drink.

Audrey's lips curled into a smile of satisfaction. "Going to give up at last and join us, George?"

"So it seems," George grumbled. Drinking his drink, he turned toward her, coughed, wiped his mouth with his handkerchief, glanced at the chess table. "Finished your backgammon?" There was the irritation of stung pride in his tone.

"Yes. Permanently," said Reggie. He was near the garden door.

"Sounds like a row," said George hopefully. Here was diversion.

"What would Reggie and I have to row about?" asked Audrey with sharp innocence.

"What indeed?" added Reggie. "Don't you know Audrey shows only her best side to mere acquaintances? All bitchiness is reserved for those close to her. A common fault, to give that adjective double duty."

Audrey spoke to George. "And if your hardiest perennial were inexcusably rude, that still wouldn't excuse me for rowing with him. Now would it?"

"Of course not," said Reggie in a soothing voice which was

infuriating to Audrey. He went on, now tersely. "And now, if you'll excuse me, I'll just step into the garden and smoke a pack of cigarettes." He made a false start, then studied Audrey in a level way for a moment. "Audrey"—he got her attention—"you'll never be good at any game if you have to be winning to play well." He walked into the garden and disappeared.

"Pah!" She spat the expression after him. It was true. Even in the hunt, she had to be in the lead or her jumps were graceless. She always had to be out in front in everything or she began to fluff and behaved badly. And the more she lost, the angrier she got and the worse she got, until, in an effort to save face, she had to invent some pretext to drop out. She got away with it with everyone but Reggie and herself. It was true. Damn Reggie. George was speaking.

"I'm afraid you're not giving Reggie much of a break," he said.

"Why should I?" she snapped. "I gave you one. Now I know better." She took a drink from her glass, ran her tongue along the edge of her teeth. A malicious gleam crept into the green depths. "Peter plays very expertly, doesn't he?"

George's hand jerked. He, too, took a drink. "He was able to do that years ago," he said.

"Not as he does now. Technically, he's pretty close to perfect. With a little fire, he could be terrific. Even you should be able to tell that, and you don't know anything about it."

"You're not just trying to make me feel good?" asked George sarcastically.

"What makes you think I'd care how you feel?" She was in a quarrelsome mood. That was bad. She would have to keep her head if she wanted to win.

George tried to bite back. "If you think he's so good, why didn't you listen for awhile?"

"He's been playing for over an hour. I listened for three

quarters. That's enough." A sip from her drink, then a deliberate voice. "And I didn't say he was good. I said he could be."

"He should be good now."

"Why?"

Suddenly, the music was more audible. There was an insistence about it. They both listened. It wasn't right but it had color, had a quality which it had lacked before. George turned and started for the hall. Then abruptly, silence. George stopped, turned back, slowly, frowning thoughtfully. His gaze rested on Audrey and he was brought back to her.

"Why?" he barked. "Because he was brought up on music. Because he's had a musical education that can't be topped. And he's been through an experience that should have brought complete maturity. That's why!"

"And still he isn't good." Audrey was enjoying this. "Even for that brief moment, you can't think he was really good. So where's your argument? What Peter needs now is feeling and freedom. He isn't going to get that from study and practice."

"Then how is he to get it?"

"By living. I said just now that with a little fire he could be terrific. And I think I'd like to be his little fire."

"What?!"

"It can't make any difference to you—now."

George quit barking. "It makes a great deal of difference to me," he said evenly.

"Why? You've made other arrangements, haven't you?" Audrey made a direct hit on pious romance.

George's face flamed. But he stifled his righteous anger. He fell back on his best executive manner. "I'm not going to quarrel with you, Audrey. I've got enough on my mind without that."

Audrey drove on. "Do you mean your mind or your conscience?"

"All right. Out with it." George clung to his control. "You're nursing a grievance it seems. What is it?"

Audrey shrugged, perched on the left arm of the divan, her feet on the cushions. "Oh, I have no grievance," she said lightly, "unless being tossed about like a piece of cheap furniture could constitute reason for a grievance."

"Come now, Audrey," said George placatingly. He leaned against the opposite arm of the divan, went on in his best fatherly manner this time. "I haven't been well and I've had guests. And I thought you'd forgotten me in favor of Reggie." He did know about Reggie.

"You've got too much vanity to think anything like that."

"I know youth does strange things on the rebound."

Audrey bounded to her feet. "Rebound from what? Your vanity's colossal. There isn't going to be any rebound." She wanted to stomp in high tempo. She checked herself, resumed her perch. "I'm interested in Peter and I always have been."

"What do you mean by that?" asked George cautiously.

"What I told you." Another sip and calculation. "He isn't good and you're in a state about it. I'm going to help him and you should be damned glad I am."

"And just how do you think you're going to help him?"

"How does any woman help a man?"

George knew this must be the answer. But a moment before Audrey had told him the same thing. His efforts at deafness were useless as were his conscious efforts at blindness. He was thin-lipped and definite now. "You're going to help Peter, but not in the way you think. You're going to help him by leaving him alone."

"Am I?"

"Yes."

There was a pause while they eyed one another as two evenly matched opponents will. George broke it.

"He isn't good because he hasn't worked hard enough. But he's going to work now and nothing's going to interfere."

"Admit the truth, George. You've flopped on the job. But I'm not going to flop and you won't have anything to say about it."

"Look, Audrey"—George tried wheedling again which he hated—"don't attempt a crazy revenge. If I've hurt you, I'm sorry. I didn't think you could be hurt—"

"Certainly not by you," interrupted Audrey.

"—It seems I was wrong," continued George. "But you're not going to hurt Peter's work. Just tell me what I can do to put things right and I'll do it."

Audrey pounced on this. "Are you willing to give up Lesley and come back to me?"

George stiffened. His speech was brittle. "We'll leave Lesley out of the discussion."

"Why?" jeered Audrey. "Is it all too sacred? You chucked me for her, didn't you?"

"I thought you just suggested that you had chucked me. Or at least that you couldn't be chucked by me."

"All right then, if I'm willing, are you willing to have everything just as it was before?"

George sighed. This fight was most embarrassing. And it was getting feminine and involved and his head was starting to ache again. "But be reasonable, Audrey," he said. "Once anything like that's gone, there's no getting it back. You know that."

Audrey tried to sound triumphant. "Then it is gone? I'm delighted to hear it. It was never really there with me. How could it be?" The tears she fought back were tears of anger. To think she had lost her power over even an old oaf like this. She must say something to clinch it. "I've always thought of you as Peter's father." There. That was a good line to take. She had almost forgotten.

George paled. He stared at Audrey unseeingly. His lips were parted. Then Audrey came back into focus again. He moistened his lips. "As his father?" he faltered. "Why?"

"Why not?" She was watching him carefully with a growing feeling of excitement and satisfaction. "That's only natural, isn't it?"

"Perhaps."

"Why do you look so funny?" Her eyes were bright. "Of course it wouldn't surprise me. You aren't his father, are you?"

Awakening indignation brought vitality. George stood. "Audrey, you— For a young woman, you have a very robust point of view. I can't say it's attractive." He turned away.

Audrey hooted. "You Victorians slay me," she said. "What's so awful about being frank?"

George turned back, drew himself up. "I don't think I'm quite old enough to be called Victorian," he said with studied control and dignity.

She pretended to suppress a giggle. This was a sore spot with the old boy. "Maybe not," she said as though speaking to a hurt child. Then clearly, "But Peter and I grew up together. And he thinks of you as his father. Why shouldn't I?"

George was again shaken. "Are you sure? . . . Are you sure Peter thinks of me as his father?"

"Yes. Isn't that touching?" she said with heavy sarcasm. "Of course he doesn't think you really are his father," she went on and was delighted to see George flinch. "Anyway, we've always shared a great deal. And when he went abroad, I thought maybe we could share you, too, that I could be nearer to him that way. I didn't know you'd have other ideas."

"I should think you might since you gave them to me." George had been hit hard but could still strike back however weakly.

"Say what you like to comfort yourself," said Audrey scornfully. "But your avid reaction came as a shock." Of course the truth was that she had engineered the whole business. George had to be 'made' and made to think he was doing it all.

He had one thing only—money—for her, at any rate. She rarely felt revulsion with a man but she had felt it with George. He had never been in her bedroom, nor had she been in his. His poor outbursts of passion had always occurred in the car on some dark lane after they had been at a party at the Club and he was more than a little drunk. The antique idiot had no idea that he had never really possessed her. Through all his puffing and snorting, he thought he was giving her a hell of a time. And she let him think so. Why not? It was a lucky break. The first time had been accident. She had been quite surprised. It was a revelation to find that a grown man could know so little. Grown man? Old man. She had kept it that way. It was a simple trick which she had learned at a very early age, possible only because of the magnificent form of her legs at the pelvic bone. Of course, it was messy and hard on her beautiful clothes—she smiled at the descriptive phrase—but much to be preferred to actual contact with George. Naturally, marriage would have changed all that. But she had been willing to accept the ordeal in view of the reward. Now she could forget it.

"Now that Peter's back," she continued to George, "now that I've seen him again, I know what I've always known. I know that no one else will ever do and that's that. I hope he'll marry me."

George settled slowly back against the arm of the divan. "Audrey, I don't know what your idea is in all this—but if it's to hurt me, you'd better find some other way. I'll fight for Peter to the last ditch. And you won't like what I'll do to you." Native underlying menace was unmistakable.

"I can believe that. But I'm not afraid of you, George," she retorted. And there was sure-footed defiance in every word. "And suppose it's what Peter wants? Are you going to do things to him, too?"

"Yes, if it comes to that. I think I can tell him enough to kill any feeling he might have for you."

"If you do, I'll tell him everything. That should kill any feeling he might have for you." She had him now. "And there's one thing I could tell him that would take him away from you entirely."

"Really?" George was cautious again. "What's that?"

"Try to fight me and you'll find out." She flung the words at him with amused contempt. Then as a whip, "It's a little something you told me just a moment ago without meaning to. Clever of you."

Fear was creeping around his heart in spite of himself. "I don't believe you, Audrey," he said angrily. "And I'm sure Peter won't believe any wild story you tell him, either."

Audrey smiled. "Maybe not," she conceded. "But Peter's a sensitive boy. Once plant a doubt in his mind and it sticks —especially if he doesn't want it to." Unbeatable feline wisdom. "And you might find it hard to deny what I'd have to tell him."

The menace was back as George spoke. "If you're wise, you'll tell him nothing. The boy comes first with me. Before I see him hurt, I'll sacrifice everything and everyone else, including myself."

"And Lesley?"

George was on his feet. "I thought I said—!"

But Audrey was not to be intimidated. "And Lesley?" she repeated.

"What's Lesley got to do with it?" spluttered George.

"Lesley is the crux of the whole situation, to use a polite word in a delicate phrase."

"What do you mean?"

"I mean you're going to lose Lesley to Peter if you don't watch your step."

"What are you talking about?" he demanded.

"Peter and Lesley, Lesley and Peter. They've got a terrific crush, at least Lesley has. So if you want to keep her, you won't stand in my way with Peter."

George was startled. He was confused. His headache was getting worse. "What sort of nonsense is this?" he growled.

"Nonsense?!" Audrey laughed a high C. "Men are a riot. They either see nothing or imagine they see much more than is there. If you'd had your eyes open just now instead of closing them and frothing at the mouth, you'd have seen Lesley dangling on every note with the love-light in her eyes and Peter just eating it up. I tell you they've got it, George, and it's got to be stopped."

"But that's ridiculous," said George lamely. "Peter's been home only a few hours."

Audrey swung down from her perch, stood facing him. "So what? They're both young, you know."

There it was again. She was twisting the knife. He took a step toward her. He had never struck a woman. It was only life-long observance of that convention which stopped him now. He stared at her fixedly for a moment, then drooped almost imperceptibly. In the back of his mind he knew he was no longer young. If he were, he would have found her irresistible at that moment, standing so close to him, fire in her eyes, flushed with the beauty and appeal of young life. But he felt no urge toward her. Perhaps when he was strong again, all that would be different—perhaps.

"And it all has its roots in the dear old bygone days anyway," she continued. "Don't be a fool, George. She probably liked you for the same reason I did."

He winced under the sting of this. Then over his anger and confusion came suspicion, suspicion of Audrey and her motives, to give him fresh courage. He straightened, the cloudiness and pain in his head receded, he almost smiled as he spoke to her. "You're the fool if you think you can trick me with your vicious nonsense, any of it. I simply don't believe you, Audrey."

Taken aback by this sudden transition, Audrey rallied

quickly. "Of course you don't," she said chidingly. "You don't believe anything you don't want to. Who does? But you will. You'll see for yourself soon. And I'm surprised even you missed the sparks in the air during dinner. They weren't from the champagne. The dear children must have managed a moment together somehow before that."

Henry walked into the room. He gave them barely a glance, went to the fireplace. Half turned away from them, he prepared and lighted a cigar. He disliked 'scenes' and sensed that one was in progress or had been. He saw so much of that sort of thing. He could take it but tried, when possible, to avoid it. And he had just indulged in a happy interlude.

He had left the music room on George's heels and gone to the library. It was next to the music room toward the rear of the house. It had metal lamps with down-shooting light and was a silent room. The desk and chairs were club-like, forest-green leather and dark wood. The tall bookcases were lined with the great classics of the world, all excellent editions, stoutly bound in well-kept leather. Here was the essence of earthly intelligence in Greek, Latin, Sanskrit, Norse, German, Chinese, French, English and good English translations, Italian, Bengali, all languages, the so-called living and the so-called dead. Not that the modern works in the living room had not much to recommend them, not that many of them would not one day find a place here, but this was rich stuff. Henry did not 'browse.' He dipped deeply and quickly into every volume he removed from the shelves with the skill of one practiced in research. He was familiar with most of them and a glance was sufficient to revive full experience. Through the years, on his visits to 'Cragie,' he had spent much of his time in this favorite room. He handled the books with almost physical affection and deep gratitude to the artists who had created them. He would have liked to spend the evening there. But devotion to courtesy made him replace the last volume and move on to the living room. He wished now that he had stayed longer.

Audrey, after appraising both men and acting jezebel indifference, went to the little bar to 'sweeten' her drink. George watched Henry, looked toward the hall, then back at Henry.

"Where are Lesley and Peter?" he asked.

"I wouldn't know," replied Henry. "I left them shortly after you did."

George looked at Audrey and his brows contracted. Audrey lifted her chin and smiled at him. She was biting her lower lip gently but she was happy. She had gained an unwilling and dangerous ally. George glanced back at Henry, glanced from one to the other several times, then back toward the hall again.

"Damn funny," he said.

X

GEORGE HAD STALKED OUT. AND WHEN HENRY SLIPPED AWAY, Peter knew, without thinking and without raising his eyes, that only Lesley remained in the room with him. The cold current in his blood was replaced by a surging warmth. He abandoned his mistress and began to make love to Lesley. It was neither truly musical nor unmusical. It was unorthodox playing and it was arresting, provocative. This was the bit to which George and Audrey had paid special heed in the living room. Lifted from her chair, Lesley crossed the room to the piano and stood looking down at Peter. He held a final chord and looked up at her. His hands came away from the keyboard. He got up and took her into his arms.

"Don't say anything," he whispered and kissed her.

They stood in close embrace for fully a minute. Then he held her away from him a little and searched her beauty with desperate hopeful love, a half-smile on his lips.

"I want to see the farmers." He spoke eagerly, huskily. "Can you walk in those shoes?"

"I haven't used a wheelchair all evening," she confided.

"I think they're chic and exciting. I should hate to have you ruin them."

"What with tractors and trucks, the wheeltracks from here to the barns are as smooth and hard as a rock, my sweet. And I thank you and I wouldn't take time to change in any case."

Peter hugged her. "Let's go," he said.

They went from the music room to the north side entrance

and out into the drive. Reggie was just coming around the corner of the house.

"Hi," called Peter softly.

"I've just promised to smoke a pack of cigarettes," said Reggie laconically. "Do you happen to have a pack of cigarettes?"

"We're going over to the cottages," said Peter. "Come on." Reggie was ever a prime favorite with the farmers as well as the staff.

"Swell," was Reggie's only comment. No reference was made to the little recital just completed.

Peter tossed his cigarette case to Reggie. "Catch," he said. A first-aid, quiet, sure feeling of exhilaration was sweeping away the weariness of depression. "And let me have one, too," he added.

They all lighted up. Then Reggie held the case out to Peter.

"Please keep it, Reggie. You always liked it."

"Liked it? It's super. But I couldn't, Pete."

"Please," said Peter pushing it into Reggie's coat pocket. "And there's something that belongs to you, Lesley. But it's in the vault in town. I'll tell you about it later."

"Peter, it's not what I think?"

"It is."

"I can't accept it." But she knew she would. Peter had once loaned his mother's tiara to a charity art exhibit. Later, at the show, without knowing whose it was, Lesley had gone into ecstasies over its regal simplicity.

They swung along the lane toward the cottages whose windows were squares of welcoming light. The farmers were still up. Lesley, Peter and Reggie were happy, happy in revival of old communion. They breathed deeply of the salty-earthy air and drank in the surrounding scene aglisten with a supernatural yellow frosting supplied by the harvest moon. The stars were very close. The sea gave off answering flashes of blue and gold as it shimmered and rolled in its ceaseless motion. Started by Reggie, they sang 'It's a Great Day To-night for the Irish' in low-voiced harmony. The first cottage was occupied by Miss Mary, Mr. Ed and Frank. Here most of the other cottage residents and their neighboring friends gathered on Saturday nights. Peter used the wrought-iron knocker. Miss Mary opened the door. She peered into the darkness for awhile, then clasped her hands.

"Why it's Peter," she said as though she were witnessing the Resurrection.

There was a general shuffling of feet and furniture on the plank flooring to the tune of pleased though modestly muffled exclamations.

"Come in, come in," cried Miss Mary. "And little Lesley and Reggie, too." Miss Mary was five feet in height but those she loved must ever remain little. She and Mr. Ed were sister and brother. They were as old as Mrs. Williams or older. Ostensibly, they ran the farms. Frank, whom they had adopted, was in his forties, a huge bronzed fellow, shy and awkward away from the livestock and the fields.

Peter handed Lesley into the room, bowed Reggie in, and then stepped into its sampler homeliness himself. Miss Mary closed the door. Peter took both her hands, as gnarled as Mr. Ed's, and kissed a withered cheek

"You look well, Miss Mary."

General greetings were going on around them and Lesley and Reggie were being made to sit down while all eyes constantly returned to Peter.

"And you look well, too, Peter. But you could do with a little weight."

Peter grinned at her. "We're two of a kind then, I think."

"Oh, I'm fat enough. If I got any heavier, I'd be as lazy as Eddy." She had practiced this well-meaning shrewishness on her brother from the time they were children. She said it was like water on a duck's back but she would never give up trying. Miss Mary was a strenuous worker. Her brother had ever sweetly enjoyed a casual acceptance of life. They had been orphaned at an early age. There had been enough money to see Mr. Ed through an obscure Franciscan college. A classmate who was his best friend had become the leading steel magnate of the country. He had asked Mr. Ed to join him not once but many times. The answer had been invariably the same—'Charlie, I love you and I know I'd be a very rich man down there in the city. But I belong up here.' This unconcern with worldly gain was the quality in her brother which Miss Mary respected and which drove her mad. Peter studied her closely and swiftly. All was well. Her coarse Victorian dress was draped over a scare-crow figure which was surprisingly agile. Her face was pinched and lively, her eyes were dark and darting and bright, her hair was still jet black and drawn tightly back into a small knot. She was bird-like as ever and nervous as ever. And at the moment, she was gloriously, reminiscently flustered, 'all of a twitter.'

"Well, Eddy," she turned to her brother standing just behind her, "aren't you going to say hello to Peter?" She stepped aside and whisked imaginary crumbs off the 'special company chair.'

Mr. Ed and Peter shook hands with a spontaneous, strong, firm grip. There was a kinship of understanding between the two men in which age played no part.

"It does my heart good, Peter." There was grateful sincerity in the kindly eyes behind their battered gold-rimmed spectacles. And the leathery features were lifted in a secure and gentle smile.

"You haven't changed a bit," said Peter. His left hand rested on a powerful, drooping shoulder. He punched Mr. Ed lightly in the chest. "And I've missed you like hell." He knew a love and respect for this young-old man which was as mellow as Mr. Ed's own nature.

And Mr. Ed had not changed. The sparse white hair was

awry. The same front teeth were missing, the remaining ones stained with tobacco juice. He needed a shave, the white stubble grew from Sunday to Sunday. He wore no coat. His shirt was a faded blue denim. The black string tie was askew. the dark wool trousers had no crease. The belt looked like a piece of old harness. A blue bandanna, pipes and a package of Five Brothers tobacco protruded from the hip pockets. The work shoes had been treated with neatsfoot oil and would never take a shine. The long sleeves of a cotton undershirt extended below the partially rolled-up shirtsleeves. He had the wholesome man-smell of the farmworker and weekly bather. And he had never seen fit to try to excuse all this even though he was more than familiar with such standard Metropolitan explanations as artistic pretensions, the shortness of valuable time, deep thinking, or philosophical intolerance of conformity. Mr. Ed was Mr. Ed. And Peter would not have had him otherwise.

No, Mr. Ed had not changed. Nor had the cottage. The same pegged, plain and sturdy wood furniture—the bleached rag rugs, the porcelain clock and figurines, the frilly curtains, the ship lights, storm lanterns and oil lamps, the big brass one with the circular wick burning on the main table, the white Dutch fireplace now almost obscured by Frank's bulk—all the same.

"Well now, come and sit down and have a bit of ale."

"You tempt me," said Peter. He went about the room greeting everyone. Frank was blushingly inarticulate. 'Honey Boy' Lait and his parents, Tess and Tim, had not lost their Arkansas humor and twangy drawl. Abe Corn looked like the young Lincoln for whom he had been named, his father like Franklin and his mother and sister like woodcuts. The dark Framer girls, school-teachers and nurses, had grown into very pretty women, their brother Joe was a rustic Clark Gable, their fine, erect father, with his full beard, a biblical picture of Noah. The seven Noels, down to the youngest aged eleven, were blooming and blonde and handsome. Seth Maple, hollow-cheeked and full-mustached, should have been on a bicycle built for two but he could never have pushed his huge chortling Amy along the road. Some of the younger ones in the top teen-age bracket were out driving or at a dance or the 'movies.' Peter dropped into the chair selected for him. Everyone else present, over sixteen, had a cool-looking pewter mug of good if startling ale. Peter was given one forthwith—and a plate of morsels of the 'free-lunch' school set beside him. Lesley and Reggie were, of course, already served.

Before anything else, Peter wanted to know everything that had happened to everyone and listened attentively to each least incident retailed while telling them all a little about himself here and there.

"We were going to stop by to see you after Mass tomorrow," said Miss Mary when there was finally a pause.

"I hoped you would but I couldn't wait that long. And I wanted to thank all of you for that beautiful case of Scotch."

"Oh, tush, tush." Mr. Ed and others all protested that it was nothing.

Peter interrupted them. "I'm just back but I know it's practically impossible to get. I not only appreciate the gift but also all the thought and effort and possible sacrifice behind it. You must help me drink it. Even so, I shall probably be happily crocked for at least a month."

They all roared at the idea of Peter ever having too much. He could have told them there had been many times. Mr. Ed was drawn into philosophizing about world conditions. This he did with an eye on Peter for confirmation and approval. He got both. Peter liked nothing better than to hear Mr. Ed expound his views. There was an unaffected soundness about them.

Many of the happiest hours of Peter's early youth and young manhood had been spent with Mr. Ed. He had worked in the barns and the fields with him. He had gone with him for the cattle and helped him with the chores. He had assisted in the cleaning of the lamps, seated on the bench outside the woodshed, in an atmosphere of amusingly penetrating comment, kerosine and tobacco juice.

But the best times had been when they had gone to pick berries in the clearing in the woods. Miss Mary had always scolded, saying she knew blessed well very few berries would be picked. And she had been right. But they had both conscientiously carried pails. After picking a few berries and perhaps having an exciting adventure such as killing a poisonous snake which had escaped Bull, the big pet black snake, Mr. Ed had invariably suggested that it might be time for a pipe and Peter had given the standard rejoinder that that sounded fine. They had then withdrawn to the cool shade of the woods and a favorite resting place, a fallen oak which had two natural armchairs in roots and branches. Peter had never been very fond of a pipe. But with Mr. Ed, pipe-smoking had had the significance, permanence and comfort of an accepted ritual. Once, when he had replaced a walloping wad of tobacco, which he had been chewing, in its paper pouch, he had told Peter that 'you chew it first, then smoke it, and then use the ashes for snuff—practical economy.' After smoking in silence for a time, Peter had always introduced the problems which were troubling him at the moment and had then sat back and listened to the rich and peaceful discourse which Mr. Ed had never failed to deliver.

The problem of good and evil, for instance, had been one with which Peter had wrestled in his young mind over a long period. He had been able to talk to no one else about it except Lesley. And they had been of an age, stumbling about in the dark together. Mr. Ed had told him that there was no answer, at least, no satisfactory answer, from a worldly viewpoint. The great minds of the ages had struggled with the same enigma and come up with only metaphysical solutions.

But those metaphysical solutions while lacking the constant workaday warmth of mother love which we all crave could still be proved in physical results.

Mr. Ed had gently guided both Lesley and Peter to the discovery of the bed-rock on which they had built their characters. No matter what storms threatened the superstructure, no matter how time seemed to change it, that solid base must forever remain the same, an absolute faith in the all-power, the onliness of good.

Watching and listening to him now, after all the years, Peter felt a return of the suspended reassurance which Mr. Ed's calm had never failed to evoke. There was wisdom here. But it was not to be captured and set forth in words—or music. Or was it? Or was it hypnotism? Or was the commonplace hypnotism, and this level sense the reality which broke the spell for a time? Was it not, perhaps, art in a pure form and unrecognized as such? And was not all of art, as Mr. Ed had said, the medium of truth? Peter listened once more with the increasingly sharp langor of undisturbed concentration. Here was the contentment he had known that he remembered.

General conversation was resumed and, directed by Peter's interest, turned to the farms and their trials and victories. Despite a late frost and heavy rains, the crop had been a particularly rich and heavy one. Peter took pleasure in noting how grateful to God these earnest souls were for what they considered His blessing, especially at a time such as this when they felt a starving world needed it so badly. The livestock came in for a generous share of the talk. The character and temperament of individual animals were gone over in detail. And everyone chimed in with the recollection of a breaking, run-away or some other adventure in which Peter had been involved in the past. It was like folk-lore.

Peter was purring. But it was getting late for the older ones. Reggie made the break. He stood up.

"Pete, old son, you may want to risk your life for the thousandth time but I'm getting back."

Peter was loathe to move. It was all as though he had never been away. These generous people had seen to that. But he, Lesley and Reggie spoke their thanks, said good-night and stepped out under the stars once more. The night air was light and clean without the chill of early fall. Clem Noel, one of two gardener-chauffeurs, went with them as far as the garage where Peter picked up his car.

"She's all tuned up," said Clem proudly, "and a lot better than the stuff they're turning out today."

They drove back to where the lane opened into a tree-lined parking circle near the house. Here they left the car and walked across the front of the house to the living room but not without certain misgivings which they knew must prove to be well founded.

XI

LESLEY, PETER AND REGGIE WERE GREETED WITH SULLEN silence from George, a warning look from Henry and flippancy from Audrey. Peter quickly explained what they had been doing and was enthusiastic in his praise of the farms. George was somewhat mollified and began to think he might have been stupid to allow Audrey's indictment to influence his judgment. But he watched Peter and Lesley closely.

Audrey knew that Lesley had stolen a march for the second time. But with Reggie along, it could not have resulted in a coup. There would be no third time before she invaded the field herself. Peter must be snapped out of this absurd infatuation. There would just be no third time.

Peter was talking to George. "You must have had to face impossible shortages in all supplies and yet I understand, and could see, that the buildings, the stock, the machinery, everything, is in top flight condition and the farmers are enormously pleased with the harvest. I hope I can have them over for a little billiard tournament some evening soon. They get a kick from that and it will give me a legitimate chance to break out their Scotch."

Across the hall from the living room was a drawing room, long and wide, tastefully furnished and with a dais at one end where the orchestra could play at the big parties. Immediately below this room and equally as large, was the game room. Here, in the well-lighted basement, were billiard and pool tables, bowling alleys, games of chance, a television set and a long, perfectly appointed bar. It was traditionally understood that when members of the household or their guests were not using it, this colorful chamber was at the disposal of the farmers. George disapproved but would not break the tradition. The farmers sensed this and rarely took advantage of their privilege other than in the winter months. But they loved the casual, carefree quality of the place and Peter knew that the evening his contemplated would be a very happy one.

"That's a very nice thought, Peter," said George with an effort.

"Why did you stop playing, Peter?" This from Audrey as she posed against the edge of the console table. "It sounded lovely out here."

"When distance lends enchantment," remarked Peter, taking a packet of cigarettes from a heavy humidor at her side.

Henry interposed, "I couldn't have listened all that time and wanted more if it hadn't been good."

"If it had been good, you wouldn't have noticed the time," countered Peter. "What did you think, George?" He might as well ask.

"I enjoyed it," replied George coldly. "I'll tell you what I think another time."

"You won't have to, really."

"Don't be silly, Peter."

Lesley lighted his cigarette. "You weren't giving a concert, Peter," she said. "You were entertaining the family and you did it beautifully whether you think so or not."

"Thanks," said Peter as he exhaled. Then, "So beautifully that my audience walked out. That's a record even for Peter Drake."

"A short walk-out and just for animal comfort," said Reggie. "We never stopped listening."

"Oh, please forgive me," said Peter. "I'm behaving very

badly." He turned away. The topic had to be met. And it would be Audrey who had to introduce it. Well, that was that. He turned back smiling. "I'm glad you liked it," he said.

George bestirred himself. He had been brooding over Peter and Lesley and had not missed the intimate business with the cigarette. "And what would you like to do now, Peter?" he asked.

"Reward you all for listening," replied Peter, "but since I can think of no suitable way, I'll have to do the next best thing and do nothing."

"That's it," said Henry. "Relax. It's a good trick to learn. I've been trying to teach it to George but he learns very slowly."

"Nice of you to insinuate that I'm an old dog," said George dryly.

Cross-purpose and tension took refuge in formality. It was suggested that they should be using the terrace on such a fine night. At that season and with a breeze from the sea, there would be no mosquitoes. A few garnered drinks and they all strolled out into the garden.

Peter and Henry walked slowly back and forth in front of the house and then down to the dock and out to the end. They listened to the water lapping against the piles, sniffed the strong, fishy, sea smell and looked out at the various craft which, under their riding lights, had assumed sharp silhouettes against the rays of the moon. The 'Betsy,' a seaworthy yacht named in honor of Mrs. Williams, stood out amongst them. She spelled fishing, swimming, cruising, party, fun of the first order. Peter wished she were cutting her way through the Mediterranean with Lesley and him aboard. On the horizon, a liner was plying southward. Southwest Ledge Light flashed rhythmically. Peter flicked his cigarette into the waves.

"Now they all know, don't they? It was a hell of an ordeal but I suppose it had to be gone through sooner or later."

"What seems to be the trouble, Peter?"

"No faith. I can't believe in music or the love of music. And perhaps worst of all, there's almost no person or thing I believe in. And certainly, I can't believe in myself."

Henry knew Peter was letting off steam but he also knew there was intense fire behind the steam. "Do you know why?" he asked sympathetically.

Peter nodded. "I used to have a strong faith. It was simple enough—just that good would always win out no matter how it seemed doomed to lose. Lesley and I used to prove it—or thought we did. The first real blow came when I got out into the world. An experience common to most young people. So many things, little and big, were blatantly all wrong and no one seemed to care very much. The few who did weren't able to do anything constructive about it, and try my best, I wasn't either."

"And that was the beginning?"

"That was the beginning. I started to lose faith and I lost steadily from then on. I clung to it stubbornly but, oddly enough or naturally enough, the more I fought, the weaker it got. Then the war came along. That was the end for me and for the work, too. I can't expect George to understand but I hope you and Lesley do."

"I hope we do, too." Henry's smile was tight-lipped as he continued. "As for George, you must realize by now that he doesn't believe that understanding and discipline mix."

Peter laughed shortly, mirthlessly. "George will never know what discipline is, not now, or that it's no good when there's no heart in it. I've disciplined myself so that I can play well but there's nothing in it." He paused and the loveliness of the night invaded his mood. "I don't know," he continued, "there's so much beauty in the world, so much beauty in people. At least, I always thought so, but I can't have faith in it now because something ugly always kills it."

"But that's your job, Peter—to see that it doesn't."

"And I fail."

"You can't fail. You can only seem to. That's the agony of it, I know. But you're working for perfection and that's the soul of Man, Peter. There are passions in all men far deeper than those which lead to violence and they're passions for beauty and peace."

"Then why aren't they the ruling passions?"

"They are when aroused. But they're deep and sure and the appeal to them has to be deep and sure. The artists make that appeal and that's why the artists are the great of this world. Of course, they needn't paint or be musicians. They may just labor or think or live. But their gentleness teaches them patience and patience experience and experience wisdom so that they're able to help us ever more and more on the road to the sky. And they never fail and they never die. And you're one of them, Peter."

Peter breathed deeply. "I'd give my life to be," he said. "But I can't lie to myself, Hank. It would have to be real. One old teacher I had used to say, 'If you can't be a virtuoso, give it up.' I think that could be a very sound philosophy of life, don't you?"

"Yes, if you knew you could be a virtuoso."

It was good of Henry to be Henry. He was always to be relied on. Peter smiled. Their talk was lifting him out of the angry doldrums. He took a new tack. "Well, Hank, you'll be glad to know that something's happened just tonight to give me new hope. That's what I need so badly. And a very real hope it is."

"Wonderful," exclaimed Henry.

"It is. It's Lesley."

"Leslie?"

"It's meant everything seeing her again. I love her, Hank.

Of course, I always have. But this is different. I lost her for awhile, or almost. That's when I lost everything. But tonight I got her back—maybe."

"Why the 'maybe'?"

"I think she wanted my love at one time. She may not now. I have some reason to believe she does but she hasn't told me in so many words. Until she does or gives me some clear sign, I can't be sure. But I'm already half-sure. So much so, that when I'm not knocked down as I have been several times since I got back, I'm walking on the clouds. That hasn't happened for years."

"Then you think it's okay?"

"God, I hope so," said Peter.

"I hope so, too."

"Thank you, Hank," he said. Then his smile was replaced by a frown. "But from the little we've already said, I know she has certain reservations. She wouldn't say what they were and they came as a distinct shock. We've always been so close. Of course, that's silly. It was a long time ago, all that. Lesley will always love me. Of that I'm sure. But I want her to be in love with me. I don't want to share her with others in that way. If there's someone else, I'd prefer to bow out rather than try to enjoy my bliss in doubt. I don't want sympathy and sacrifice. I want love." His face cleared. "But what am I grousing about instead of being grateful? I'll cross that bridge if, as and when. I love a great spirit and my chances look good."

"I'm sure they're very good, Peter—somehow I'm sure." What had Lesley said? Henry was perturbed by this new development.

Peter was encouraged. "I can't but believe that a complete and perfect love would prove all the beauty I want to work for. I don't think I'm grasping at straws exactly either. I know that love is one thing and work quite another. Naturally, I've got Lesley in my blood and can think of nothing else very clearly. But I think the spirit that makes such a love possible is the basis of everything. Without that spirit I feel I'm a dead duck because I can't feel. And I'm scared, Hank, just scared as hell."

"But what are you afraid of?" asked Henry thinking meanwhile that he was the one who was really scared.

"You must see," said Peter almost reproachfully. "I've failed every way. And now this—if I can't make a go of it, then I'll really be through, the most dismal failure who ever lived, or pretended to."

"Is that all?" said Henry with some relief. Earlier in the evening, he had known beyond any doubt that Peter must be the love of which Lesley had spoken. In fact, he had always known it in a way. "You and Lesley will have a wonderful life together, I feel sure. I don't see how anything can prevent that. And I congratulate you both. I'm very happy about it. I can tell you now that I've always hoped that you and Lesley would marry. It seemed obvious that you were destined for one another from childhood. Anything which blocked consummation would have been the deepest sort of tragedy. You say you love one another. Don't ask for more Peter. You say you want more but don't ask for it and it will undoubtedly be yours. I'm very happy about it."

"Thank you again, Hank, thank you. Lord, won't it be wonderful? I know that, in time, I'll be able to do all I should with my life and my work. It's the first real inspiration I've had since I left years ago. And it's more than great enough to meet a great need." Peter felt highly exhilarated.

"Peter"—Henry hesitated—"you haven't said anything to anyone else about this?"

Peter looked at him questioningly. "Of course not," he said.

"Then don't. Let it be your secret and Lesley's, for a time at least. Don't talk to others and be particularly careful not to say or do anything that might give George a hint of what's up."

"But, good God, why? He'd be delighted."

"No. Believe me." Henry was serious. "There's a very good reason why he should know just at this point. I can't tell you what it is now but one day I will. You'll have to trust me in this. You do trust me, I hope?"

"Of course." Peter was completely mystified.

"He'd be anything but delighted. George's case is a very peculiar one. I'm familiar with his plans and ambitions—hallucinations in mild form if you like. Whether right or wrong, they're all—important to him. You know how he is when he's crossed. We don't want him to have a relapse. This particular bit of news could have dire results just now. Please promise me you'll make sure that he doesn't find out, Peter, at least for the present."

Peter regarded him searchingly for awhile. Then, "Okay, Hank," he said. "But I don't like it." More reservations. And he could not fail to notice that Henry had not denied the existence of a possible rival. It might not be a serious rivalry but obviously it was there. And where did George fit into the picture? Peter could not believe that George would favor another over himself regardless of what project he had in mind. Then why the secrecy? Quick, burning thoughts passed through his mind. Perhaps George was the rival. Perhaps George was the other man. He considered George as elderly, as a sort of parent who was almost a stranger. The idea of his being in love with Lesley was repulsive beyond belief. He put the thought away as too ugly to contemplate. He had arrived at that sorry stage where he was ready to accept any outrage as possible. He was heartily ashamed of the thoughts which flamed from this state. It was all the result of the hardening process he had been through. His fleeting reactions had taken but a second. He shook himself free of them. It was strange. Everything was strange, and everyone. He would simply have to accept the situation. But he did not like it.

"I don't like it either," Henry was saying. "But we do have

to consider George. Why we have to consider others at such a time, I don't know. But it seems we always do." Henry sighed.

"I hate secrecy, lying, especially about anything so marvelous. But I'm as bad as any general. If it happens, nothing will bother me much. I'll be too happy."

"It needn't spoil things, Peter. It may even add a little color, not that romance of such a high order needs any additional color. But there is a special intimacy in shared secrecy. It can be fun if it doesn't hurt anyone and in this case the reverse holds true. You'll be trying to help someone. In time, you'll be very glad you did it. It will add to your happiness then. To be trite, it's all for the best, Peter.

Henry could readily appreciate how heavily Peter was counting on this new-old love even though he knew it was but one bright step along the way that he must follow. It could not make him an artist. But through the maze of circumstance, it was absolutely essential to the release of the artist already there. And Lesley would derive from it all the great happiness she so well deserved. George must not be allowed to introduce any harsh discord which might jeopardize or destroy it.

Peter refused to be put down by further unpleasant conjecture. "I still don't like it," he said. "But I do trust you, Hank. So I know it's all right." He stretched his hands toward the sky, then let them drop back to his sides. "Gad, I'm really sailing. I remember I always used to think that anyone living a life without love, from choice, was playing a fool's game at best. Now I know I was right."

"You were," said Henry.

Audrey gained Lesley's ear. She talked clothes for awhile. Then, "If I were you, I'd be a little more careful, Lesley," she said brightly.

"Careful?" This abrupt turn in the conversation made

Lesley wary. She knew the danger signs with Audrey too well.

"You're going after Peter too openly. George is bound to see what you're doing and that'll be very awkward." Audrey did not imagine for a moment that Lesley could really be frightened off. But she might become a little nervous and confused. Every little bit helped. It was worth a try.

Lesley glanced instinctively at George seated at the other end of the terrace talking to Reggie. She knew they were discussing economics and the chances were very slight that they could hear what Audrey said even though Audrey's tone clearly indicated that she would like to have them catch a key word here and there. Still looking across at the men, Lesley began a rapid estimate of the situation and how best to deal with it. Audrey's clear laugh interrupted her.

"Don't worry. They didn't hear me, darling," she cried softly.

Lesley looked at her narrowly. "I don't think I know what you're talking about, Audrey," she said in level voice.

"Balls, my dear." Audrey laughed again. She considered Lesley hyper-sensitive, believed she was easily shocked by open personal discussion and vulgarity. "You're not satisfied with George. Not that I blame you. You're probably as cold as ice. And as a lover, George might as well play with himself once or twice a year. So you're not satisfied with him and now you want to make a fool of Peter, too. Well, I, for one, won't stand for that, darling."

"I see." Lesley was actually shocked by Audrey's cheap attack. She felt that was stupid of her because she knew that was its purpose. It was a common trick used by many men and women to achieve what they called a 'psychological effect.' It could never sway her in the least but the shoddiness always caused her a little mental nausea. But she was away ahead of Audrey and outwardly calm. "You want Peter for yourself. Is that it?"

Audrey started a denial, then checked herself. "That's it," she said arrogantly and lifted her glass to her sultry lips. Any serious contest with Lesley always made them dry. No use pretending here. No, the thing to do was make the most of it. The drink was good. "And Peter wants me," she continued. "Of course, he's in a blue funk and isn't sure what he wants. But I am."

"That's nice for Peter," said Lesley ironically.

"Very nice," agreed Audrey mockingly, "but not so nice for you. Peter needs a woman who's a woman, not a perennial virgin. So if you don't stop your little campaign, I'll stop it for you."

Lesley was silent for a moment. She knew that Audrey was capable of almost anything where her selfish interests were involved. But she must try to learn what the 'anything' might be in this particular instance. Audrey's desire to boast often loosened her tongue. Lesley feigned a concern which was partly real. "Just what will you do?" she asked.

"Tell George what you're doing, for one thing."

Lesley had expected that. "Then he wouldn't have to see it for himself, would he?" she asked innocently.

"No. And if that isn't enough, I'll tell Peter about you and George. That'll do the trick I think." There was a hard, triumphal note to all this.

Lesley was learning nothing which she had not anticipated from the moment Audrey declared herself. Probably there was nothing to learn. Audrey's craftiness might be unscrupulous but it was rather limited. And she had imagination, too. Very odd. But one need not be a genius of intrigue to spread havoc. Lesley returned to the fray. "And will you tell him about you and George, too?"

Audrey was rocked inwardly. "But there's nothing to tell," she said sweetly.

Lesley let it go at that. She had simply wanted to jolt Audrey a little and she had. She had no intention of fighting fire with fire. That might be all right in the forest. In the delicate business of living, it left permanent scars. She must test Audrey on one more point of which she was as sure as the others. "Wouldn't it be much more effective just to give Peter a demonstration?" she enquired.

"I'll take care of that, too," said Audrey defiantly.

"I rather imagined you would." Lesley's manner was close to meek. "Well, this has all been quite interesting and it's very good of you to warn me, I suppose, but I still don't know what it's all about."

"Oh, for God's sake stop it. We're the same sex, you know."

"Now and then I wonder," said Lesley tartly.

"So do I, in a way," retorted Audrey. "And I know Peter will never really fall for your lady-like frigidity. But you do seem to have a certain nuisance value for the moment. You're playing the old tricks in a new way. But if you're as smart as I think you are, you'll stop now. I'm in love with Peter, you see. I always have been. And I'm going to marry him."

"Really?" Lesley was deeply disturbed but carrying the whole thing off very well. "You seem to know a lot that I don't. And it's all pretty sordid, isn't it?" There was a definite tone now. "But I don't believe that you love Peter or that you ever have." She saw Audrey flinch slightly under this simple truth. "You've always treated him badly. And I'm glad you've put me through this mucky business. Now I'll be able to save him from whatever you're planning to do. And your childish threats won't stop me either."

Audrey laughed with less assurance. "You're stealing my thunder, darling," she said. "I'm doing the salvation work around here. Just remember that. It may save you a lot of grief." She set her glass down on the garden table and wandered off in search of her quarry.

Lesley dropped into a nearby chair and discovered she was trembling a little.

Audrey stepped onto the dock and hailed Peter and Henry.

As she joined them, Henry excused himself. He was anxious to find Lesley, tell her what he knew and peg her promise before any more damage could be done. He tried to appear casual as he hurried off. Peter and Audrey looked after him, then at one another. Peter, strongly aware of Audrey's sex appeal, wished that Henry had not left him there with her. Audrey, equally aware of her appeal and determined to use it, was elated.

"Thank God," she said, "alone at last."

"What do you mean?" protested Peter. "I'm here."

"Don't I know it," said Audrey emphatically. "What's wrong with that? Can't we be alone together? Isn't that possible?"

"Sounds impossibly intimate or highly insulting, to one of us."

"I'll admit it hasn't seemed possible tonight." Audrey forged ahead heedlessly. "I haven't even had a chance to tell you I think your playing was thrilling." She stepped very close to him.

Peter stepped back and almost toppled into the water. He regained his balance and some of his poise. "Now Audrey," he said guardedly, "you know enough about it to know that my efforts tonight were simply dithering."

"Not at all," said Audrey, pressing her advantage. She placed a hand on his arm. Her breasts were touching his body; her right knee, his legs. "A little nervous maybe but good. You've improved a lot and that's saying a lot." She straightened a little and most of her body was against him. "What do you plan now? Concerts here?"

"I don't know," said Peter uncomfortably. He edged away from her, moved to the corner pile and leaned against it. Whew. He surreptitiously removed a light film of perspiration from his forehead and upper lip. "What have you been doing all these years?" he enquired politely. "Have you been a good girl?"

"Certainly not," scoffed Audrey, crossing to him.

"That's good," said Peter and quickly held out his pack of cigarettes. To his intense relief, Audrey took one. He lighted it, held the light and took one himself. "How's your golf?" he asked.

"So-so. I play very little," she lied. Never tell the truth when a falsehood will serve just as well. And Peter must not get the idea she was all froth. "I've given up practically everything but hunting. I find that most sports addicts are otherwise damned dull fellows." That was true enough.

"But you still play bridge, I suppose?" He must try to keep this thing on what was known as a 'sane footing.'

"Not when I can help it," she replied with some feeling. Cigarette between her lips, she lifted her skirt and adjusted the seams of her stockings. As she leaned over, her breasts, tenderly full and smooth, and her midriff, modishly flat and smooth, were brought into full view. As she stood erect again, she glanced in the direction of Peter's thighs, then looked to see if his lips were parted. They were, she thought. "Women don't like me, you know," she continued. "And most of them play such bad bridge." She squinted, removed the cigarette from her moist lips. "You gave some recitals in Europe before the War, didn't you?" Not that she cared but she must find an approach.

"A few." Peter remembered his cigarette and took 'a long drag.' He looked on the straight physical urge he felt toward Audrey with some consternation. He felt no deep desire for any woman but Lesley, had not for some time, but there was no sense in trying to deny that Audrey excited him, obvious as she was. Perhaps it was the drinks. Or was it something out of the past? Did he like to be hurt? Hardly. Or had he been hurt so far beyond anything Audrey had ever done, or ever could do, that he just didn't give a damn for any conventions, inhibitions, restrictions? Did he consider them merely superficial? Did he wish to overcome old hurt, all hurt? Did he consider his dearest hope-beliefs birds of passage to be ignored when a well-cooked goose was on the table? He chuckled to himself, thought of Mr. Ed. This was all the rankest kind of tommyrot but it did serve to calm him.

"Well, at least you do play backgammon," he said. "I heard you were playing tonight." Reggie had volunteered this confession on the way to the cottages.

"I only did that to be nice to Reggie," said Audrey wheedlingly and moving closer to him once more. "I could listen to you at the same time. And Reggie needs the money, you know."

"I see." Peter was bitterly amused. Audrey believed in letting her left hand know what her right hand pretended to do. He knew Reggie. And he knew Audrey. "I take it Reggie isn't a sports addict," he said pointedly.

"You wouldn't have me be a nun, would you?" explained Audrey pointedly.

"Indeed not. And I shouldn't think the nuns would either."

She pouted coyly, then gave that up scornfully. Other methods were better. "What's a girl to do when you men are off playing pianos and fighting wars?"

"Be a girl, I suppose."

"If she can find any good material." What could she talk about? She had just mentioned the war and that was taboo, more or less. And while it was sure-fire interest, it might just make him moody. She was sure he felt a definite attraction. But she wanted to strengthen that with something close to his heart. "George tells me you've done some more composing. I think that's exciting. What sort is it?"

"No sort, really. As yet, anyway." What did George mean by spreading a story like that? Or had he? He could easily believe that he would but Audrey might have just invented it. "Tell me, Audrey, how are you on the gay night round in town? Of course you must be terrific."

"Cafe society's nothing but an alcoholic joke in bad taste. I like a little tradition with my fun."

Peter smiled to himself. No one liked night life any more than Audrey. He had grown to like it himself when he was feeling low, which was most of the time. Of course there was no way for Audrey to know that. She evidently had reached the conclusion that, because of the war and his work, he must be on the heavy or stuffy side. Well, let her think so. "You've changed, Audrey, grown very serious," he said with a twinkle.

"I've just grown up, that's all. Some people never do. They're afraid to probably, afraid life would be very dull. If they only knew what a rich and interesting experience life can really be." Peter did not seem to be too impressed. "And you're being very difficult, Peter, and you know it." She had to laugh at her own expense. "How is a woman to listen adoringly to a man if he refuses to talk about himself?"

Peter laughed, too. "You know you're not the least bit interested in my work or my plans for my aesthetic problems, if any."

"Oh but I am," she objected. "But since you won't talk about them, I'll tell you I'm even more interested in having you interested in me."

"Now we're getting somewhere," he said. "And you know I am, so everything's all right." He turned and looked off to sea, a faint smile on his lips.

"But it isn't all right." She took his arm and again brought her body close to him. "You know what I mean. I think you're just as lonely as I am." She was being a little dramatic but effective. "At least, you're not happy. And I'd like to do something about it if you'll let me."

Peter decided she was a good actress. "That's very sweet of you, Audrey," he said unctuously. "But I seem to vaguely recall going through a lot of hell with you in the past."

Audrey made an effort and stayed in character. "I'd like

to make up for that," she said simply. "It was only because I was jealous, wanted you all to myself. You'll think that was a strange way to show it but that was it. I know it was stupid and childish but you must remember that I *was* a child." Had she ever been a child? "But I'm a woman now, Peter, much softer and—oh, that sounds awful but I have to make you understand." She hugged his arm hard and wriggled as though with impatience.

Peter felt he was in some sort of pleasant half-straight-jacket. He looked down at her over his left shoulder. "I think I do understand, in one way," he assured her. "But in another, I don't get it at all."

"But there's no mystery about it," she insisted, turning him, making him face her. She put her hands on his sides. In looking up at him, she bent back so that the lower part of her body was pressed against his legs. He was backed against the pile. There was no escape. "It's just that I want you, Peter, and I always have," she went on with assumed intensity. "There's something about you that's enough to drive any normal woman mad. And I'm pretty normal when it comes to that."

"I can believe the last statement, not the rest." Peter was getting very warm. "I'd like to but I haven't got it. I know what physical appeal is. It's what you've got too much of. In fact, you're one of the most luscious bits of femininity I've ever seen or ever hope to see."

"Peter, if you mean that, that's marvelous." She hugged him impulsively. "And let me be the judge of what you do to me. I don't know how much love means to you, darling, but if it means as much as it does to me, I think you'll find I've got a lot to give to it." She moved her hips slowly as she spoke.

"Gently now, Audrey," Peter admonished her. "You're much too fast for me." He shot his cigarette into the water. Audrey's followed as she clung to him with her left hand.

They made red arcs against the night before they spot out. Peter made a tentative effort to change his position. Useless. He was trapped.

Audrey tried to sound properly wistful, earnest. "Do you love me, Peter? Or are you fond of me, at least?"

"Why, uh—of course. You know I am." What else could he say?

"Darling!" She hugged him again. "And I'm mad about you. I really am. If you have any doubts, you won't for long." She must clinch things somehow, and quickly. "But we can't really talk here with all this mob milling around. Are you very tired after your trip?"

"No," said Peter doubtfully.

"Then why not come over tonight after everyone's gone to bed?" Audrey was doing her best job of selling. She played the dependable, confident, quietly exuberant conspirator of a situation rampant with fleshly desire. "We can be cozy and have a drink. And maybe I can help you to forget all that's troubling you. In fact, I'm almost sure I can."

"I'm sure you can, too," said Peter with complete conviction. "But it can't be." He took her shoulders and made her stand back a step. "It's all very tempting, mind you," he continued, "too damned tempting. I've got a very clear picture of what I'll be missing. But, you see, well, there's someone else, Audrey. And it wouldn't be fair. It wouldn't be fair to her or to you, or even to me, for that matter. Now would it?"

Audrey was taken aback. She had expected something of the sort but not at this juncture.

"Why not?" She parried petulantly. "She isn't making you happy. That's obvious."

"She hasn't had a chance," explained Peter as lightly as he could. "But she will—if she wants to. I know that."

"Then it must have just happened." Lesley had made even greater headway than she thought or would have believed possible in so short a time. How the hell had she managed it? "It isn't Lesley, is it?"

Peter replied coolly. "It can't be talked about, Audrey. That's all I can say."

"You sound like George," said Audrey with a harsh laugh. "Then it is Lesley." She laughed again. The sneaky, sanctimonious, two-timing bitch. "Good Lord, Peter, that's crazy. And anyway, she's already taken. Of course, you couldn't know that, I suppose, and you'll never guess who it is."

It was coming. The abysmal ugliness he had no wish to hear, was determined not to hear or believe. "I don't want to guess who it is and I'm not interested," he said angrily.

"Oh, yes you are," she crowed. "You've no idea how interested you are. You couldn't be more so." The great green eyes were flashing, the pouting mouth close to a sneer. She was out to hurt now. "And he's right here with us tonight. The dean of lovers, or maybe I should say the last of the clunk lovers. Be prepared for a shock, ducky!"

There was but one way to silence her. Peter grabbed her and forced his mouth down against hers. That took care of it. Audrey did everything but wrap her legs around him by way of response. Her hands were everywhere and finally clutched the back of his jacket. Peter held it as long as he could, then broke it.

"Now will you shut up?" he whispered.

"Oh, yes," breathed Audrey.

"Then let's get back before there's a lot of talk at both ends of the line. I hate talk. It's so superfluous." He shook his clothes back into normal drape. His lips were oily. He purloined a tissue from her evening bag and wiped them clean.

Audrey retouched her makeup rapidly. She was inordinately pleased with herself. This had been her greatest victory. "Oh, Peter darling, you're marvelous, *marvelous,*" she said with a groaning sort of drawling throatiness. "And so *strong*—and so *big*. Mmm!"

"Let's go," said Peter. He often caught himself using such expressions as this when upset, GI phrases which he disliked intensely. He must get himself in hand.

They started up the hill.

"And you will be over, won't you?" It was more a statement than a question.

"We'll see," said Peter shortly.

Audrey was in seventh heaven. She had said enough. Peter had guessed the rest. Of that she was sure and also sure that he was her prize. What a night it was going to be after all. George and Lesley would just have to suffer the consequences. They had no one to blame but themselves. They had been fools to try to defeat her intentions. They deserved what they got. She had to trot to keep up with Peter.

Peter was deeply distressed, writhing inwardly, fighting his thoughts. George again. Everything pointed to George. Lesley's reason for leaving, Henry's warning and request for silence, Audrey's description, eliminating any other possibility, all these bespoke George and George alone. And yet it could not be. It simply could not be. The whole idea was too repugnant to be borne. But why should it be? He had never analyzed his feelings toward George very carefully. He only knew that he was often restless and unhappy around him. And there were obvious reasons for that. Did he hate the man? Surely not. Then why this feeling of revulsion?

He had seen the depths of degradation and lived through it all. And what was degrading in this? Was he jealous? Possibly. Probably. Certainly he was jealous for Lesley. He had enshrined her in his heart and in the world in which he wished to believe. He and all men should kneel before her in spirit and in gratitude. It was sacrilege for an arrogant old man who had smothered his own soul to aspire to the love of such a divine personality. But that could be whimsical nonsense. He aspired to her love himself and he had no soul at all. He laughed shortly, bitterly. Then he forced himself to pull out of such hurtful thinking. He had no proof of all this. And even if it were true, it was none of Lesley's doing. Her attitude made that clear, that and all that he knew so intimately of her character. It need not be an unbroken rule of attachments that a woman must encourage a man. If George fancied himself in love, it could be the natural result of proximity. No man could be near Lesley very long without conceiving a great fondness for her. He thought of his mother. She must have been something like Lesley. George had often spoken of her with a sort of awe-struck reverence and a deep regard for her memory. Peter had gradually come to assume that George had been secretly in love with her and could never care greatly for any other woman. He was sure he was right in this. Also that George's attitude toward him and his life and his work was based largely on that secret love. This relationship between George and Lesley, if there was any 'relationship,' could be a very fine and sympathetic one. The mad idea that others had put in his head would be simply how it seemed to an outsider. He silently apologized to them both. His spirit lifted and happiness returned to his heart. And surely he was not just talking himself out of a self-evident fact too darkly unpleasant, too wildly savage, to carry for even a moment. Why look beyond that which was all? He loved Lesley. And he had every reason to believe that Lesley loved him in return. That was everything. He gave Audrey a whack on the fanny.

Henry found Lesley on the terrace and got her aside.

"I have news for you," he began.

"Oh, Hank, it's so good to talk to you. I'm terribly worried."

"What's wrong?"

She gave him the substance of what Audrey had said.

"Drastic steps should be taken with Audrey," he said grimly.

"I'm in love with Peter, Hank. I always have been. You knew, of course."

"I had an idea."

"If he should marry Audrey, I honestly believe she'd just make him unhappy. She always has. That mustn't happen to him now. What am I to do, Hank?" she asked desperately.

"Take it easy, Lesley. Peter won't marry her. He's in love with you."

"What?" Could she trust her ears? She must hear it again.

"He just told me. That's what I wanted to talk about."

"Oh, but are you sure?" she asked feverishly. If Peter had said it, then she could be sure of what she had already known and scarcely dared believe.

"Quite sure," said Henry. "Of course, he isn't sure of you. But I can see now that he soon will be. And, as I told him, I'm very happy about it. It's what I've always hoped for."

"Is it? You're a darling." She kissed him enthusiastically. "But I still can't believe it," she added hungrily. "What did he say? What did he say?"

Henry smiled. "Oh, a great deal," he assured her, "a great deal that bases all his hope on what he hopes is true between you. But he'll tell you himself."

"I wish he'd hurry," she said plaintively.

"And something you said has given him the idea that there might be someone else."

"Something I said?" Lesley frowned. "Oh, that must have been about having to get back to town. That was because of the George business."

"That's what I was afraid of. You must be more careful of what you say, Lesley. Peter wasn't very happy about it."

"Do you think he was jealous?" she cried, pleased in spite of herself.

"I don't doubt it," said Henry dryly. "And about George—this is the last thing he must learn. Without telling him why, I got Peter's promise to keep it secret. If George learns about it gradually, in the course of a year, say, he may be able to adjust himself to the idea and, in the end, be quite happy about it."

Lesley was stunned. "Oh, but a year, darling! A year's forever. And what about Audrey? She might get him, you know. I think maybe she could. I made a great show of being brave with her but I was bluffing horribly. And what if she tells George?"

"We'll try to see that she can't before we leave," he said soothingly. "I don't think he'd believe her anyway." But Henry was by no means certain of this. He talked now to reassure himself. "And the suggestion might serve us well later. And you know Peter won't believe her if she says anything about you and George."

"Oh, I hope not," she said fervently.

"I suppose you couldn't explain to Peter?" suggested Henry almost timidly.

"Good Lord, no," exclaimed Lesley. "Peter must never know. He'd be miserable about it. And he'd never get over it. And this year business, I can't risk driving him away from me. I might drive him straight to Audrey or some other woman."

"You can be together all the time in town," he said placatingly. "It'll be easy there. You could even be married secretly if you like."

"I don't like. I want a big church wedding, a tremendous do. I'll only be married once."

"Well—well—a month or two may be all the time we require. I'm sorry you have to face all this mess just when everything should be perfect. But there's a life at stake. We know the shock would finish George and we have to think of things like that. But then, too, we know it'll all come right, don't we? It has to."

Lesley's spirits rose. "Yes, yes, if we stick to the right, no matter what, it's got to be," she said gaily. "It's always stood by us, hasn't it? Oh, Hank, I'm so happy, so happy. I hope you're as happy about Zara Moore. If happiness like this comes to anyone, it should come to you."

"Should it?" he asked musingly. "No," he answered his own question. "You're the one. I'm all theory. You put the theories into practice, prove them. Maybe I'm afraid to. Or maybe I'm too busy telling others what to do to do it myself. But I get my happiness from that if it does any good."

She kissed him again. He was such a dear. "That's all love, too," she said feelingly. "You always sacrifice yourself for others. I do wish you wouldn't quite so much."

Here was his chance. "That's my profession," he reminded her. "But it's not yours. It's more than enough to save George from himself by hiding your great happiness for a little while. In the matter of his obsession about you, you must do only that which can't hurt you in any way whatsoever."

"If he broaches the subject, I'll do as you asked—let him down gently."

"That may not be easy."

"There are always nice but definite ways for a girl to let a man know where he stands, even a man like George. The solemn and touching 'I'm terribly flattered and I'll always be fond of you, you're like a father or brother, but it can never be more than that and I do hope we'll be great friends' routine, for example." Lesley laughed lightly.

Henry was serious. He knew George. "Promise me you'll do no more than that, no matter what sort of act *he* puts on."

Lesley became serious, too. "If anything happens, whatever I do will have to ge governed by circumstance and I'll know I'm being guided in the right. That's our way, isn't it?"

"But in this particular case—"

She patted his arm. "Don't worry about it, darling."

But he was worried.

XII

THEY WERE ALL BACK IN THE LIVING ROOM.

The inevitable badinage, or polite insult, were the order of the moment. There was a growing feeling of restlessness in the air.

"Let's do something exciting," said Audrey suddenly. "What can we do that's exciting?"

George was seated in his favorite armchair. Audrey half-sat on the arm of the other. He looked at her with something very like hatred in his eyes.

"I think this is exciting enough," he said.

"Let's go over to the Casino," suggested Audrey, nothing daunted.

"You do get the damndest ideas, Audrey."

"But I think it's a wonderful idea," interjected Peter. "I'd love to do a bright spot. Is it a lot of fun?"

"Fun? It's noisy," grumbled George.

Audrey was determined. "Then let's go over to the Club or somewhere else where we can dance. It's such a beautiful night and I'd love to give Peter a party."

"Can't you dance here?" asked George irritably.

Peter interposed again. "Stars and an orchestra do make a difference, George." He was standing near the fireplace with Reggie and Lesley. He turned to her. "What do you say, Lesley? Wouldn't you like that?"

"Very much," said Lesley, then addressed herself to

George. "Don't you think you and Hank would really enjoy it, too, once you got there?"

George sulked. "I'd enjoy staying here much more," he said.

"George and I are conservative," supplied Henry from the depths of the divan. "He, because he has to be, and I, because it's my nature."

George was getting very angry but trying to hide his feelings. Nothing was going as he would wish. With the possible exception of Lesley, they were all against him. "Why not have some bridge?" he suggested desperately with an effort to be off-hand.

"Bridge?" hooted Audrey. "What have you against us all?"

He ignored her, spoke to Peter. "In any case it's getting late and I should think you need your rest, Peter."

"But I want to play for awhile, George. I want to play hard. And not the piano. I need it."

"Then I can't induce you to stay here?"

"You're really the one who should get to bed, George. I've been very thoughtless, I'm afraid."

"I'm not an invalid, Peter," said George sharply, "and I had rather expected to go to bed late tonight."

"Then why not come with us?" asked Audrey maliciously.

Henry was quick to speak up again. "He hates to admit it, Audrey, but he does have to be a little careful."

Reggie sympathized with Henry and was also with him in that, he too, liked his storm clouds only in the sky. "Then suppose the youth contingent gets the hell out," he said and moved toward the garden door.

"Right," said Peter. He walked to Reggie's side. "Come on, Lesley." Then, as she joined him, "Good-night, in case you're asleep before we get back."

Lesley turned to George and Henry. "We may not be long. Why not wait for us?"

"Maybe we will," said Henry.

"Good," said Peter.

He and Lesley walked out into the garden. When they reached the drive, Peter turned, looked back at the house and then at Lesley.

"Let's duck," he whispered.

"All right," agreed Lesley excitedly.

He took her hand and they ran lightly down the black, hard gravel path, which wound through the old orchard on the lee side of the hill, until they had dropped out of sight of the house. The path led them to Runsheep Run, the stream which flowed through the valley. Here they stopped to rest, laughing and panting.

Audrey lingered to tease George some more. She was angered by Peter's seeming preference for Lesley but she was also pleased because she knew the effect it would have on George. "It's a shame you won't come, George." She smiled smugly, spoke with mock courtesy. "You do enough strenuous things at other times."

George managed to speak. "That may be why I feel this sudden restraint."

"Please don't be too strenuous about that. Young ideas make you attractive." She was delighted to see George getting purple. "I had a lovely time and I hope you'll still be up when we get back."

Henry intervened once more. "We'll have a little chinfest," he said. "Look for us here."

"Right," said Reggie and dragged Audrey from the room.

George got up, started for the garden door and stopped at the liquor cabinet. He gulped a straight drink, then mixed a very strong highball. He felt Henry's disapproving look.

"I can't think of anything better at the moment," he snapped. "Will you have one?"

"No thanks," replied Henry quietly. He forced a yawn.

"As a matter of fact, if you don't mind, I think I'll hie me up to my room soon."

"I mind, of course. But you mustn't mind that. And please be good enough to stop that damned yawning." George walked back, shoved himself down into the armchair, lighted a cigarette, inhaled deeply several times and drew on his highball.

Henry punched pillows into a corner of the divan, stretched out, locked his hands behind his head and lay back against the pillows in an effort to relax. He was nervous. He disliked all this tension and hoped there would soon be an end to it. "I seem to be losing some of the old magic lately," he said.

"I suppose you mean about burning the candle." George was scornful. "I think it was damned selfish of them all to run off like that."

"Henry sighed inwardly. Now he would have to calm the old coot. He wondered just how much George knew or suspected. He was almost certain he had noticed nothing during dinner. But while Lesley, Peter and Reggie were at the cottages, he had behaved very strangely. Henry had hoped that was merely pique over fancied neglect just as he thought his present mood was. He devoutly hoped that was all it was. "All that energy must have some outlet. You know that," he said as though by way of apology for the younger element. If George did have any suspicions, he must get them out of his mind.

"Of course. 'Youth must be served, Youth must have its fling.' Don't you think there's been enough talk about youth around here tonight?" George's whole attitude was one of sarcasm and anger.

"I'm sorry, George. But you can't expect them to have settled ideas at that age."

"Don't forget the rubbish about wild oats. That's all you've missed. You may be getting old ahead of your time, Henry, but I'm not."

"I am not getting old. I didn't intend to suggest that for a minute."

"Then don't suggest that I am. Normally, I feel more than equal to anything they might want to do."

"So do I if it comes to that."

"Then why didn't you go with them?"

"Because, although I'm not getting old, I'm old enough to know what I like."

"And why do you like what you like? Because you're getting old. Isn't that it?"

"It certainly is not it." Henry sat up. This was good. It was distraction, argument apart from the chief concern. "But there's not much romance for me in a merry-go-round. I'm a little past that, I think."

They heard Audrey calling Peter's name. George squirmed in his chair.

"But you think there is romance for them and that we'd just be in the way?"

"I think they're young enough to think they find romance in champagne and popular music."

"And why not? We do, too. But that isn't the kind of romance I had in mind."

"It's the kind they like, I'm sure. They're still susceptible to brass and tinsel hypnotism. So were we at that age."

"Were we? Funny I don't remember that."

"A year makes a great change in the point of view. Thirty years make a change thirty times as great."

"Why don't you just bury me and get it over with?"

"I'd rather wait another thirty years, at least."

"Always the doctor no matter how painful." George halted the rapid interchange with this poor mimicry. He worked moodily on his drink for a moment, then gave voice to his thoughts. "I wish I knew just what's happened to Peter. He's changed. Not just in the ways you'd expect. He's a different person entirely and I don't like it. He's acting like a spoiled child. I suppose, except for the Army, he's been on his own too long. No one to keep him in line. But I thought I could trust him."

The sound of a heavy car door slamming, followed by the diminishing roar of a motor, cut through the silence of the night.

"What's the matter with young people today?" barked George to drive the noise from his consciousness. "No integrity, no honor, no anything. Peter's been given every chance to be good and he's fallen down on the job. And that's not all. He's proud of it. Talks a lot of rot about the War and what it's done to him. You don't hear the other boys talking that way. The truth of it is he's been dishonest. He didn't work before the War and he hasn't worked since. Now he wants to cover up his failure with the best excuse he can think of. Others might be impressed by it. I'm not. He knows that. So he acts as though he resented me and everything I've done for him. I tried to talk to him and he looked as though he pitied me. He wants to slide out from under. But he's not going to. He's not going to let his mother down after all these years. Not if I can help it. It means too much."

"It means just as much to him," said Henry quietly but firmly. "He'd give his life to be good. And he will be. But that may take time. And you've got to try to be a lot more understanding, George."

"How you do love to harp on understanding."

"It's rather necessary in dealing with an artist. There isn't one of them who hasn't gone beyond his work in a search for truth. Peter wants to know the meaning of things and the only answer he's got so far has made him unhappy. That's held him back. But it's got to be gone through. And out of it all, the artist will develop. In the meantime, he needs gentle handling and help."

"I don't think he is an artist," said George shortly. "But he's going to be, and quickly, or I'll know the reason why."

What Peter needed was discipline, not wishy-washy understanding, and he was going to see that he got plenty of it—the kind of discipline that made a man keep driving on regardless of how he happened to feel.

"You'll only hurt him and hurt what you want by trying to force things," warned Henry. "I should think the homing instinct that made him so anxious to get here would make you want to give him a hand."

George grunted, looked at Henry steadily for a moment. "There may have been another reason for that, something we haven't mentioned," he said significantly.

Henry was mildly startled. Again he wondered just how much George knew or suspected. "What's that?" he asked as casually as he could.

"Never mind." George was rather abrupt. "The whole picture is wrong, Hank, and it's got to be put right. I might have known something like this was going to happen."

"Why?"

"The 'why' will amuse you. A dream. Go on, laugh. I dream a lot without remembering. But a short time ago, I had a dream I've been remembering very clearly. I dreamt I was asleep and was wakened suddenly by the phone or something. I jumped up and started across the room. But after I'd taken a couple of steps, my legs gave way and I fell. I managed to get up but then I fell again. I got on my feet a number of times but each time I'd crash to the floor or against some piece of furniture. I knew I was wrecking myself but I couldn't feel anything. Still I could think of the pain that would come later and I was afraid I'd probably be disfigured or crippled for life. I couldn't reach the wall button and I couldn't call out for help—you never can in a dream. In the end, I couldn't move at all. I just lay there on the floor in a sweat of fear like the death panic. It was all damned ugly and terrible and it's still very vivid as I think of it." George laughed flatly.

"I fail to see where that's very amusing, George."

"Oh? Why not?"

"You must know. An attack such as you describe could easily be the first stage of the illness we discussed this afternoon."

"Then I was right!" There was a hint of madness in George's eyes. "I didn't know that and I'd have no way of knowing it. So you'll see why I knew something wrong was in the offing."

"My God, George," exclaimed Henry, "you're not going to add superstition to everything else are you? That dream was nothing but telepathy, a clear indication of the closeness of our relationship through the years and the depth of the concern I've felt for you lately. All very interesting, I grant you, but it means absolutely nothing."

"Of course a psychologist would know," said George skeptically.

"Don't call me a psychologist. My colleagues refuse to."

"Yes, I know. The brilliant heretic."

"Heretics are rarely brilliant. They're just thoughtful and sincere."

"And they're usually wrong. Don't forget that."

They were interrupted by Reggie's entrance. He came into the room from the garden, went to the cabinet bar, poured a triple Scotch into one of the tall Continental highball glasses, added ice and a little soda, turned, and beamed on them.

"Hello," he said. "Still up?"

"That's all in the point of view," replied Henry. "You didn't stay long."

"We didn't go."

George was all attention. "Really? Why was that?" he asked.

"Lesley and Peter disappeared. I entertained Audrey magnificently for thirty seconds or so but she seemed preoccupied and finally drove off in a fury." Reggie sipped his drink lovingly.

The lines around George's mouth hardened. He threw the cigarette he had forgotten into the fireplace, set his drink down on the end table and gripped the arms of his chair. "Where are Lesley and Peter now?" he asked in a choked voice.

"Climbing moonbeams for all I know," said Reggie cheerfully. "Well, I'm off." He crossed the room to the hall door. "Life in the country is too much for me."

Henry laughed a little distractedly. He had been keenly aware of George's reaction. An explosion was imminent. "It is if you drink yourself into a stupor," he said brightly.

"I don't have to drink to achieve that state, Doctor," Reggie informed him. "Good-night."

"Good-night, Reggie." Henry was resigned. There was no holding Reggie, no way to stop George. But his mind was working at high speed. He must be prepared for any eventuality.

Reggie went into the hall and on up to his room. George could scarcely wait for him to get out of earshot.

"Well?!" he roared in release of pent rage.

"Well what?" Henry set himself for the blow.

"Maybe you'll try to explain that away? I was right, you see. I knew." George leaped to his feet unmindful of a twinge in his heart and a cleanly sharp pressure behind his eyes. As he ranted and raved under the best cover of formidable strength he could assume and the liquor began to work, these pains disappeared, warning lights which passed unheeded.

Henry used words. "What are you talking about?" he shouted.

"What do you think?" George snatched up his drink. There was crazed force grinning through the pretended power. "That's what I meant, what we hadn't mentioned. And Audrey was telling the truth after all." He walked jerkily about the room interrupting himself only at intervals to gulp some of the drink. "She told me about Peter and Lesley. She wants Peter herself and isn't getting anywhere so she blames Lesley. But it isn't Lesley. It's Peter. My God, I'd never have believed it. My own son, to do a thing like that. I wish I could get my hands on him right now. It wasn't enough to cheat on everything I've done for him and then laugh it off. Now he has to go after the woman I love. But, by God, he'll be sorry." He brought his fist smashing down against an arm of the divan.

Henry jumped. He had been partially absorbed in his rapid speculation. And though he had tried to be ready for it, to learn so abruptly that George knew the one thing he wished him not to know had shaken him nevertheless. Audrey had been cunning enough to make good her threat before she made the threat. There was double-edged cruelty in that bit of treachery. Audrey worked on the emotions of her victims so that no matter what developed, there were bound to be doubts, misgivings, distrust. Too bad he had left her alone with Peter. She had probably said things to him as well. But while Peter might be profoundly disturbed, he would not be easily swayed. George was another matter. He would have to do the best he could with him. "George, George, this is all nonsense. Get yourself in hand," he pleaded.

"Do you want me to take it lying down?"

"That's the way you'll have to take it if you don't calm yourself, try to see things sanely and clearly. How do you know Peter's going after Lesley? And even if he were, does he know how you say you feel about her? Have you told him? You haven't even told Lesley, have you?"

"I haven't had a chance. But she knows. She must. And Peter knows, too. You can be sure of that. He couldn't miss it. But that doesn't stop him. He doesn't care. He doesn't care about anyone but himself now. He wants to 'play.' He 'needs it.' So he plays with Lesley, a fine girl like that. You've seen a lot of rotten things. Did you ever know of anything as cheap and low as that?"

"You're not even making sense. It's absurd to assume that they know how you feel. And I don't like your insinuations. If I didn't know that you're not yourself, I'd resent them more than I do." Henry saw that this reigned George up a bit. All his protestations to the contrary notwithstanding, George still respected the old-fashioned standards of chivalry. "Just because you're hurt, annoyed with Peter, yes, and with Lesley, too, you're ready to believe any impossible slander, ready to make a mountain out of nothing at all. You never believed Audrey before. Why believe her now?"

Somewhat abashed, George looked down, kicked at the carpet. "I'm not a fool, Hank. I watched them. I saw it myself," he numbled stubbornly.

"Saw what?" Henry was still trying to think as he talked. This new development not only made the general problem almost hopelessly complex but at the same time demanded its quick solution. The endless ramifications held deadly harm for all concerned. The expedient thing seemed to be to delay, to prevent, all action. Any action at the moment, would be wrong. "All attractive young people feel a certain spark when they're together. That's only natural. And it's nothing to get in a rage about. It's charming."

"Charming?" exploded George.

"Yes, charming." Perhaps he should have put that differently. Too late now. "There's certainly nothing ugly about it. Unless you've got that kind of mind."

"Thank you, Hank. You're a great help." George was not to be stopped twice in the same way. "There's nothing ugly in what Peter's doing. He's only hurting me and Lesley. That's all. How many times have you said the ugliest thing any man can do is to deliberately hurt someone else?"

George was not being clever. He lacked the facility. He carried the argument to an opponent at the first opportunity simply because he could not bear being on the defensive. Henry knew he would have to use some other means to pacify him. Fortunately, there were any number of ways to some degree effective. The thing was to select the most effective in time. "But Peter doesn't want to hurt you. Can't you realize that? He wouldn't want to hurt anyone. Neither would Lesley."

"You're talking like a child," scoffed George. "Why did they do it? Why did they leave us here? Why did they run away from Audrey and Reggie?" He gave Henry no chance to answer. "Go ahead. Hand out the routine banalities, the placating folderol. Ask me, wide-eyed, why they shouldn't want to have a little time together. Tell me they're two old friends. Tell me how they've always been close, how they're bound to have a lot to talk about, how that's only natural. Everything's 'only natural' to you. You don't have to disappear into the night with an old friend. And we're all old friends. Where do the rest of us fit in?"

He rushed on again without waiting for a reply. "Now patronize me a little, explain simply and tolerantly that they've always been more intimate with one another than they have with the rest of us and I should realize that, that you'll bet they've been dying for a chance to be together for the last five hours—and why not? Why not indeed? No, Hank, I know what you're trying to do but you're wasting your time. I'm not afraid of the truth. I want it, welcome it. That's the only way to deal with a thing like this. Now give me a sample of your sarcasm," he continued without taking breath, "throw jibes, say that I'm quite right, that people are ugly, life's ugly, so's the world, and it was all made that way just to make things tough for me but that I can handle it. Then enquire why I don't grow up for God's sake? If I did, maybe I could be insulting and stupid, too, then. At least, I've got the guts to face things. I don't shut my eyes and try to make pretty pictures."

"No, I'll give you that," said Henry, at last allowed to speak. "The pictures you're trying to make of Lesley and Peter certainly aren't pretty. Why they waste their affection on you, I can't see."

George could never anticipate Henry. Just when he was sure he was going great guns, Henry would always introduce a new thought or a variant to give him pause, ever a mortifying experience. "I don't blame Lesley," he said sullenly. "She'd never want anything like this to happen. It's all Peter's doing."

"All what? He couldn't do very much without cooperation, could he?"

"Very funny, Hank." George was offended by this insinuation that he was short on sophistication. "What about this spark you speak of between young people? If Lesley should happen to feel it, Peter would make use of that, you can be sure." Not a very strong rebuttal. Damn that smirk of Henry's.

"Oh, George, you're simply jealous, a bad case of hurt pride. And that makes you more than a little ridiculous, I'm afraid," Henry summed up cuttingly.

"I see," said George with assumed indifferent superiority and a flushed face. "You seem to be quite happy about the whole business, quite different from your reaction to my suit." He wanted to shock Henry, to say something to hurt him. "If you weren't so damned generous with Lesley where others are concerned, I'd be inclined to think there was something Freudian in your strong opposition to me." He stood watching his old friend, whom he did not entirely trust in this matter, to see if the barb found its mark.

Fury rose instantly to Henry's throat but was as quickly choked back. Habit. He would have been justified in cutting George down for this clumsily overplayed insult and he could have done so easily. Instead, he pondered the possibility of bias affecting his judgment.

Blocked by convention and inhibition from having Lesley himself, was he determined that she should go only to the one most eligible and possessing the greatest number of his own qualities? Hardly. Henry had no faith in the cant of the psychoanalyst. He did not believe, for example, that at some point in their lives all men suffered the Oedipus complex, perhaps without cognizance but also without exception. He had loved his parents dearly in the little he had seen of them. And he had been well aware that apart from a few isolated instances of injection, copulation was essential to conception, his own included. But he had never been able to associate the idea of sex with his mother or father. And he had learned that he was not an oddity in this. George and other of his intimate friends had been guilty of the same absurdity.

Nor, to return to the moment, did he believe that particular fondness for any other member of the family was consciously or unconsciously based on physical desire. Again, for him and for others, these relationships remained sexless. It was rather sickening stuff to contemplate but he was eminently fair. The contentions of the dogmatic were always worthy of open consideration. They were mental soporifics but they still might secrete enough truth, as well as venom, to have some bearing on a particular case. Not here however. Lesley was all of heaven and earth but she was also family. She occupied no other place in his thought or affections. When he appraised her as strictly a woman, as he had earlier in the evening, it was at once apparent that she was completely desirable. But he had to force himself to do this the better to understand complications such as those which had developed. Henry was both right and wrong in all this. Like all artists, he was capable of egregious blunders. They sprang from his simple humanity and natural humility, the very qualities which gave him stature that far outstripped his fellows. The error at issue was not important except in that it was preposterously human. But if Lesley had not been his niece-daughter and had not been so young, she would have been his wife. Of this, he was happily unaware. Only Lesley knew in the silent depths of her womanly wisdom without ever giving it thought. While quite unburdened with convictions, Henry believed beyond the shadow of doubt in everything of significance which he thought, said or did at the time he thought, said or did it. To this extent, then, was he absolutely right and to this extent must he ever remain so.

He looked on George coldly for awhile, then the doctor softened his attitude. "Perhaps the ridiculous is your stock in trade, George," he murmured.

George was livid, ashamed and defeated. "And I suppose my dream was ridiculous, too?" he bellowed. "I know what I know, Hank, and I don't need your help. I've had warnings like that before and there was always a reason. That's why I can't be fooled by this, any of it."

"That's pretty feminine reasoning for a man," said Henry chidingly, "especially a strong man."

"Is it?" George resorted to mulishness once more. "You can't kid me out of it, Hank. I've told you you're wasting your time."

Henry spoke with professional earnestness, "George, if that's so, if there's nothing I can do, then you'd better do something yourself, you'd better kid yourself out of it, and quickly, too."

George was interested. "Why so?" he asked.

"Because it's nothing but hysteria, part of all the hysteria you've banked up inside yourself somewhere. And if you don't throw it out right now before something happens, if you let it get you, then your dream will come true in a hurry and in a way you won't like."

George knew this. He jerked erect. His pulse fluttered. But he remained adamant. His one age-old fear had been supplanted for the time by another even more terrible. Or perhaps it would be more correct to say that the one had been greatly augmented by the other. The new was so closely related to the old that they could be the same. His synthetic confidence, based on his will, had been shattered. He was furiously determined not to waver in his purpose. But his heart, with that insistent voice which is never to be denied, told him that he was going to lose, told him that he was going to lose Lesley to Peter before he ever had her. He was afraid of Peter, he was afraid of youth, and he was afraid of the future. But he was no longer afraid of himself or for himself. At least, not enough to be cowed into giving up. There could be no giving up. He knew now more than ever that he must win. If he lost, he was lost, he was not, he had never been. His outraged ego inflamed his heart, consumed its voice. He could not lose. "If I have to live in a fool's Paradise to survive, I'm not interested," he said with only the faintest trace of a quaver.

Again was Henry moved to admire this courage which could face a fear that recognized almost certain death. "You prefer to live in a fool's hell. Is that it?"

George dropped into his armchair. "Oh, go to bed, Hank," he said flatly.

"Right." Henry got to his feet. He yawned, stretched, let his arms drop and stamped to shake himself down again. Rather convincing, he thought. Might have some suggestion potency. "Bed is just where I'm going. You, too, if you have any sense left."

"Then I haven't," said George shortly. "Good-night, Henry."

Henry feigned incredulity. "You're not going to make the mistake of waiting up for them?" he expostulated. "That'd be too embarrasing for all of us."

"I'm not going to 'wait up for them' as you put it with such holy horror," replied George exasperatedly, "neither am I going to bed just yet."

"George," Henry continued with this old attack which usually won and never failed entirely, "don't do something you'll regret and never be able to explain. If they come back and find you here, they'll think it's damned odd. Peter will really begin to pity you if you start doing things like that."

"I know you're anxious to get your rest, Henry. Don't let me detain you." Irritation dulled the edge of simulated boredom.

Henry was getting results. When George began to call him 'Henry' and use a taunting tone, he was trying to conceal, even from himself, the fact that he was impressed. Henry carried on in the same vein. "Then you're determined to make an ass of yourself? I can't understand you. I should think you'd at least want to keep Lesley's respect if not Peter's."

George believed that he could ill afford at any time to appear ridiculous to even an infinitesimal extent. Ridicule was a fatal weapon and one against which there was no defense. He had seen world leaders and key politicians fall before it never to rise. The idea that his conduct might make him appear quite ridiculous before Lesley, of all people, was untenable. He spoke harshly. "Hank, I'm a little fed up with all this. And I'd like to be able to feel at home in my own home. So, if *you* don't mind, I'm going to have another drink and do a little quiet thinking."

"There's nothing quiet about your thinking."

"Is it violent as well as vile?" asked George with solicitous sarcasm. "I'll see what can be done about it."

"Then change your mind and do what I ask."

"No."

"I give up," said Henry exhaustedly. He walked toward the hall door. "I don't think I'm lacking in stamina but I give up."

"You're getting old, that's all," jibed George.

Henry stopped in the doorway and turned. "Yes, thank God," he agreed. "At least I'm old enough to know the value of intelligent self-government."

"Oh, I don't think you're that old. Good-night, Henry."

"Good-night!" snapped Henry with a good approximation of hurt annoyance. He turned on his heel and marched to the stair.

As he mounted the steps, he hoped his ruse would succeed. Left alone, George would begin to mull things over. Once convinced, as he was surely likely to be, that the position he had adopted might well seem far from admirable in the eyes of others, especially in Lesley's eyes, he would follow along and retreat to his own room as soon as he felt he could do so with some show of dignity. To have remained with him would have been to give him a legitimate excuse to satisfy his morbidly covetous curiosity, perhaps even to confirm his rapaciously jealous suspicions, a consummation to be avoided at all costs. He would have been quick to realize the face-saving value of another presence and would have drawn the discussion or argument out with pointless digressions until Lesley and Peter returned. And while George was not inventive, he was adept enough at that sort of thing. He was like some woman in argument—antagonistic, personal, skittish, illogical, evasive, unreasoning, elusive, hypersensitive, deceitful, inhuman and unbeatable, vainglorious and a poor winner—any means to any end. How did women get into this? Because it was an ingenious and paralyzing conundrum, Henry supposed. He was really tired. Much too much strain for one evening. He must relax, be alert for what the morrow might bring.

In his room, he was glad to be alone. As he got ready for bed, and after he had climbed in under the covers, he kept listening for George's footstep. When, at last, he heard it and heard George's door close firmly, he dropped off to sleep.

As soon as Henry left him, George got up and walked to the garden door. He stepped out onto the terrace and peered into the darkness in all directions. A cloud was passing over the moon. He could see but little. He listened. He heard only the cricket chorus, the croaking of frogs, the call of a whippoorwill. He grunted his disgust and returned to the living room. His mind was in turmoil and his frustrated reaction was one of revolt. He went to the bar and replenished his drink. One swallow and he blew his lips apart through clenched teeth. Too strong. He never did like the stuff. But he liked the effect.

What to do now? Applying epithets to Henry and the world in general was somewhat soothing but could not be expected to solve anything. That was what was so maddening. Visions of himself as a rather silly figure were unthinkable and terrifying. They brought a hot blush to his cheeks. But he would not be able to rest until there had been a showdown. Still there was that innate stupidity in everyone that had to be taken into account. His actions might be misinterpreted unless they were carefully planned. He was unquestionably right but he must take the precaution of making sure the offenders were placed in a position where they were obviously wrong even to themselves. If he went to his room and got into a lounging robe, he might be able to hear Lesley and Peter when they came in and then come quietly downstairs for a drink on the pretext that he was unable to sleep. But his hearing was not so keen as it had once been and he dared not leave his door open a crack for fear they might get up the stairs without his hearing them or Henry might be poking around. He always closed his door, was not to be approached, when in his room. Carefully established customs were a damned nuisance at times. If he left it open, it would be too obvious, embarrassing, make him seem pathetically anxious. He should never have let Henry get away.

There was a rustling sound in the garden followed by a slight scraping noise on the flagstones of the terrace. George started so that he almost spilled his drink, then froze with pounding heart. After a brief pause that seemed eternity, there was a scratching on the screen door. Mickey and Mike! Christ. He relaxed and wiped the sweat from his face. But that settled it. He must not be taken unaware. He moved quickly about the room and with weakened hands turned off all the lamps but one which spilled soft light over part of the divan. If the dogs would just bark, he would be given ample warning. But the chances were that they would not or that they would even remain near the house now that he had put out the lights. If he spoke to them occasionally they would stay by the door and Lesley and Peter would be bound to hail them as they approached. That would give him time. He could get to his room undetected, change and return after a decent interval. He started for the garden door but his movement was arrested by another startling thought. What if they should come back into the house some other way? They could even already have come in noiselessly and gone to their rooms. Highly unlikely but he must satisfy himself on that score. In any case, he could not remain there in the shadows. His position was far too vulnerable, even more so than it had been with the lights up. If they had returned then, he might have carried it off somehow. This way, he would look a fool indeed.

Taking his drink with him, he went into the hall. He could not sneak up the stairs. Henry would be listening. He made his step exaggeratedly natural. When he reached the upper hall, he glanced swiftly toward Lesley's room, then Peter's. Both doors were open, both rooms dark. He stepped into his own room and flicked the light switch. He closed the door with a definite thud but instantly, silently, opened it again. He set down his drink and took off his shoes. He stepped back into the hall. All was silence. He went to Lesley's room. There was enough moonlight to make it clear that no one was there. The same with Peter's. He went back into his own room and closed the door gently, with infinite care.

He took off coat and shirt and donned maroon velvet smoking jacket, matching scarf and slippers. Wild-eyed though he was, he could still think of dressing the part he was to play. Now came the ordeal of the vigil. He left the small lamp on the bed table burning and switched off the others. He lighted a cigarette, took his drink and sat down near one of the windows. But not for long. He was on his feet again in a matter of seconds. The natural night murmurings of the old house sent him to the door to listen. He opened it quietly. Nothing. He went to the head of the stairs. No sounds from below. He returned to his room, closed the door and resumed his seat by the window. But the longer he waited, the more restlessly impatient he became, the more his inflamed thoughts seethed with righteous anger.

He got up and paced the length of the room. With frequent stops to listen, back and forth, up and down, back and forth he went until his feet threatened to wear a path in the deep nap of the carpet. The nerves in his back and his neck were aching. The strain was beginning to tell in his head, throat, chest and stomach as well. His fury mounted. He cursed Peter and Lesley and a fate that was injuring him at a time when he should be supremely happy and taking the best of care of himself. Perhaps he could go down to the library. He would be able to hear everything from there and if they should discover him first, he could pretend to be reading until he felt sleepy. Many people did that sort of thing. But they knew he never went near the library. God damn it! He must content himself with occasional excursions to the living room. He made one forthwith.

Thereafter, at intervals of ten minutes or less, he could not endure an interval of more than ten minutes, he would slip downstairs and approach the room cautiously but with seeming freedom in case he should be observed. Finding the room empty, he would stall about in the chaos of indecision and, at length, force himself to return to his own room.

Once back there, his thwarted indignation would provoke increasingly damning thoughts of Lesley and Peter. His gorge choked at pictures of the girl in Peter's arms, receptive, responsive to his caresses, acquiescent to his desires. The sex thing was unimportant but it was a symbol. Sexual intercourse was terribly overrated but the woman of his choosing must be completely inviolate to all save himself, a sort of Puritan princess. Lesley's marked indifference to the importance of matters material might be unique and amusing, but in this instance, it was most unfortunate. Peter was young, there was no denying that, but too young to have any character, too young to hold any interest for the discerning. He was a heroic figure—the veriest nonsense that, the backwash of propaganda. His artistic pretensions made him romantic perhaps. He might even have better than average physical appeal. But that was doubtful. The injured-little-boy-needing-to-be-mothered quality certainly should not intrigue any woman of Lesley's perception. Against this bargain-counter outworn adolescence was arraigned his own far from insignificant maturity. No woman who thought as a woman should, could think twice in making her choice. But Lesley refused to think solely along accepted lines.

Here he was, a man of great achievements and, indubitably, a handsome and virile man when his health was right. A highly respected and powerful figure, he operated, with outstanding success, one of the foremost banking institutions in financial history, had contributed heavily to the furtherance of modern civilization, commanded a great and ancient fortune and held the reins of many others including Peter's. He had coped with countless problems of vast importance to all mankind and had won every time. If he were to lose this present battle, it would be a divine fiasco. If there was a Controlling Power of the Universe, its representatives on Earth must be men such as himself, men who directed the course of the world, formed its future, dictated its ultimate destiny. He could not lose. And to have his own son plotting his downfall. Sacrilege beyond belief.

What a really filthy cheat the boy was, attempting to make love to Lesley. And of course, he would pretend ignorance at first, ask what was wrong in that. Wrong! George refused to believe it, would not have it. Peter was not going to kill his mother's hope in him. George would crush the boy completely, kill him, before he would allow even an approach to such unthinkable crime. Let him understand *that*. He had come whimpering to him with his hymn of failure and expecting understanding. There was only one thing to understand—integrity. You made good your bond with your life if you had to. Peter did not even know the meaning of integrity, honor. But he was going to learn and he was going to learn tonight. He would protest that he had honor, that he had proved it. False pride would drive him to that. Was he all cheat and liar? What had he grown into? What sort of hideous joke was he? He would have to show fight at that, show fight for the first time and to defend weakness, the lowest kind of weakness. But he was not going to get away with it. He was not going to escape by claiming he had done his best.

George's brain was in a whirl of madness and anger. Peter would say that he was acting as though he were insane, that he could almost wish he were. Well, by God, he might get his wish but before he did he was going to learn a lesson he would never forget. And he was going to stay away from Lesley. He was not going to hurt her. Did he *understand* that? No. Peter would claim he did not, that he did not know what George was talking about. He would dream up some quick lie such as that he had always wanted to understand George, to know him, but that George would not permit it, had never wanted to know him. George would give his life not to have known him. He had given it to see him fulfil his mother and he had cheated them, lied to them. And now he wanted to cheat him of the only happiness he had known since she died. But he was not going to. He was going to stay away from Lesley. Peter would protest innocence again, ask what Lesley had to do with it. He knew damned well. He would like to kill their love with his rotten selfishness. It was not enough to kill everything else. Now he wanted to take Lesley away from him. He wanted to finish him off. He had tried hard enough. But there was an end to it.

When they married, George would have his life again in spite of all Peter had done. He was not going to kill that. And he never wanted to find him near Lesley again as long as he lived! George was overtaken by a wave of nausea and vertigo but he fought it off savagely.

XIII

WHEN LESLEY AND PETER HAD RECOVERED BREATH LOST IN their mad happy dash for freedom through the old orchard, they moved to the bank of the stream. They stood looking down at the hurtling life of Runsheep Run below where it broke free from the woods and was picked up by the moonlight. It was no more than eight to twelve feet in width at most points but was rather deep and swift. And it carried Peter swiftly back to his childhood.

He saw a fascinated little boy there on the bank. He was lying on his stomach under the great maple and was talking to the water. The stream was seductive as it swirled and eddied around its gaily mellow rocks, leaped from bright, leafy sunlight to deep shadow where the trout could know siesta dreaming away the afternoon, and slid and tumbled into the dam which formed a beautiful, rustic, lily-patched swimming pool with its softly uneven frame of aging trees and tender grass, then over the moss-trimmed sluice of thick, rotting boards, to crash at its foot with a jolly, shouting roar and rush on to a larger stream, the Thames River, the Sound and the open sea.

"What's the rush, little fellow," asked the little Peter.

The reply was happy and lilting. "I'm away, I'm away, I'm away to the sea."

"But why not stay here? All your friends are here. Everyone, everything, loves you here."

"I'll be back, I'll be back. But I'm off to the sea."

"But such a long trip, thousands of miles of water and no land. And then to get back, you have to be drawn up by the sun and put in a cloud and blown over here and dropped down as rain, and if you're dropped on the hill, you have to seep through the earth to get back to the stream—a long hard trip."

"A lovely trip, a lovely trip, and I love to seep. It helps the earth. It helps our friends. I'll be back."

"Well, a pleasant journey to you, then."

"Thank you, thank you. The same to you, the same to you."

"But I'm not going away."

"You will, you will, far away, some day, far away, far away. But you'll be back, you'll be back. We'll both be back. We'll meet again."

Lesley took his hand. He returned to her and to the moment.

"Are we back, darling?" she asked. Her insight was mystic.

"We're getting there," said Peter hopefully. "If inspiration would flow as faithfully as Runsheep Run, we'd be a cinch."

"Dam it up, sweetie, like the pool, hold it until it spills over, then hold the fresh flow the same way."

"I tried that but the damn dam broke." He was reaching for lightness again. No good. No use. "I've never had the strength or courage to build a new dam. I could now but there'd be no point. The stream has dried up."

"It's spring-fed. It can't dry up."

"I wish you were right." A sigh escaped his lips. He covered it with a deprecatory chuckle.

"I might as well tell you what happened. It was one of those things that just can't happen but do. I've never told anyone."

He took a deep breath, then spoke quietly. "Before the War, after I'd been in France only a few months, I was hit with a flood of inspiration. A symphony flowed into me. I was wildly excited, miserably happy, feverishly exhausted, all at one and the same time and from then on, all the time. It must be like giving birth and it goes on interminably. I held it and began to set it down—when I could see—my eyes were usually burning from lack of sleep and the fever, the good nervous strain. But it went well. It was always running through me even when all I could do was walk and walk for hours. In less than a year, I had better than half, almost two thirds of it, on paper and in final form. Then I was called down to Italy for a few weeks. When I got back, the maid had gathered up the manuscript and burned it."

Lesley gasped and cried aloud. She was shaken to the roots of her being. Peter's staggering revelation had been so abrupt and completely unexpected. Here was personal tragedy of the most pitiful sort. Here was soul-shattering experience sufficient to throw the greatest artist who ever lived off balance. Here was loss to test the faith of the most seasonedly devout. And it had come crushingly down on a hopefully eager and most sensitive youth. And it had been but prologue to an insane series of even more harrowing crimes against spirit. The tears welled into Lesley's eyes, her throat was dry, the world was spinning about her. She grasped Peter, clung to him.

"Take it easy, darling," said Peter consolingly. "It's all over now. I just wanted you to know how the bad times started, why, up to now at least, I've felt dried up."

"Oh, dearest," she managed to whisper.

"I naturally went berserk for awhile," he confessed, "and I've never really got over it. All that followed didn't help. But it's all right now—I hope. When I could whip up enough spirit, I tried to recapture some of it. Then when I found I couldn't, I stayed drunk most of the time until I went to England." In Paris, Peter had lived in the Latin Quarter. His apartment had been the second floor of an old house run by a fat, grasping, middle-aged, falsely jolly and maternal Lesbian. During Peter's absence in Italy, she had given the pretty young maid too much cognac and the maid, in a burst of energy, had cleaned Peter's studio thoroughly for the first time and, in doing so, had gathered up all loose papers and destroyed them. Peter related all this to Lesley as casually as he could.

Lesley was sickened with grief.

Peter had been fortunate in having a circle of very talented friends including several of the leading musicians of the day, men of the genius genre. Many of their evening gatherings had been spent in Peter's studio where they always insisted on hearing his work. The consensus had been that it was really pretty super. He could not honestly claim credit for it. It had simply come through him.

But with the destruction of the manuscript, the flow had stopped. His friends had never been able to understand why he had dropped an effort of such great promise. But it had been an unspoken rule of the group to accept each other's conduct without question. So Lesley was the first to know.

For some time now, he had indulged the opiate practice of lying to himself, telling himself that, at some distant date, the flow would return. But this had been little help. He had always ended by laughing at himself rather bitterly for such fearful weakness—a deliberate, false effort to assuage his suffering. But tonight, the more he talked to Lesley, the more he knew the memory of Runsheep Run was true. Beyond any doubt, there was a crystal trickle threading its way through the old parched channel. He would not have burdened her with his tale otherwise.

Lesley could do little but hold him close to her. She was completely his. Yet she knew full well that this was not enough. Would she had a thousand lives, a thousand loves, to give him. But she knew, too, that one can actually give no least part of oneself to another, no matter how desperate the longing to give all and more. In time of great trial, this was the unbearable block to expression, this knowing that, with all the heart in the world, the crying need cannot be met. All one could do was love and hope with the will to give. The loved one must help himself. And his help could come only from God. In trying to give, one might help to supply the inspiration which would lead the one loved to make the needed effort. Thus one might be an instrument in his redemption. There was much to be grateful for in that chance. But it would be such sweet heaven, no matter what the cost to her, to give that which her agonized heart was bursting to give but could not, might not even have to give if it could. She had to work hard to summon what assurance she might from her old, dear belief in the power of good.

"Come on, darling," said Peter. "We're allowing one dark moment to ruin the beauty of the night."

"You're right," Lesley whispered agreement, her eyes compassionate and proud. "Let's explore the night. Maybe we'll find the answer there."

They walked along the bank of the stream toward the pool. The night shadows were deep and mysterious and soothing and imaginatively stimulating. Tree and shrub, highlighted by the moon, cast sudden, blue, impenetrable, silhouette patterns beyond them which were hypnotically alluring. Lesley and Peter walked breathlessly along the edge of the pool and out onto the sod-dopped dam. The water glimmered invitingly.

"Let's go in," cried Lesley.

"Now that's a tremendous idea," said Peter. "I'll be with you in a second." He sprinted across the bridged sluice and on to a log cabin backed against the woods on the other side of the dam. This was the bath house. He grabbed two huge, fluffy bathtowels, hesitated fleetingly, to relish the clean pine smell of the place, and dashed back to Lesley.

Lesley had slipped out of her gown and was working on

shoes and stockings. Peter dropped the towels and whipped off his jacket and tie. As they chatted and laughed, he pretended to race her but really could do little but look on her golden loveliness being revealed to him there in the magic light. She stood, dropped her petticoat, took off her garter belt. Only the black 'bra' remained. Peter had managed to get down to shorts, shoes and socks.

"I beat you," she said as she unsnapped the 'bra' and her superb breasts stood forth.

Peter swallowed hard. "You cheated," he objected. His hands trembled as he worked on the shoe laces.

"Only the dress," she teasingly protested in turn. "I can put it back on and still beat you."

"I concede you the victory," he articulated froggily, "but you're not in the water yet." He was at last free of shoes and socks. Standing, he stepped out of his shorts.

Lesley pulled her gaze away from him to look at the water doubtfully. "I'll let you win there," she said. The chill of night had not yet settled through the lingering warmth of the day but the first contact with that water was bound to be a shock just the same. Her gaze swung back to Peter. His sweet face and his scarred, gracefully erect body were the most ecstatic vision in desire she had ever known. She yearned toward him so violently she swayed where she stood.

Peter's eyes travelled over her entire person. Here was perfection of the madding, gasping, blood-whipping sort which must either devour or be devoured. Confused by the pounding in his ears, Peter was startled to discover that he was extending himself to the tightly drawn point of orgasm. With a supreme effort of will, he forced himself to turn abruptly and plunge into the relative iciness of the pool. Whoosh! That took care of it! Panting frantically, he regained his breath and struck out.

"Wow! it's cold!" he called out shudderingly. "Come on."

Lesley was excited. To think she could do that to him when

he had not even touched her! She stepped uncertainly to the edge of the dam and, with palpitating heart, started to ease herself into the water to escape getting her hair too wet. My God. It *was* cold. As soon as she could, she shoved off into the killing breast stroke. After a short time, that helped considerably. But she was still cold. She swam with a rhythmic series of yelps while Peter laughed shiveringly.

Neither stayed in too long. As they climbed out onto the dam bank, snatched up the towels and dried themselves vigorously, talked and laughed chatteringly, they felt sparkling stirrings of exhilaration replete with the joy of life. Looking across at the shadowed mystery of the virgin woodland, Peter could visualize the fascinating network of tunneled or cathedral-arched pathways originally broken by big game and later kept clear by the livestock, along whose brown carpeting of needles he had so lovingly and enchantedly trod countless times, both alone and with Lesley. His eyes sought hers. She, too, was remembering the romance of the forest. Her perfectly beautiful face and figure, with their firm flesh and aura of pale glistering gold, were straightforwardly irresistible. And this time, as she returned his gaze, Peter made no further effort to resist. He moved over to her and she was in his arms. He kissed her and, bending her far backward, lowered her to the satin grass. His lips moved over her, explored each sensuous secret of her sweet sanctity, then found her lips again. Her dark eyes, smoldering, flecked with shooting sparks, smoothly sultry, clear to his vision in the lighted dark, were savagely possessive, wildly sensuous, barbarously happy. Lesley's head was singing, the rest of her ablaze. She was ready, had been ready for ages. There was a lip-biting, suspenseful moment of sweet pain. But she was so lovingly, liquidly, entirely receptive that all was quickly well.

Peter's consciousness was whirling. A thousand tiny fingers were tapping inside his skull, along his spine. He now knew all he had longed for, lived for. He knew love. They were both flooded with the dazing, unbearable, white frost-light of reality. There could be no greater life. They cried out in thrilled anguish. They spoke in husky, gasping, fervid whispers.

"Oh, darling, it's so wonderful, so wonderful."

"I love you."

"I love you."

All of Time thundered through them.

Lesley's whole body shook madly, convulsively, ecstatically. "Oh, I shall die. I know I shall die. But I mustn't die. I must live now. I've never lived before. I don't want to die so soon."

"Angel."

"It can't be right, all this happiness. But of course it's right. I don't mean that. It's only because my head feels so light."

"Darling—this—just this—it's—it's so right—so perfect. Don't you feel that, too?"

"Oh, yes, sweet. I know. But it's so perfect I can't believe it can be. But it is, isn't it? Say it is, Peter dear."

"It is, darling."

"Oh, darling, darling, darling!" she almost screamed. Again! He sobbed into her mouth. He, too, then!

And again and again, the mad impossible, glorious dream repeated itself. And each time, its wonder and beauty grew.

Lying side by side, they floated with alert listlessness through the far reaches of infinity. Each held for the other the invincible, romantic peace of utter satisfaction. They were steeped in excited contentment. Lesley's hands glided lovingly over Peter's body, traced the scars tenderly.

"Darling—you're so beautiful," he said.

"Oh, dearest—no."

"So beautiful I can believe again, believe in beauty and good and love, all I've needed so much to believe in. Thank God. Thank God for you, Lesley darling."

"You really mean that, Peter dear?"

"With all my heart. And you know all it means. I can see all the perfect things in you, all the great things that are called soul. I can. That's why you're so beautiful, so lovely, so perfect, my darling."

"Oh, my dear."

"You're all I've ever wanted. I've been half crazy through these years, looking, looking—looking just for you. It's so funny, so terrible, that I couldn't see that. But now, now I've found you at last."

"I've always known it could only be you. It's been my very special secret dream for years. You were always the hero of the novels I read, always the great love of the poems. And now, now in everything lovely, the sunset, the trees and the stars, in kindness and warmth, in all beauty, the sweetness of the beauty is you, Peter dear."

"Oh, my darling." He lifted his head quickly, kissed her lips lightly. "Sweet angel, sweet, we must be married at once.

"It'd be crazy to wait. At once, darling."

"Oh, dearest." Lesley faced the ultimate practical purpose of life. The unattainable was hers for the taking. Life was a skittish business. One could not live others' lives. Others could not, would not, work out one's salvation. What was this roundly abused motive, this smugly nourishing risk, of self-sacrifice? In the overall scheme of things there was but one move to make. Yet she must bow to the conscience that had brought her here. Madness. "Oh but no. No, we can't. We must wait. Oh, darling, how awful."

"But we can't. Why must we wait?"

"Because. The woman's reason. We must. We can't even say anything. That's because of someone else, someone close to you, someone you love."

"Then you mean George. Hank asked me too. And he's asked you. But I can't see why. Do you know?"

"Yes. But I can't tell you now. I wish I could. But Hank's right. Please believe that, Peter."

"I don't like it. It almost sounds as though— I told Hank that. I don't like it." What possible objection could George have, other than the one he had refused to accept? "I want to shout our love from the house tops."

"I know. I don't like it either. But it has to be. It's our way, isn't it? We have to think of others. And we know it's all right. We'll have our love, our life, just the same, just you and I."

Peter was struck with the terror of impending tragedy. He was very intense. "Lesley—nothing could happen—there's no way that I could ever lose you now?"

"Never, my dearest!" She reassured him with the whole warmth of her great sincerity. "How could you lose me? I've always been yours, darling, all yours. Don't you know that now?"

"Sweet. Thank God." Relief poured over him. "I wouldn't just die. I'd despair. I would. It'd be the most horrible death. And it would never end."

"You'll never die, Peter."

"I can believe that now, with you. And I know I've found my work again, too." He lay back and looked deep into the night skies, happy in life, happy in life millions of light-years away, as Man measured openness, freedom. A full song was on his lips. It took form in his main theme. That main theme of his symphony had haunted him constantly and he had as constantly fought away from it, stubbornly, frantically denied its utterance, ever since the Paris incident. Now, suddenly, he gave it voice. Without words but with mounting joy, he sang and hummed it from a soft beginning to a surging end. Lying atop the dam, the sounds of the waterfall and the rapids below were muted. They blended in soft, bell-like accompaniment with Peter's warm tones. The strains floated across the night world and lingered in tier on tier of rapturous harmony.

And Lesley was raptly silent until the last sweet sound

died far away. Then she spoke her breathless ardor, "Darling, how beautiful!"

He blinked back happy tears, turned back to her, thanked her with a hug.

"What is it?" she asked tremulously.

"It's for you. That's the main theme. I'll play it for you later if you like." Here was complete release.

"How wonderful!" she whispered and gave her thanks in silent prayer.

"It's for you, for all that you are, for beauty and good, for love." His voice was as deep as the skies. "I love you, my darling."

"Oh dear God, I love you, my sweet."

They kissed and kissed, lingering excited kisses. Peter was thrusting to life again. She drew him toward her.

Lesley and Peter walked into the living room and fell naturally and happily to the softly lighted divan. George was just starting the ninth belligerent pacing of his bedroom.

Peter reached over and took Lesley's hand. "Dearest, dearest," he sighed joyfully, "you're so lovely, so lovely. It's murderous. It's wonderful. There's such loveliness in every bit of you. And I can feel you close to me. You'll always keep me close to you, won't you, darling?"

"Always, my sweet, and all ways." She squeezed his hand rapturously, the music lifting through her. "Oh my darling, my beautiful darling, you're mine, all mine. We're one, you and I."

"One. One now, now and always." Dropping close to her, he kissed her hair, her shoulder.

She leaned away from him a little, fingertips at her temples. "Oh, darling, I can't stand it. I can't. You don't want to kill me, do you? You don't want me to die, now that you know I'm all yours?"

"Dearest. If only we could—" He sat up suddenly. "But,

of course. That's it. We *can* be married, married secretly. Then we'll truly be one. We'll walk with the angels, have our dream with the poets. No one need know."

"How perfect!" She could not go on refusing her dearest, impossible wish, her universe, her eternal life. But she must. "But we mustn't, Peter. How could we? We might hurt those we love, those who love us. We can't do that."

"We must." Peter's mind raced the arid stretches of common acceptance. Their friends would understand, could not be hurt. Who would be hurt, then? George. And why? Could the cold stranger, which was George, aspire to that which was completely foreign emotionally? Peter could recall no trace of the affection he had always looked for in George. Did George fancy himself in love with a child? Did he dream of marrying Lesley himself?—and with a sly wink of approval from a knowing world?

Peter realized that as much as he hated such rotting conventions, they were a part of daily life. It was all too revolting and frightening to endure. Lesley could not be ensnared by such ugliness. She was a free spirit. And they had always loved and lived as one, even though he might not have always known it. Nothing must be permitted to destroy their life. He went on talking. "How could it hurt anyone? Anyway, whoever 'they' are you speak of, they wouldn't know. But they can hurt us by keeping us apart. We can't allow that. Please, please say you will, Lesley."

"I want to so much. But I can't." This was torture. "And they would know. They'd have to know sometime. We've waited so long. We can wait a little longer. And they can't keep us apart. I am your wife now. We are one. It's only the wedding that must wait. Be patient. Help me, my darling."

"It isn't fair. *It is not fair,*" Peter protested teasingly. "I have to do anything you ask. Anything. Oh, my sweet, I do adore you, idolize you, love you."

"And I, you, darling, with all my heart and soul and might,

with every thought, every breath, all I do, all I say, with all of me, all, darling."

Tenderly passionate, he kissed her. "Lesley, my Lesley. Your eyes, they're so deep, so dark, and your mouth, it's so beautiful. All I want is to lose myself in you, to feel your lips making love to me." Again, his mouth was on hers.

Lesley drew back a little from his bewildering kiss. This was foolhardy. George might appear, becloud perfection with sordid drabness. "Oh, darling, darling. We must try to be calm now. We must."

"I'll never be calm again, never."

"Aren't you going to play for me, Peter? You haven't forgotten?"

"No. But I wonder. I don't know."

"Please." Then with sudden inspiration, "We'll drive to the chapel. Old Andy and Meg still take care of it and live in the rectory. They'll let us in and be so happy to see you. It'll be wonderful there tonight, Peter."

"Yes, marvelous." Before he left for Europe, Peter had often given organ recitals in the middle of the night in the almost-ghost village of Cragie. Seated at the little chapel organ he had happily played his heart out for just Lesley, Andy and Meg, played all those things of his own which he could play for no one else. "It's just that—I know I'll play well. I know that now. But no matter how well I play, I won't even begin to say all I want to say to you."

"Oh, how sweet. But don't love me too much, Peter darling. Love the music more. I must help you. You must love the music above all."

"No, Lesley. I must love you above all." Desire swept him along. But he was sincere with the intense sincerity of one drunk with poetry who may speak a part of his soul. "It's all one, in you, the music, the beauty, everything we believe in. The more I love you, the more hope there is that I can be an artist, really an artist, and a person, too."

Lesley feared the danger of hurt in such abandon. She was a unique woman, her view simple. She could not believe that woman made men great or that men inspired the soaring artistry her own sex had, at times, achieved. "But you are an artist, Peter, a great artist, to your sweet fingertips. I love your love, dearest. I'm insane with the joy of it. But it's all your own beautiful thought. You must know that. You must know you could stand alone if I didn't exist at all."

"But I couldn't. It's only because you do exist that I can believe and hope again. No man, no artist, could dream you, my dearest Lesley, my beautiful love." Again he kissed her passionately.

Lesley was a picture of disheveled loveliness. Peter had lifted her legs to the divan. Seated on the edge, he had been leaning over her earnestly. Her hair was tumbled about her divine face, her breasts were exposed above the richness of her black gown, her skirts were thrown back to her hips. All the creamy perfection of her was startlingly clear, wildly beautiful, savagely alluring, there in the soft light. It was almost impossible for her to resist the caresses she hungered for so madly. But, dimly now, she knew she must. She forced Peter away from her a little, arched her body, pressed her head back against the cushions.

"Oh, my dear, my dear—wait," she whispered. She fought for control, gained a little. "We must go to the chapel. *Now,* darling."

He took her into his arms, strong insistent arms. "Yes, dear, yes," he agreed hoarsely, without thought. "But just for this moment, only that, let me hold you so." He kissed her lips, her eyes, her neck.

George stepped into the room. Then, for a moment, in a frozen, apish attitude, he stood staring at the scene with flaming eyes.

Lesley had found some voice. "No, no, please, Peter my

dear, please," she was saying. "I can't bear it. I can't. You must stop. Please, Peter. Unless—"

"Peter!" George's voice had the impact of a bullet.

Lesley's and Peter's hearts stopped as one. Then Peter turned slowly and stood.

"George," he said.

George came into action. With panther swiftness, he moved to the fireplace and grasped the poker which Peter had used earlier in the evening in play. Then as swiftly, he turned on Peter.

"God damn you," he rasped and, with the strength and rage of a maniac, struck hard at Peter's head.

But Peter was quick. Both arms were up to ward off the blow. His right wrist took most of it. He felt a blinding flash of pain. The blood rushed into his eyes. This was the sort of thing Peter had come to understand without thinking about it. Postgraduate Commando dirty fighting over old Fulton's early boxing lessons. With his left hand, he grasped George's jacket and as he drew him toward him, drove a hard right to his chin. George dropped like a stone but with his jaw unbroken. The pain of contact had thrown Peter's timing off a hair and the elbow which followed the fist had but grazed its target. Nor had Peter driven his right knee into George's groin. That was just lucky, unthought restraint. Panic-stricken, Lesley had got up from the divan as she automatically, incongruously, adjusted her gown and brushed the hair back from her face. George staggered to his feet but without the poker which had slithered away from his nerveless fingers. He raised both fists above his head as though he would crush Peter to the ground. Peter was about to drop him again as Lesley stepped between them. She clutched George's lapels, shook him violently.

"George, George!" she cried. "You don't know what you're doing! George!"

Both men stood transfixed. Gradually, George became

aware of Lesley looking inploringly into his eyes. Then, slowly, he lowered his arms, sagged perceptibly. Dazedly, as might a frightened child, he put his arms around her waist, let his head sink beside hers. She patted him soothingly, crooningly. "There, there," she said. "You're all right now," then turned in his arms to look at Peter, hoping for the sympathetic understanding she knew she could not hope for. Pale with pain, Peter was staring at her fixedly, unseeingly, unbelievingly. His left hand was graspingly working on his right wrist. The buttons had been torn away from his dinner jacket taking material with them. The right sleeve had ripped open at the shoulder seam. Unconsciously, he tried to adjust it, a wistful, weird movement in this nightmarish moment. Then, aburptly, he stepped aside and moved rapidly from the room into the hall.

"Peter—Peter, please wait," called Lesley with the pleading of despair.

No answer.

XIV

SHORTLY AFTER PETER LEFT THE ROOM, GEORGE BEGAN TO shake. Lesley guided him to the nearest armchair and his withered bulk obediently collapsed into it. For some minutes, he said nothing. His eyes held the vacancy of mental and emotional anguish. His breathing was throaty. He scarcely moved. He was old. Lesley was at a loss. It was all so absurdly melodramatic. But she knew she was dealing with a man already half mad. And she was filled with horror when she viewed what she had done. For she had done it. Then remorse swept through her and washed away the horror. Nor could she allow herself to think beyond that which was necessary to the moment. She must save George. All other whirling, slashing fears must not be allowed to make her lose sight of that. Her darling Hank was deeply embroiled in all this. He would be hurt. But he must not be allowed to be hurt beyond recovery. He must be carried to secure heights at all costs. All costs? What of the probable cost to Peter? And to herself? That must be made right somehow. But later. That must come later. Peter did not know what could happen to George. She did. Nor did Peter know what it would do to him should it happen. George must die a natural death. Right must triumph. She started to giggle at the cheap expression then quickly overrode the temptation to hysteria. She pushed her burning panic back. She certainly was not thinking very clearly. But she had no wish to think clearly. She wished only to hold and be guided. George was speaking. His words were slow, slow and hollow.

"I tried to kill him—tried to kill my own son."

"You didn't mean it."

"I struck him—struck him with hate—cursed him—her son —my son—my son, too, Lesley."

"I know," she said softly.

He lifted his dead eyes to hers. "You know?" She nodded. "Hank told you then. I'm glad." He dropped his eyes. "To try to kill our son. But he drove me to it. He shouldn't have done that. He knew—surely he knew that you're everything to me—and he tried to make love to you, forced himself on you."

"No, George. You mustn't say that. I wanted him to."

"Don't defend him. I saw it all, heard you tell him to stop and he wouldn't listen. I can understand you might think him attractive. You're both so young. And he has a kind of charm and fascination, I suppose. But don't be fooled by it, Lesley. He's cruel and heartless. He'd only hurt you. You'd know that if you could know what he's done to his mother and to me, and the cold-blooded way that he's done it."

"Please. You mustn't say things about him that I know aren't true. You're going to know they aren't true, too. He's found himself again, George. Just tonight. He really has. He's going to do great work, I know. He's going to be a great man. You'll see you're all wrong about him. You'll see."

"Are you in love with him?"

"I've always been in love with him."

"Then you plan to marry him?" George spoke more and more as from the grave.

"George—you say I'm everything to you. You've never told me that."

"I thought you knew. I was going to ask you to marry me—just tonight—but you gave me no chance."

"But—but Peter's mother, George. I thought—you speak of her as though she were all of love that you could ever know. How can you care for me other than much as you might care for Peter? I don't understand."

All the rancor he felt for the implication in Lesley's innocent question could not pull George out of his ennui. "It doesn't matter now," he said. "Nothing matters."

"Can't you tell me?"

"No. There's no way to tell you. For years nothing mattered but I kept driving on. I don't know why. I accomplished a great deal but in the end, it meant nothing and I wanted to quit—once I saw Peter on his way. Then you came to me, made me want to live again. Peter might have done that, too. Instead, he killed all I'd ever lived for. But I hoped I still had you. Now I know I haven't. And nothing can ever matter again." There was much withheld and distorted in this incoherent recital but there was also some truth and a feeling of genuine distress and a hopeless seeking for sincerity.

Lesley was almost overcome by resurgent thought. She frowningly moved her shoulders and shook her head to free herself. There was only one thing to do. George must be saved. She looked at him for a long moment. Then, "I think we'd better be married, George, you and I," she said. She heard her own voice as though it were coming from another.

Lesley's words startled George from his torpor. His eyes glinted to life. His voice gained in strength. "Lesley, you—but you can't mean it!" he said incredulously.

"I do mean it, George."

"But you—you love Peter. You told me that."

"Don't you want to marry me?" Her voice was still far away.

"My God! Of course I do! It's all I want." Sure of defeat, his realization of victory was almost tearful. His enthusiasm was pathetically child-like and with a disturbing touch as of premature senility. "And you're just as fine and great as I thought you were. You won't regret it. I'll give you everything, everything. You'll be happy with me, Lesley. You're too young to know how happy you'll be. I'll have you with me always, in everything I do. I'll conquer the world for you. And I can, you know. You'll have my protection, all I can give you. You'll know nothing but happiness, Lesley."

"Yes, George," said Lesley, uneasiness tempering the weariness of her tone. "And you'll be happy when you learn that I was right and you were wrong about Peter, won't you?"

"Perhaps. Yes, even that. Even that can be right with you." He would be magnanimous as became him.

"And now I must find Peter, George. There's so much I must try to say to him."

He held out a hand to her. "You won't be long?"

Lesley accepted the hand. "No," she murmured.

He drew her to the side of his chair, put his arm around her legs. "You don't know how happy you make me, how much you make me believe in myself again."

"I'm glad." There was a sickness in the pit of her stomach. She straightened to dismiss it, drew away from him gently. "I must go to Peter now." She walked out of the room and into the hall with as much composure as she could simulate.

When Peter walked out of the living room, he went straight to his own room. He wanted to go to Mrs. Williams. She would know what to do about his wrist, know what to do about everything. But he could not disturb her at that hour. The only thing was to get away. He would have liked to ask Reggie to go with him. But Reggie's door was closed and Peter had grown accustomed to carrying his burdens single-handed. A peculiarly appropriate analysis. He smiled grimly. If only he could laugh. There was always saving comedy if one could but ferret it out. He never could. That was not his temperament. His right hand was useless but he managed with fair, labored rapidity to change from his dinner clothes, dress shoes and black tie to his gray suit, new shoes and tie. The tie required about ten painful minutes but it was finally presentable. He looked blindly about him. He had money. That was all that was really necessary. He went downstairs, out the side door, on to the parking circle, and climbed into his car.

Lesley went to Peter's room. The lights were on. His dinner clothes were on the bed. His new suit was gone. He was going away. She heard the sound of a motor. She ran downstairs and out the side entrance. Peter's car was coming toward her. It swung wide to avoid hitting her, caromed off a garden bank back into the drive and sped away. Lesley stood in the drive for a long time praying that Peter would come back, knowing he would not.

Left alone in his triumph, George glanced at the liquor cabinet and decided that must be his next move. But first, his eyes turned into his own mind. As on a pathotype in blazing letters that spoke, he read and mouthed, 'You're a liar, Hank. Do you hear me? A liar!'

His eyes traveled back to the cabinet. His brave words were boastful and idle and fearful. He got up slowly and started for the little bar. After a few quick, uncertain steps, he spun about and went hurtling to the door. He lay there for a time without moving, then rolled about a little, unable to manage more movement. At length, he started to rise, still bent on reaching the liquor cabinet, and almost succeeded in getting to his feet before he fell again. This time, he lay shivering and panting. Now he gave up all thought of the liquor and planned only to get back into his chair. He made the effort, fell again. After two more such unsuccessful attempts, he was back near the chair. Each fall had been hard, terrifying. If only he could reach the wall button. That was a ridiculous demand. He lay at the foot of the chair for some time summoning all his poor strength and then, with the supreme effort, dragged himself up into it. He sat there breathing hard. Then his eyes rolled upward. His lips moved but he made no sound. With all the will he could command, he tried but it was useless. After a number of minutes, he suddenly settled into a rigid position, his features drawn into a weird, pained grimace.

Lesley came back into the room, her personality blanketed with a truly weary listlessness. She sank into the armchair facing his but scarcely noticed him, spoke as to herself in a convent cell. "He's gone." Her words carried the simple, great weight of eternity. "He almost ran me down. He wouldn't stop. I wanted him to listen. I wanted to try to make him understand. But he wouldn't. He just rushed on past me. I wasn't even there. I don't think he even looked at me really. He didn't even see me, except as a person in the road. He was hurt, George. I know he was hurt. I wanted to run after him but it was no use. He went so fast. I tried to call to him but I couldn't. I could have helped him. He needs help. I think I could have helped. I don't know where he's gone. He shouldn't have gone. I don't know what to do. Hank will have to tell me. What am I to do now, George?" She looked at him through her glazed eyes and those great eyes suddenly leaped to life. She saw the horrible, set expression on his face. She was on her feet instantly. She rushed to his side. "George, George, what is it? What's the matter?" He looked at her but could say nothing. "George, tell me." Still silent. She ran to the hall door. "Hank, Fulton," she shouted. She pressed the wall button rapidly a number of times. She continued to call. "Fulton, Peter, Reggie, Hank!" She turned on all the lamps. "Oh, hurry. Hurry!" she begged.

Peter drove through the night until he became aware of The Sea Horse, a roadside bar and grill with an impersonal but kindly atmosphere. He pulled in and parked sloppily. The proprietress was a casual dipsomaniac of whom he was very fond. She was nowhere about, probably on a tentative binge. Her binges were always like that. Good enough. The bartender remembered him vaguely, welcomed him warmly. No one bothered him. He had a double Scotch, had several. The pain in his wrist was severe, had been getting worse. The Scotch helped him to forget it, eased the pain of everything. The temporary comfort of dullness was good. He could even muse a little in a semi-detached way. His world had fallen away from him, his universe had tumbled about his ears, leaving only the no-world of the 'realist.' His dire premonition of clinging years had proved true. To all intents and purposes, he was still alive. Death would never find him less so. And a man was supposed to stand up under such denuding onslaught. God alone knew why. But he would abide by the moronic code until his grant of escape. Life was a lie. There was only loneliness. Here was pain indeed. But Peter had learned to suffer. Crushing experience had taught him a kind of stoicism. He had struggled through interminable, relentless sand until too weakened to move farther. He had lain there for eighteen hours without water through the freezing night and blazing day of the desert unable to escape his crumbling thoughts and the pain of a partially shattered shoulder before he lost consciousness. He had been pinned to a beach, five hours behind schedule, using two corpses as cover, a piece of steel in the flesh of his leg, his uniform soaked with brine, and not daring to move to the assistance of the wounded, the dying, at his side. A hole in his left side, below the heart, he had pitched into the oozing mud of northern Europe. Half delirious, he had come to in time to avoid suffocation in the mire or drowning from the black pools the weight of his body kept forming. For he knew not how long, he had kept creeping his head from side to side before he was lifted away. And now nothing but emptiness.

He had another drink. The conversations around him were not loud but he could hear them clearly. They seemed banal. All conversation was banal. He pushed erect at the bar to test his condition. He was feeling better. That could not last long. But he was feeling better. With a quirk of a smile at his self-centeredness, he returned to his drink.

He remembered Audrey. He finished his drink, went out, got into his car and drove to 'Stoneleigh.' On the way, he knew only regret for the way he had handled the surprise situation with George. He should not have fought violence with violence. After the first unexpected blow, he could have avoided further injury and, with but slight hurt to George, made him drop the poker or any other ad lib weapon he might seize. Then if George insisted on continuing the attack with his fists, he could have let him go on until he exhausted himself. Too bad he had not thought of that. But it was too late now. And Lesley would probably have stopped it quickly just as she had. Lesley. Her chief concern had been George, not himself. He would think no more about it. There would be endless hours to think. And in the matter of regretting, why pause over one isolated incident where he had done no real harm? There was so much in the past where the hurt had been great, incalculable, unknowable, so much he should regret to the death of his burning soul. But the sackcloth of regret could not make him forget. He looked forward to Audrey and 'Stoneleigh.'

Peter swung up the wide drive and parked across from the main entrance. 'Stoneleigh' was well named. There was a great deal of stone, hundreds of huge blocks of quarried stone rising to a slate roof and running off into wings. It was a moderately modern house with a strong medieval influence. It was un-gabled, many-windowed, sumptuous and hospitable. It was not ornate. And Peter rather liked it for what it was. With its simple lines, it looked cool bathed in moonlight. The extensive grounds, carefully landscaped and forming a small coastal point with a low reinforced bluff and white beach, also looked cool in the moonlight.

Audrey was storming about the great hall which served as living- and drawingroom at 'Stoneleigh.' She had sent the servants to bed and had been reliving recent scenes at high speed, an untouched drink clutched in one fist. A string of curses streamed behind her. She had been over the whole lousy problem scores of times and had hit on no solution that would make everyone involved wish he or she were dead. She had rehearsed everything she might have said and done, everything she was going to say and do, and she was still raging. None of it was any good or bad enough.

When she heard the sound of the car in the drive, she stopped her seething excursion abruptly. From where she stood, she tried to see out through the leaded casement windows. If Reggie bothered her in this hour of trial, she would kill him. She saw the car. It was not Reggie's car. It looked breathtakingly like Peter's old car. Could it be? Of course not! But she must know at once. She quickly winked back angry tears, set her drink down and rushed out through the great arch into the reception hall. As she swung the big iron-bound door wide, Peter was coming toward her across the drive. Her heart leaped.

"Hello, Audrey."

She practically hurled herself on him. He had to give a couple of steps and put his arms around her to keep his balance. She had her arms around his neck, pulling him down to her, laughing into his ear.

"Darling! You did come after all!"

"Yes. Careful. I've hurt my wrist." He held it away from her.

She released him, stooped to examine it. "How? Let me see. Is it bad? What happened? How did you do it? Does it hurt very much?"

"Never mind," he chuckled. "Just don't try to climb onto it."

"Oh, you're impossible," she pouted and herded him into the house.

Peter went to an upholstered oak bench before the fireplace in the great hall and sat down while Audrey closed the front door, came into the room and drew the drapes over the casement windows. The fire was lighted but had not been built on a large scale and gave off more cheer than heat. The fireplace was one story in height, the room, two. A vast room. Little galleries opened onto it from halls on the upper floor. Great beams swept across it. Smaller beams met and crossed in the center of the room to support an iron-wrought chandelier of electric candles. More electricity in high standing iron candelabra on either side of the fireplace and across the room. But only two nearby table lamps with giant maroon shades were lighted. Although there were shadowed corners, the room was not dark. Two suits of armor were eerily visible as well as the elaborate crest over the fireplace. The floor was flagstone relieved by Persian throw-rugs. There was a lot of maroon velour in drapes, runners, covers and elsewhere. The long divan which faced the fireplace at a safe distance was maroon velour with a tarnished gold-braid trim and drop-ends tied off with tasselled, thick gold cord. There was more maroon velour in the cushions, held in place by more gold cord, on the backs and seats of the big carved oak and walnut chairs placed with matching coffee tables and side tables in open units facing the center of the room or the fireplace. The tables carried lamps similar to the two now lighted on the big table behind the divan. The polished stone walls were adorned with exquisite tapestries. Everything was big and heavy, the ornaments, the ashtrays, the books and bookends, the cigarette boxes, the footstools, everything. It was comforting to have a sure haven in a storm not yet passed but Peter was only half-way glad to be here.

"It's so wonderful to have you here. I can't tell you. I'd

just about given you up. And I was feeling terribly low and lonely. And if I'd known you were out doing something silly like injuring yourself, I'd have been out of my mind." Audrey finished her tour of the windows and came and sat beside him, hands clasped in her lap. "Now. Tell me everything," she said eagerly.

"Dow te' me eve't'ing," he mimicked her teasingly and rubbed his nose against hers.

"Please," she pleaded.

Peter had intended to say it was accident, that Reggie had slammed the car door not realizing his arm was there, and lucky it missed his fingers as he had instinctively started to draw it away. Instead, he told her the truth.

Audrey was delighted and sympathetic. "My dear, how simply awful for you. I tried to warn you, tried to make you see the light, do the right thing, but you wouldn't listen. It wasn't just that I wanted you for myself. I wanted to protect you, keep you from getting hurt. And now you've gone and done it, poor darling. But at least now you know what they are. I—"

Peter interrupted her tersely. "Let's not talk about it." There could be no doubt he meant what he said.

"All right. I'm sorry," said Audrey meekly. Her heart was gloating and filled with kindness. "But shouldn't we do something about your wrist, compresses or call the doctor?"

"No," said Peter, again firmly. "It's only a bruise. The best thing to do is forget it.

"Then you must have a drink." She jumped to her feet. "What'll it be?"

"You sound like a bartender," he said with mock severity. Then, "I've killed a bottle already, I should think."

"Well, it didn't take. Was it Scotch?"

"I think so."

"Try brandy. That's what I'm having." She walked on air

to a tray of bottles, vase-like glasses and ice on the big table, mixed a strong brandy and soda and returned to Peter.

"Thank you," he said and sipped the drink tentatively.

Audrey retrieved her drink and sat on the divan. Peter joined her. They put their feet up on the bench and stared at the flames licking around the small logs. It was a moment for dreaming. But Peter was not in the mood to dream. He squirmed about and took a long draught.

"Happy?" she asked.

"Of course," he protested none too convincingly.

Well, if he would not talk, she would. She must get him into a lighter mood, keep him from thinking of anything but herself. Not that she was to be taken lightly after the snare had sprung.

She launched into a long, bright and frequently amusing account of all she had been doing during the years he had been away and how much she had missed him in everything. She garnished the whole with choice tidbits of scandal well remembered. As she chattered on and on, with his twinkling reception ample encouragement, she climbed about him puppy-fashion and plied him with more and more brandy. The brandy gradually settled in and Peter became headily at peace with the world.

He was vaguely aware that something had been amiss, very much amiss, but he had reached that mellow stage where he could view all human problems, however grave, with benign indifference and a stomach of deep content.

Audrey's voice had become very dim when he suddenly realized she was tugging at him and almost shouting.

"Are you hungry?"

His tongue was lazy but he got it to work. "After that dinner?"

"Are you hungry?"

"Yes."

"Come on." She pulled him up off the divan and led him across the reception hall, through the long dining room and out into the kitchen.

The kitchen was a dazzling testimonial to modern science. Audrey snapped open the door of one of the big refrigerators. There was a beautifully lighted, sensational display of tempting viands. They pounced on fried chicken, apple pie and milk, sat down at the kitchen table and literally wolfed the chicken and then the pie, laughing and choking and washing it all down with the smooth, rich milk. It was a riot of satisfaction and left them momentarily exhausted.

Afterward, Peter could never remember the trip up the shallow stone steps which curved away from the reception hall to the parquet modernity of the second floor.

Audrey's bedroom was big and had eight big windows overlooking the water. It was done entirely in red and white, even to the delicate flowered wallpaper. The wall-to-wall carpet was white. There were squares of red carpet under the various pieces of furniture including the really tremendous white bed with its cerise cover folded back. Across from the foot of the bed and in front of the red fireplace, was a polar bear-skin rug. The fire was dying down. Audrey poked it to life. Chill air was drifting in from the sea. Only one lamp was lighted, near the bed, but with the help of the moonlight and the brightening fire,

Peter could make out everything clearly, or as clearly as was possible in that hazy hour. The little tables, dressing table and desk were white with red tops. The lamps were white with red shades. The small straight chairs were white with red cushioned seats. The upholstered boudoir armchairs were red with white pillows. The white was very white. The red was neither bright nor dull. It was simply alive. Peter whistled to himself. He had never seen anything *quite* like this before. Even the toilet articles were red tinted crystal.

Audrey got soft dance music on the radio beside the bed. The phone rang. She answered it.

"Hello . . . oh, hello . . . that's all right. What is it? . . . Why no, no he hasn't . . . Well, I should hardly think so now . . . Oh . . . Oh, that's too bad . . . Yes, of course, if he does—immediately . . . Not at all. I was just reading and listening to the radio. Is there anything I can do? . . . Right . . . Good-night." It was a very sweet 'good-night.' She walked over to Peter.

"They're worried about you."

"That's nice."

Peter pulled off his shoes and they danced. And as they danced, Audrey began to undress him. They stopped. She completed the job. Peter's right hand was more or less useless. It amused him to be helped. Audrey's gown came off much more readily than it went on. She staggered slightly as she hung it carefully in the dressing room. She stepped out of her shoes, peeled off her stockings and struggled free of her girdle. She wore no 'bra.'

When she came back into the room, Peter was standing at the foot of the bed. She was jarred somewhat by the scars. They stood out in the firelight. She liked a man's body to be perfect. But no matter. He was pretty perfect otherwise. And those scars had probably cost the poor devil a lot of suffering. She was going to speak of them but as she opened her mouth to do so, fuzzy intuitiveness told her she should keep silent. She raised herself onto her toes and walked toward him.

Peter became slowly, strongly conscious of her standing impudently before him. A soft red glow diffused itself over her body, highlighted its curves. Her back arched seductively. She stepped close, put his arms around the blazing silkiness of her amazingly slim waist. She slid her hands over his shoulders, up the back of his neck, clutched his hair, pulled his face down to hers, pushed herself up against him. Her breathing was harshly throatal. Peter was dismissing serpentine landscapes. Something important was demanded of him.

Guardian comedy is no respecter of situations.

Peter blacked out.

Gradually Audrey became drunkenly furious. She pounded and slapped the form on the foot of the bed. Useless. Still ungraspingly angry, she shoved and pulled Peter to one side of the bed and threw the covers over him. Exhausted, she made her way all the distance to the other side and flopped. As a dreamy strong reflex, she pulled the blanket to her.

In less than an hour, Peter, with damning perversity, came to drowsy consciousness. Within a minute, he knew mistily where he was. He turned his head. There was Audrey; he thought. He was right. She was sleeping. Good enough. Let her sleep is she wanted to be rude. Was that fair? Let her sleep. It was her house. Strong background wounds sobered him somewhat. He was in his own land. He settled back, lay awake, listened to the old familiar sounds of the night. Good, good. He was duller than he liked to be. No matter. The thing was to take and love what was given him. The smell of the sea, the trees, the earth and the flowers drifted up his nostrils, a sweet soothing incense. The cricket chorus was less strident. The fog was creeping about the house. But the moonlight still filtered through, vaporously mysterious as, in darting reflection, it seemed to move by. He could hear the throbbing bass whistles of the big ships, the dreamy monotony of the lonely fog horns, the mournful warning of the bell-buoys. It was all so dear to Peter's heart. And vaguely heavy though his heart was, he felt a growing warmth within him. He seemed to remember that his life was no more. But it began to matter less and less. There was light reflection on the bed table. He squinted as near-sighted. It looked like bottles, ice, yes, ice, too. Audrey had brought the 'bar' upstairs. His left hand reached the brandy. He splashed out a big drink. He was drinking it when it crashed to the floor. A train whistled in the distance. He slept.

At 'Cragie' all was quiet. Henry and Lesley sat by George's bed. George slept peacefully under the effect of an opiate.

The rest of the household settled down to such sleep as might be gained after so rude an awakening.

XV

SUNDAY MORNING DAWNED CRISP AND CLEAR.

Peter wakened early, his heart pounding violently. His sleep had been troubled by scattered dreams. He had been on a night patrol. While he was pressing his throat to stop a cough, a flare had gone up from a Very pistol. He had stood motionless in the sickly greenish light. Then all hell had broken loose around him. He had been spattered by the flesh of the whole detail. Lost because of him. Again he had been creeping over jagged rock and getting nowhere, his energy going, his woolen uniform in ribbons over his lacerated flesh, caked with sweat and driving him crazy. He could not reach his objective and the battalion could not move without him. Again he had been crouched on the sump of a foxhole a quarter filled with water. Tanks rolled overhead. He had peered over the edge. The monstrous creatures from another world were everywhere, crushing and roaring through everything, tracer bullets ricocheted crazily, the beautiful, devastating, slow-motion puffs of bursting artillery fire in the too-near, dust-filled background, strafing planes zoomed and crackled, he was deafened and buffeted by the volcanic reverberations of detonated bombs. Cursing madly, Peter had hurled a Molotov cocktail. It had missed and struck a rock and one of his own men had leaped screaming to his feet, face and body a mass of flames. Again, in hand-to-hand combat, his right forearm had been broken, then shattered, then torn away.

Peter knew he was very sick. He tried to drive these false, fiendish glimpses from memory. He lay very still, his heart still pumping hard. The light hurt his eyes. They were on fire. He had to squint to focus on anything.

Gradually, he remembered where he was and the events which had led up to his being here. He turned his head to look at Audrey. She was still sleeping blithely. His slight movement had started the room spinning. His right hand flew to his forehead. He uttered a choked cry of anguish. The pain in his wrist was unendurable. With his left hand, he lifted his right away and placed it back at his side. His head was splitting and he was nauseated. He knew what had to be done and he hated it. Through the veil of his illness, he realized that his energy had been dissipated to the minimum. He spent some time gathering such faint strength as he could. This was nonsense. His muscles were still there somewhere. He worked his way into a sitting position, dropped his legs off the side of the bed. A fine film of sweat covered his face.

Urgency drove him to force himself to his feet. He did a swooping stagger for several steps and grabbed the back of a chair with his good hand. He closed his eyes and did not open them again until the vertigo had subsided. The blood began to move through his veins. He made his way jerkily to the bathroom, closed the door as quietly as he could. A grisly half hour followed. One way and another he got rid of the poison. As a finale, he leaned over the wash basin for five minutes, coughing and gagging. This simply made his throat sore. His stomach was empty.

When, at length, he straightened, he stood there until his breathing became less labored. He found the door and went back into the bedroom. Weak and quaking, he dropped into the nearest armchair. It was inadequate but expedient. He sat there thinking of nothing, growing relatively calmer. He was completely unnerved, unfathomably depressed. His eyes fell on a bottle of brandy. Well, why not? He trembled to his feet, made his way to it, and, after several grabs, weakly secured it. He went back to the bathroom, drew the cork with his teeth, held the bottle against his left side for control, and poured a drink. He got the cold water running, got some into another glass. There was some waste but he got some water down, followed it with brandy, got some more water down. He hurried awkwardly into the bedroom, breathing through his mouth, frantically found a cigarette, got it going and stood leaning against the wall.

In a little while, he went back to the bathroom. More water, more brandy, more water, more cigarette. Each time he almost knocked his teeth out, finally thought it funny. He repeated this performance a half dozen times and topped it of with milk of magnesia. He sank back into the armchair and drew heavily on the current cigarette. He supposed he was drunk but the pain and the shaking were in limbo.

Peter knew he had been drinking too much but he was not yet on dangerous ground. His reasoning, when acknowledged, had undergone no change brought about by alcohol. But he was in tenuous territory, the gloomy-lonely realm of the desperate yearning, brain-scarring, over-nurtured hangover. He must proceed with care, cautious, calculated care. He would do that. Overcome with a great drowsiness, he got back into bed. He slept soundly.

Four hours later, he was awakened by Audrey's kiss. It was a more relaxed awakening until she spoke. She was seated on the edge of the bed in a rich white robe, her makeup already accomplished.

"Good morning," she caroled with grease-paint gaiety. She kissed him again, then drew away a little and looked into his eyes with what she hoped was earnest enquiry. She had gone headachily through the first part of her toilette with a growing feeling of humiliation. Either the whole world might one day know and laugh or no one but she would ever know and any laugh was doubtful. It all depended on how drunk he had been. The suspense could not be borne, She had to know. "Can you believe now that I'm going to make you happy?" she asked with measured will.

Peter floundered, summoned words. "How could I doubt it?" he countered with disciplined gallantry. How the hell should he know? He had evidently committed himself. Christ. But what matter? He still felt lousy in a way. He still felt lousy and his spirit was still sick around his heart.

Audrey flushed scarlet. That was all right. He remembered nothing! The breaks were still with her! Watch it, watch it. Easy. She lowered her eyes to hide the intense relief and triumph which must be revealed there. She gave him another quick, girlish kiss. "You're hung over," she chided, pouting coyly, "the traditional bridegroom. But you're not alone in skipping originality. The bride's hung over, too." She swung up and away from him and went to her dressing table.

Peter's heart pumped. There was no giving a damn now about anything but necessities. Necessities were blessedly temporal. He got up. He got into his shorts and into the bathroom. Cellophane-wrapped toothbrush and razor were on the shelf.

After a stout breakfast of kippers and bacon in the Dorothy Draper-English Country House dining room, they piled into Peter's car. Audrey's maids had packed a bag which was placed in the back of the car by her butler, Garden. A tall, lean, lugubrious, mortuary figure with a perpetual 'edge' and a semi-covered cockney accent, he had a kind heart and an outstanding talent for loyalty and calm service.

"You're looking very beautiful this morning, miss."

"Thank you, Garden." She was wearing a dark green gabardine suit, grass green alligator shoes, gloves and bag, a pert grass green felt hat, red silk scarf and weighty emerald jewels. Her eyes were extraordinarily green and bright, her lips vermillion, the skin of her sculptured face and neck marble flesh against the blue coal of her hair. She was emptily determined to be excitedly pleased with life.

"I may be in town for a few days. I'll let you know when I know." Uncertainty kept servants alert. "Going to 'Cragie' first."

"Very good, miss."

On Audrey's insistence, they drove into the village to see Dr. Thompson before doing anything else. It was a perfect early fall day. As the colorful countryside flashed by, four excellent cups of coffee percolated anew and Peter asked Audrey her preferences in the matter of the wedding. Audrey would have revelled in spectacle. Those who witnessed it, saw the pictures or read about it would never cease to talk about her marriage to Peter Drake. But arrangements for a formal wedding would require at least a month. She could have cried in her disappointment. But the opposition she must face was strong and unscrupulous. She dared not add the element of time risk. And there was romantic glamour in elopement. And there was triumphant security in the dotted line. Then New York had that silly adultery law.

"Would you like to drive to Elkton?"

"Is it far?"

"Not after we get to New York. And I think the justices of the peace accept fees seven days a week."

"Done," said Peter.

They found Dr. Thompson at his Georgian home on the lovely old tree-lined main street. The old gentleman was back from church and seated with the *New York Times* awaiting his Sunday noon dinner. He was delighted to see them. After the usual exchange of pleasantries, Audrey apologized for disturbing him and explained she was worried about Peter's wrist. Peter told him the car door story.

Dr. Thompson examined the wrist at some length and with the greatest care. His strong, gentle hands held the penetrating wisdom of experience. His unhurried attention to detail carried the solid conviction of the consecrated professional. He completed the examination and sat back.

"Are you going home when you leave here?"

"Well, not exactly," replied Peter. "I'm stopping only long enough to pick up a few things and then I'm driving on into the city."

"You'll want an opinion other than mine and that, of course, you'll get in New York. I think you'll find my diagnosis correct, however. In any event, my recommendations should help and certainly can do no harm. I'm satisfied that there's no fracture, but there is a nasty bruise, and, I'm afraid, a very serious nerve injury." He went on to explain and advised certain care and treatment. Peter would not hear of a sling or even carrying the hand over the top button of his coat. If the blood flow should be on a level with his elbow, that would have to wait until he got started to town. Those who would see him at 'Cragie' must not be alarmed. He wanted no fuss. He pledged the doctor and Audrey to secrecy. As a poor substitute, the doctor slung the hand in Peter's right coat pocket, told him to keep it there and gave him a shot to ease the pain. To impress the need of early attention, he revealed the possibility of paralysis through delay, neglect or carelessness.

Peter groaned lightly through his nose. In a flimsy epilogue, he had sustained the greatest shock of his life. The emotional low had been activated, the one physical injury which exceeded darkness had wiped him out. Bizarre anticlimax to everlasting fury. Audrey, watching him narrowly, had no idea what he was thinking. But she wisely decided she should say nothing until he did. It was sufficiently damning of George, and Lesley too, as it stood. Dr. Thompson would accept no fee. Sunday cases were emergency only. He asked them to dinner. They declined with thanks. He saw them out to the car.

As they drove toward 'Cragie,' Audrey casually, but with

bitter irony, introduced the subject of the line their loving adversaries were likely to take—the ruse of fractional-truth appeal to sympathy to quickly quell all anger and animosity and place them on the defensive. Then she cagily coached him in the adult reaction which must surely make impotent such time-honored, routine, selfish subterfuge.

Meanwhile at 'Cragie'—

Lesley was moving restlessly from the living room to the garden to the living room to the side entrance to the drive and back to the living room. There were shadows under her seemingly enormous, dark eyes and there was little color in her hollowed cheeks, save for a bright red flush at the cheekbones. Her arching brows were drawn into a frown, her full, affectionate lips atremble. Her light reddish hair glinted in the morning rays, every nerve in her strong, exquisite person was tensed, her heart was flooded with prayer. Thrown well back over a sky-blue toreador-type wool jacket and black skirt, she wore a very full black, blue-lined, cape which swirled flag-like as she strode from point to point. She would have been surprised to learn how strikingly beautiful she was at that moment.

Henry was staring at the floor of his room trying to decide what he should say to Lesley. George had just shaken him badly by telling him that Lesley had agreed to marriage.

Behind his locked door, George was getting dressed with Fulton's assistance. His irritation over needing help and embarrassing recollection of his collapse was tempered by frightened thoughts of the happiness which lay ahead.

Reggie was out.

Henry caught Lesley in the living room, halted her, halted her roving, confused loneliness through immediate concern for him.

She put a hand on his arm. "Hello, darling. How do you feel?"

"All right, I guess. Hope you are, too. Have you had your breakfast?"

"We had it together, didn't we?"

"So we did." His preoccupation was giving him away. Her defense of decision would be forceful without benefit of preparation. Now she must sense what was coming, must know that he knew. He ran his finger along the edge of the console table. This was no very real help to his search for words.

"Where have you been?"

"Nowhere. In my room." He was rather worried. She was so unconsciously magnificent.

"Have you seen Reggie?"

"No. He's resting, I imagine, just as we should be."

"He was wonderful last night, wasn't he?"

"Yes. A little difficult to be hysterical with Reggie around."

"How's George?"

"He's staged an amazing recovery, thanks to you."

She turned away to the garden door, looked out to sea. "I wish Peter would come back or call or something." Peter was not at sea.

"I wish he would, too. I'm going to need him."

She walked back, held his eyes. "That's not fair," she said quietly.

"I'm not going to let you do it, Lesley."

For once he must quarrel with the admirable, the motivating force of the strongest sweet personality he would ever know.

"You're doing it simply to save George. And me. I should never have asked you to help me there. And I'm not going to let it happen, Lesley."

"It's got to be. You should help me instead of— Oh, darling, you've got to help me."

"I want to. That's all I want."

This was killing, toe-to-toe fighting against heart.

She carried on her plain plea. "Then help me to keep faith with all you've taught me."

The light of his teaching had been her reflection. "You and Peter are in love." Here was solid finality.

"And if we think only of that, what becomes of George and you *and* Peter?" The pangs of desperation were liquid in her eyes and voice. "Peter doesn't know it but he could never take George's death through this, much less his living death. There's little we can say to him. But if he'll just listen and play along with us, I know it will all come right one day. It must. If it doesn't, we've been wrong all along. But we can't have been that wrong."

"No. Nothing that wrong can be. Nothing that wrong is going to be."

Her Hank was still not with her in this. He was thinking only of her. How very dear of him. And how much harder he made her lonely struggle. Her responsibility was three fold, no, four fold. Hank, Peter, George and almost doubting loyalty to her always cherished faith. Peter had sustained a great hurt. But if she wavered here and he indirectly killed George, Peter would never rise to life. And the depthless misery of it was that it could all have been so easily avoided. But could it? Should she condemn herself thus? Could anyone outline the right of a given moment?

As Henry in this impasse resorted to the cigar readying and lighting formula, she made conversation.

"I hope nothing dreadful has happened to him."

"I'm sure nothing dreadful has happened to him."

"But where can he be? Audrey promised to call if he turned up there." She hurried away from that thought as Henry studied his cigar in embarrassed silence. "Every place we tried, they said they'd let us know. And we haven't missed one possibility."

"He may just have been driving around alone all night," suggested Henry with poor helpfulness.

"I hope he hasn't been drinking." She gave up blind talk and turned away again. Her eyes travelled the sea. And she was alone again. Why was she being so damned noble? Was she as George had often platitudinously said all women were? Was her great love for Peter not absolute but capable of substitution? Was she attracted to George far more than she would admit? And secretly enamored of the idea that she must shortly become a very unique and romantic figure, a young and beautiful widow of vast wealth? Rot. She snorted derisively at her childish attempt to be hardboiled and analytical. She had best stay within the bracket of herself. Very well. She did not believe in hurt. But she must ride with it in the face of greater hurt. Nor did she believe in martyrdom. But she must be able to take it, take it and see it through.

If she could not, then the backbone of her philosophy would snap and life would be paralyzed, empty, meaningless and miserable indeed. She would marry George. She would stay with him until he was entirely well and fed up with her. Then she would divorce him. Ghastly. Every fibre of her being, every nerve of her body, cried out against it. Yet it was not in her power to speak or move against it.

She laughed harshly. She was doing what she was doing because she could not do otherwise. She turned back to Henry, saw his startled look.

"Don't mind me." She laughed again, lightly this time but without heart. Then, "I think I'll take a turn around outside," she said quickly.

"Yes, dear. Do that."

His eyes were troubled as he watched her go. She had never walked out on him before. This was going to be even tougher than, in careful, scientific, frank fear, he had known it would be. He picked up the extension 'phone at the end of the divan.

"One five, one five, please . . . Hello, Miss Audrey

Smyth's residence? . . . Could I speak to Miss Smyth, please? Henry Curzen calling . . ." A respectful Garden informed Dr. Curzen that Miss Smyth was, at that very moment, en route to 'Cragie' with Mr. Peter Drake. "You're quite sure?" Garden was sure. Miss Smyth had informed him that was the plan. "I see. Do you—" Henry knew the question should not be asked—"do you happen to know how long Mr. Drake had been there?" Garden was sorry but he had not seen Mr. Drake when he arrived. "I see," again. To try to get other than a routine correct answer from Garden was as futile as are any and all attempts to shake the poise of a telephone operator. "Thank you, Garden." Garden thanked Dr. Curzen. Henry cradled the phone. He must find Reggie.

Unable to disguise the fact that he was leaning heavily on Fulton for support, George moved slowly into the room from the hall.

"Here, what's all this?" cried Henry sternly and hurried toward him.

"This is George. Remember me?" He looked at Henry quizzically. "And what's all that? You, isn't it?"

Henry and Fulton got him into the nearer armchair.

"Thank you. And thank you, Fulton. Forgive me if I've overtaxed you. I keep forgetting that we're both getting older."

"You're as young as ever, sir. And I can still manage. Will that be all, sir?"

"That will be all," said George gently.

Fulton gave Henry a worried glance and retired.

"I don't want to be in bed when Peter gets here."

"I can't see why. He'd prefer to find you alive, I'm sure."

Peter had just come back after eight long years. Surely, George reasoned stubbornly, he could not really go away again no matter what had happened. "He'll be here. I'm sure of that."

"So am I."

"I don't know what I'll say to him, Hank."

"I'd suggest you let that take care of itself."

George visualized a scene of mutual forgiveness. Then all that remained was for Peter to get back to work. With that and Lesley his happiness would be complete. But it might not fall out just that way. He wondered what he would do should he meet with reverses. This was a new approach for him. He noted with pride that his thinking had been following new and strange lines this morning. It might be a result of his attack but he had moments of relaxation when he knew he could play the resignation of the great man convincingly. Even now was he looking on this hypothetical problem of further difficulties musingly, without rancor. Of course there would be no problem. But it was curiously comforting to know that, if need be, he could now meet even death through defeat quite gracefully. George did not realize that dreams of tolerance could be the backwash of victory.

He looked up at Henry and remembered he was afraid of what Henry would think of that attack. "Was I—was it very bad last night, Hank?"

"I don't have to tell you how bad it was."

George smiled to himself. Hank was so serious about this sort of thing. After all, supposed conclusions in such cases as his were purely surmise based on incomplete experience. The field remained an unsolved mystery for the most part. And his collapse had proved to him that he knew more about himself than anyone else ever could. He was invulnerable. And even if he were not, there could be nothing very harrowing in any phase through which he might pass. He suddenly saw the immensity of the relief this unchallengeable knowledge brought him. Now he smiled on Henry.

"Hank, you made me a promise yesterday." He paused

for effect. "I want to release you from that promise." Then a shade frantically as Henry failed to answer, "I mean it, Hank. I've changed my mind."

"That's very kind of you, George." Here was an amusing George, a light, a novel George. Henry studied him closely and knew the case was out of his hands. The balance in these matters was extremely delicate, the tilt of the scales so microscopic it defied exact detection. But the outward manifestation was always temporarily broad. This new brightness could mean a real and lasting improvement or the sudden flashing lift before the end. Either way, he could do nothing about it. George had taken the play away from him. Henry was familiar with this odd phenomenon. There was nothing now but to hope for the best.

Incredibly, the physical injuries George had sustained through his falls were relatively negligible. There had been no injury to his jaw as a result of his brief encounter with Peter. There was no help a physician could give him. George had been open for the first time. He had freely discussed the details of his dread experience of the night before. And he knew it had been brought about by the strain he had imposed on himself. No one else was to blame for his reaction to normal incidents. This momentary George could admit his condition, confess his age, even be fairly, slyly witty.

Henry knew that even now George was playing with him. He decided to take up his part of the game. "You're quite sure you won't change your mind again?"

"Quite. And if I do, I want you to ignore it."

"But you exacted that promise in such a way, I don't know that release is possible now."

"Good God, Hank," said George with mock indignation, "you don't think I'm not perfectly normal now, at this moment? You don't think I don't know what I'm talking about?"

"There wouldn't be anything unusual in that."

"Don't carp, Hank! I just want you to promise you won't

keep that promise. And please believe my first thought was of you!"

"Thank you, George. And your second thought?"

"I don't care to die, not now, not in that way, thank you very much."

"You're sure of that?"

"Of course I'm sure! Just as sure as I am that you could be mistaken. And you're so damned conscientious that if I didn't take up the cudgel on cue you might even talk yourself into what you considered a mercy killing."

"But—"

"But me no buts. I won't have you pitching gratuitous scares into my life. You just give me pills and take my pulse. That's enough for any medico."

"O.K. But the fee will be larger." Henry decided to try George's mood further. "And what about Lesley's promise? Are you going to release her, too?"

George was moved to anger which pulled him up short. But no, he was not going to allow himself to be thrown by Hank's trickery. He must steel himself against surprise moves, take them casually, outwit them. He should have learned after all these years. "Does she want to be released?" he asked almost coyly.

Henry drew his mouth down as from a bad taste. "Do you think it sporting to force her to carry the miserable load of keeping you in a phoney frame of mind until you pop off? Have you any least conception of the enormity of the sacrifice she's making?"

"George!" Lesley stepped into the room from the garden and walked rapidly toward him. "What on earth are you doing here?"

Smiling, George gave a good imitation of a turtle as he blinked and drew his head down toward his shoulders. "You didn't think you were marrying a weakling, did you?"

"Our George is in fine benevolent fettle this morning,

Lesley. He just freed me of what might be called a criminal debt to society, a promise he bled me for yesterday."

"No?!" cried Lesley eagerly. "But how marvelous. You see, Hank, we were right. You see?"

"Only because of you." He looked at her sharply, his heart skipped a beat, he threw his scarcely smoked cigar into the fireplace. "Excuse me. I must find Reggie," he said and hurried from the room. My God, he had almost forgotten.

"Now what?" said Lesley half aloud and sank onto the end of the divan near George.

Henry ran into Reggie in the hall. Reggie had just parked his little car near the side entrance after having scrambled all over the local roadmap with no results.

"Reggie! I was going to look for you. I just had Audrey's place on the wire. There's something I must tell you. I—I don't quite know how to do it."

Reggie had been hitting a gallant pace. Now he threw his hands out, let them drop back to his sides, drooped, sighed, relaxed. "You don't have to tell me," he said.

"You knew?"

He sighed again. "Of course. At least, now I know what I knew."

"I'm sorry, damned sorry. And this is a hell of a time to ask you for help. But I've got to be brutal. They'll be here any minute. And I need you, need you badly, I guess."

"That's all right." Reggie straightened, brightened. "What do we do?"

Henry reflected that here was an amazing man. "Let's go into the library."

They stood by the library window which commanded a view of the fork in the drive and hashed over facts and possibilities in staccato whispers. When they saw the car come roaring up the drive and take the north branch, they knew they were too much in the dark to foresee eventualities, knew they could form no plan or plans of campaign other than the obvious, which, weakened by foreknowledge, might prove the most effective after all. Excitement ran high between them. They tried to down it in favor of concise action.

George looked slowly on the lovely entity seated near him and knew that he loved her, a peacefully shattering discovery, knew, too, that he had loved Katherine in an obscure and fumbling way but honestly, knew that he loved her son, Peter Drake. So it went, so must it go. He was drowsy and alert by turns. Was this it? He shook himself mentally. This truly beautiful child bride-to-be had known of Hank's promise. That may have weighed heavily in her decision. Regardless of her reasons, he would hold her to her troth. He had gone enough of the full distance to see the importance of solid extracurricular factors. Both Lesley and Peter had yet to learn. Hank should have been with him. But only Audrey wanted to see him marry Lesley. The others were all against it. But through the astute revelations of those who knew, he had learned that this cold paradox always obtained. If he were more than formally sure of Lesley, it would be easier. But, no matter what the outcome, he would put up a good fight.

Technically, he had won already. And he was not reshuffling facts to prove his desire. He spoke now with calm light assurance.

"I'm afraid I'm going to have to stand alone in my fight to keep you, Lesley."

Lesley was unhappily startled from her bitter worry. "Fight? Why do you think you'll have to fight? I should think you'd stop fighting now."

"I will if I can be sure you'll stand with me, no matter what they do."

"I just don't get you, George."

"Everyone, our well-meaning friends, until they know it's no use, they'll try to keep us apart. Even then, some of them will carry on."

"Why should they do that?"

"Don't ask me why but they always do. It's human nature."

"But, George, such ideas are so depressing, and *wrong.*" Lesley was conversing distractedly. Her head was not aching really but it might as well be. This was a foretaste of what she must bravely endure if she was half the woman she would like to be. She was talking to a mental cripple whom she must treat nicely. But how dare she feel that way? All knowledge was still questionable. Her anxiety was making her stuffy. George was making sense after a fashion. Misery was touching the marrow, breaking her gait. See it through. See it through. "You know I don't think or believe that way."

"No. But you will." George did not mean to be cruel. In fact, he did not know what he meant, nor was he concerned. His thought was quietly in a future, fictitious country.

"I hope I never will." She was almost vehement. That was doubt. She must not doubt. "I believe if a thing's right, nothing wrong can touch it. At least, not so long as I can go on believing it *is* right."

"And you do believe this is right, you and I?"

Spirit deserted her. "I don't know. I hope so."

"They'll try to keep us apart. You'll see." It was as he had known it must be. His speech carried the false but impressive emphasis of certainty.

"George, friendship is a beautiful thing, isn't it?"

"It's supposed to be."

"It is. And if this is right between us, our friends will see the beauty and do their best to protect it."

"You forget jealousy, vanity, selfishness. There's too much hate in most love. I feel safer with my enemies than with my friends."

"Now, George, really," she tried to be reasonable, "suppose

you weren't in love with me and I was engaged to Peter. Would you try to keep us apart?"

His face was hot. He could feel it. His new freedom was still vulnerable. "I might. It's a little hard to answer that. Yes, I think I would."

"I don't think you would. Instead, you'd do all you could to help us and be very happy about it, *very* happy."

"I know I should be. But I wouldn't."

"I don't believe it." Lesley ignored George's jerky delivery. She took a tangent which was obscurely but closely related to their argumentative search for one another. "I think there's far more love in your heart than you know. You've just never found a way to give it. When you do, and I know you will," was she being stuffy again? "I think you'll find everything you've always wanted. That's what I think," she ended a little lamely.

George settled into his response. It was best that he should make it count. "Then you know how much hope I place in you, how I'm going to find everything through you. You see how wrong the sentimental are. You see how I can be sure now that I'll never be beaten. And why I'd give my life to fight anything that threatened us."

"No, George, I've got to be honest. I try to understand. But I think, in most ways, you're as much a stranger to me as I am to you."

"Don't say that, Lesley." There was genuine entreaty in his tone. "You mustn't be a stranger to me in any way." Here was some of the pathos of a terrified child. "You won't be, will you?"

The weight of duty was pressing in. "I'll do my best, George. I will. That's all I can say."

"But you must say more than that. You must. You must promise me."

"How can I?" Lesley got up and moved fretfully about the room. That was bad. But what else was she to do? "I can't think of anything now but Peter and what all this may do to him. If that comes right, everything will be all right. If it doesn't, if he's a stranger to me, then I'll never be anything but a stranger to everyone, myself included," she concluded on a sombre note. Impatience was bursting within her. Again she knew, less mirthfully, that she was not a nurse. "George, I'm terribly nervous." She indicated the garden door. "Do you mind?"

"Of course not." He made himself say it. His eyes held the vision of her long after she was out of sight in the garden. That girl was nowhere near him. But she would be. She had yet to learn.

Peter had insisted on doing the driving from the edge of the village to 'Cragie' with Audrey docilely handling the transmission. He parked the car at the side entrance.

Things began to move rapidly toward a climax issue.

There could never be an ending.

XVI

REGGIE DASHED INTO THE LIVING ROOM, LOOKED AROUND, gave George a quick 'hello, how you doing?', went out the garden door and caught up with Lesley on the terrace. He pulled himself together and grinned at her.

"Hi."

"Hello, Reggie darling."

"Gee." He looked at her admiringly.

"What's the matter?"

"Hm? Oh—" He suddenly touched off his own brand of light seriousness. "Of course it's none of my business."

"I don't think you should feel that way, do you?"

"Then, I think you're an idiot to do this. But I love you for it."

"That's very sweet, Reggie."

He craned at the tree tops nervously, then looked back at her. "I suppose you know where Peter spent the night?"

"No." She said it slowly, lowly.

Reggie was touched more than he thought he could be. He became elaborately casual, had to reach for his voice. "But you could guess, couldn't you?"

"I don't think I'd want to do that, Reggie."

"No, I know. But you'd be right. They just drove in."

"Oh, Reggie."

"Now don't let it get you." He took her arm in a quick, firm grip that hurt. "You're not through yet, you know. Peter went up to his room. Audrey's roaming the joint somewhere."

"But, Reggie, that—it's my fault, you see."

"In my humble opinion, nothing is your fault."

"And you—it's so awful for you, isn't it? I mean—you do love Audrey, don't you?"

"You can think of that at a time like this? There ought to be a Nobel prize for a woman like you."

"If I hadn't always known it, I'd have learned last night how really fine you are."

Reggie straightened. His throat hurt. "If I were really fine, I'd be in love with you, not Audrey." Then as though impatiently, angrily brushing away a tear, "But don't worry about me. I've had time to get tough. It's different with you. You've got to think fast, Lesley."

"Yes, yes. I'll try. I'm trying."

"He doesn't know it, but I guess he's just about one of the greatest guys that ever happened. And you, well, Jesus. I'll do anything I can to help you. And I'll be doing it for you, thank God."

"I wonder if this was what George meant?" And there was real wonder in her eyes.

"I don't think he knows what he means. What was it?"

"Nothing, nothing. But he was wrong. I knew he must be. Bless you, Reggie." She kissed his cheek and started rapidly across the flagstone path in front of the house.

Reggie went back to the living room. Henry was talking to George, looked up enquiringly.

"Oke," said Reggie with thumb and index finger.

"Thank you, Reggie." Henry started for the hall.

"You all treat me as though I were a child," complained George, still the quiet master of the situation.

Henry paused. "You should be able to deduce quite a lot from that," he dug back and was gone.

When Henry got to Peter's room, he was surprised to discover that Lesley was not already there. Peter was throwing essentials, one-handed, into a bag and telling a disturbed

Fulton that he would notify him where to send his other things later. Henry stepped across the threshhold and Peter, half-angry, half-sick, greeted him off-handedly. As soon as Henry told Peter with fine diffidence but distant response that he would like to talk to him, Fulton made his way into the hall.

Meanwhile, Lesley had encountered Audrey near the side entrance. Audrey's lips had twisted into a smile when she saw Reggie's car in the drive. That he had been out that early meant only one thing. She had just made up her mind to search him out as Lesley swung around the corner of the house.

"Well, well! Good morning!"

"Well, well. I do hope you turn out to be right." Lesley was not exactly tight-lipped. She was after breath, after life.

"Oh, come now. Don't be morbid. I hear best wishes are in order."

"Why so?"

"I hear that gentle George has succumbed at last. It's true, isn't it? Peter gave me all the ugly details."

"And you're so easily shocked. He shouldn't have done that."

What did the big red-headed bitch mean by that? Hey, hey, what was this? Was she still afraid of her? Of course not. Why should she be now? The hell with her. "You'll be glad to hear that I, too, am in line for condolences. Peter and I are on our way."

"Was Peter at your house when I called last night?"

"But of course."

"Why didn't you tell me?"

"You don't think I'm a *complete* fool, do you?"

Lesley pretended to think that one over. "No. No, not really."

"I knew you'd call with the story that George was ill."

"But it was true."

"I don't care whether you thought it was true or not." Audrey was really tough about it. "It's one of the oldest gags in the world. I certainly wasn't going to let Peter fall for it."

"And you haven't told him yet?"

"Why should I? You'll all do that. But don't be too surprised if he doesn't believe you."

"How could you think I'd lie where I'd rather die than be dishonest, really how?"

"You and George are two of a kind. You'd do anything to get what you want and then try to justify it to top it off."

Lesley looked at her for a long moment and nodded comprehendingly. "Of course. You would expect us to use your methods."

"I use only what I've got and have a right to use," snapped Audrey. "And that's *plenty*. And I use it well." She went on with exaggerated disgust, "I told you you'd hang yourself, Les. I suppose you know you have?"

"You look a little bloated this morning, Audrey."

"I told you Peter needed a woman who was a woman," continued Audrey savagely. "Well he's been saved, my dear, by little Salvation Audrey." She smiled grimly. "I really feel very happy this morning. And so does Peter. That is, what's left of him."

Audrey went into a distorted but amazingly recollective review of their lives. She remembered every least instance in which Lesley had defeated her. And, through it all, she had always known that this day would come when she would easily and completely defeat her holy, underhand machinations. There was pathetic un-self knowledge in her overplaying as she got back to her uncertain triumph. "I'll have to call him Peter the repeater. I could call him Peter the automatic or machine gun. But that wouldn't be very flattering to me, would it? So it'll have to be Peter the six-shot repeater. Or was it eight?" She looked away to hide an insidious feeling of pain.

Lesley was startled by so much vindictiveness. Her native understanding was great but could not grasp the fiery, evaporating passages of temperament. They were, to her, important. She had walked away from Henry. She had walked away from George. Now she found herself walking away from Audrey. She went into the house and into the powder room. Such sickness was ghastly and dangerously weakening. It was not Audrey. It was awareness of the whole maddening mass of unliveable incident. She miserably gained control. She went on up to her room and scrubbed her teeth. She had to see Peter.

"Cigarette?" Henry made the easy offer with Peter's own humidor.

"Thanks." Peter accepted with his left hand and, again with his left hand, lighted Henry's cigarette and his own. "I don't think there's anything for anyone to say to anyone, really. Audrey and I are on our way to Maryland. I'm just stopping long enough to say good-bye, that's all."

"Peter, could I have a look at that right hand?" Henry was firmly casual.

Damn. Irritating interference. No doubt well meant but privacy was still precious. "It isn't the hand. It's the wrist. And it's nothing but a bruise." Then as Henry said nothing but extended a surgeon's hand, "I'd like to forget it if you don't mind. At least until I get to town."

"I won't say anything—to George or anyone else here."

Annoyedly, Peter lifted the hand away from its jacket sling. Henry examined the wrist with deft alertness.

"We must attend to this at once."

"When I get to town."

"That's dangerous. Peter there are certain vital nerves in the wrist, median and ulnar, to be exact. Yours have been injured, perhaps badly."

"I know all that. Audrey's doctor told us."

"Did he tell you that you could lose the use of the hand,

permanently?" Henry saw the defensive anger smoldering in Peter's eyes as he nodded. He dropped the hand gently back into the pocket. "Go to old Sargent the minute you get to New York. He'll be at the hospital this Sunday. I'll call him. Meanwhile, don't use the hand, don't use it at all. If you're very careful, there may be every chance of recovery. God grant there is. Nothing worse could happen to you, I know."

"Oh, but it could, and has," said Peter with boyish bitterness and then pulled away from his resentment. Henry was no alarmist. But after all, what did these doctors really know, any of them? Anticipating fate was churlish quibbling. Why throw his weight around? Why expect rejected sympathy? His first job was to get better. And then, if he must think, think. He was doing no measurable thinking now.

As Henry watched this young suffering, he knew that his own spirit was weary, weary of all that part of life which was marred and disillusioned. But there was always still the better part of life to be won. There could be no retreat until the final shadow touched tired eyes with a new and soothing and only light. "You're right. There's nothing to say. You're going to see George?"

"For a moment."

"Any concession is too much to expect but I hope you'll be gentle. George was hurt, too, both ways, just as you were, Peter. He had a serious attack after you left. Another could easily finish him."

Peter had paid slight heed to Audrey's intimations but they must have registered. "Hank, forgive me, but that sounds a little far-fetched."

"I know. But it isn't."

"I'll be gentle," said Peter impatiently. He was anxious to be free of all these embarrassing entanglements.

"You see, George has always believed himself to be your father."

"My father?" Peter was startled in spite of himself. He sat down on the canopied four-poster which had couched all his sweet dreams in his early love of life. He looked at Henry, bewildered.

"Yes," said Henry quietly. High time the boy should know. With great delicacy of feeling, he told Peter the story which everyone knew but Peter, told him, too, how George had been a dying man these many years, told him of his recent bids for destruction. He was gratified to see the growing light of understanding in Peter's eyes as he had known he would. Henry's eloquence lay not only in his avoidance of any direct appeal but in the intimate, albeit tragic, picture his kindly understanding gave of Peter's mother and father and George. "That's all, I guess," he said finally.

After a long silence, Peter stood up slowly. "Thanks, Hank," he muttered and tomped out a second cigarette.

"Lesley has great spiritual wealth, just as you have."

Peter's eyes glinted. Much was happening in his mind which was revealing but brought no happiness. Honesty held his heart as in a vise. "Lesley may have it. I haven't."

"She knows you have." In less than a decade, Peter had endured more than he, Henry, and George and generations of others had touched upon. Pure sadness touched the words which Henry knew must be empty. "She has great faith in your strength."

"Her faith is misplaced."

"She's still close to you. Only you can destroy her belief."

"I don't want to destroy anything." Peter bit off the words. "I'll never create now. But I don't want to destroy."

Lesley was standing in the doorway.

"May I come in?" she had not meant to whisper that way.

"Of course," said Peter and hoped she had not seen how the sight of her had shaken him.

As Lesley came into the room, Henry moved to the door.

"We were just talking about you," he said. Had he taken unfair advantage? Did he want Lesley to have Peter and yet save George? A lifetime habit of belief and its practice were not easily foresworn. He hoped he had done the right thing. He turned and addressed himself to Peter. "Shall I tell George you're here?"

"In a little while. Is he in his room?"

"No. He's dressed and sitting down in the living room." Then to Peter's raised eyebrows, "No one must know that he's not a tower of strength." Henry smiled wistfully, turned away and walked down the hall.

Lesley still spoke with difficulty. "I'm glad you're back, Peter. I'm glad you're all right."

"Thank you, Lesley." He looked off across the fields. "Do you know all that's happened, what I'm going to do?"

"Yes." She sat uncomfortably against the edge of the bed, dropped her cape, cleared her throat nervously. "I—I hope you'll be very happy, Peter."

His eyes snapped to hers. "Don't say things like that."

"But I mean it. I do."

"You know I won't be," he said roughly. "Do you expect ever to be happy?"

"I did."

"So did I. That's when I thought it was real and the rest fake. Now I know it's all fake, for me anyway."

Lesley fought back the tears. "I wish you wouldn't be bitter, Peter. I know that sounds silly. But I wish you wouldn't."

Peter pocketed his left hand, too, and moved here and there about the room. That would look natural. He was getting jumpy again. "I don't want to be bitter. But there's nothing else to be and no reason to resent it."

"Oh, Peter, I—I suppose you can never forgive me for what happened. But I—I was trying to act for the best. I really was."

"I'm sure you were," he said tersely. Then, more gently, as he felt harshness was accomplishing no purpose. "There's nothing to forgive really, unless—I'm sorry I behaved as I did. I'm sorry for everything, most of all that there should be anything to be sorry about."

Lesley, watching him with anxious, almost frightened, eyes, swallowed hard. "It's so hard to talk, somehow, isn't it?" He said nothing, only looked away again. "Will I—will I see you sometimes, Peter? Later on, I mean?" There was a distressing pain in her heart.

He looked back at her earnestly. "You know that wouldn't be possible."

"You mean I won't again, ever?" She tried bravely to dismiss the pain.

"George won't ever want to see me again after today. And I don't suppose I'll ever want to see him."

"But you'll change. You'll both change."

"No, it's gone too far. And you and I aren't two people who could just 'see' one another. And I know you must hate Audrey and, oh, the whole thing would be impossible. You know that."

She was fighting for everything now. "But I don't hate Audrey. I don't."

"Then you must hate me, which is worse."

This lifted her to her feet. "Oh, Peter, Peter, I love you. And if you hate me, you shouldn't." She was an amazingly appealing figure. When he made no move toward her, she clung to the bed post. "I didn't know George was going to fall in love with me. I wouldn't want him to. You must know that. And I don't believe he is in love with me, not really, but he thinks he is. That's why I did what I did."

"Yes, I know." Peter was stirred to the roots of his being but felt he must clamp to his senses. "You've saved him, saved his life. And to do that, you had to take ours." As she started to protest, he interrupted her. "That's all right. I wouldn't have it otherwise. But you see what it means. Love isn't bigger than life and life isn't bigger than people." Meaningless talk but it had the saving appearance of detachment. "It's no use, Lesley."

The tears were struggling again. "Peter, if we can't go on believing when things like this happen, we can't go on believing at all. Don't you see?"

"Of course I see. We can't go on believing. I know that now."

"But," she said lowly under the tremor in her voice, "couldn't you try to go on believing, at least, just for a little while?"

Peter thought about it as carefully as was possible for him at the time. "I don't think so. I honestly don't."

"Peter, I know you've been hurt." Her words tumbled out desperately. "But we can't be entirely lost to each other and all we know it true, no matter how foul and fiendish the abuse. If you'll just try the impossible our way, try to stand by even just for that little while, I know it'll all come right. I wouldn't ask if I didn't feel sure."

Peter, who had been walking up and down, spun around. "But what is there to stand by about?" The hidden anguish in her expression made him lower his voice. "If you mean you'd have me go on loving you and all you stand for, you know I always will. But it's a hopeless kind of love because everything that it should take in stride can send it spinning. There is no love and there is no life, Lesley. Not as we know it."

She drove stars into her eyes, spoke through the choking in her throat. "If you're really ready to go on loving me and all we love, then I know I'll go on living. And I know you will, too."

"Since you seem to want to, I'm glad of that," he said bluntly. "But don't think I'm going to or that I want to. You know what my life will be."

"That doesn't matter." She held back the torrent, spoke buoyantly. "You're going to stand by. And I know you'll see and believe again. I know you will."

He paused, looked on her with something like reverence. Figuratively, he shook his head and sighed. "You're a great person, Lesley. And I love you for that, too. But you'll go through life, a hell of a life, looking for something you'll never find. And you'll probably have to go it alone. Don't look to me, Lesley. I'm not great. I never could be and I don't want to be. I haven't the heart to be great."

"You're far greater than you'll ever know," she said huskily with utter conviction.

Peter tore free of the spell. He was almost won over. He moved away again, talking as he went. His mild version of brutality was not too effective, even though directed largely at his inner self. He feared he was close to being visibly affected. And that was bad. He had to get going. And he could not let Lesley see him packing with one hand. "You say I'll never know. If you're right in the first instance, I hope you're right there, too. There's no room in the world for what you call greatness. It's a hurly-burly, rough and tumble grab-bag. The mental and spiritual are controlled by material conditions and ambitions. The emotional and inspirational are commercialized and vulgarized. Who wants to be knocked down and dragged to death through the mud, holding to idealistic beliefs?" He ran out of phrases and turned back to her. "Look, be a good girl and go down to the living room and say I'll be down in a minute, will you?"

Face averted, Lesley nodded blindly, gathered up her cape and fled the room. The tears were streaming down her cheeks now. Damn. She was being such a sissy. She had to go to her own room and bathe her eyes and wait until she gained control. She was glad no one had seen her.

Peter stood staring at the empty doorway for some time after she had left him. Then, cursing softly, he went back to his sketchy packing. None of this should matter to him now but it persisted. Lesley would not break her promise to George, or to herself. She was shouldering an insupportable burden which she need not have touched. It was a wanton disregard of self. But out of her deliberate suffering, she might gain peace. His own strivings toward happiness had met with nothing but failure. He would not dream of diverting her from her purpose. Good was her guide-on, her concept of divinity her CO. Loyalty was her life. Who dare touch such soul-born madness? From his entrails rose the shrieking protests of the eternally damned but he was deaf to them.

When Henry left Lesley and Peter in the latter's room, he had gone on down to the living room to relieve Reggie of 'the George watch.' Reggie had gratefully and gracefully retreated.

He now stood in the lower hall, pondering possibilities and hit on the library as a likely haven. Audrey, on the hunt for him, came around the corner from the passage to the side entrance just in time to see him enter it and close the door. Thus Reggie's anticipated breathing space was short lived. He stood for a moment and drank in the luxury of his hideaway, then crossed to the desk. On it stood a small chrome tray with a chrome thermos-carafe of ice-water and two glasses. And Hank usually kept a bottle of good whiskey in the second drawer. The whiskey was there. Good. Reggie was tired of being light about being low and George's new casual morbidity had been getting on his nerves. The hell with the whole mess. He would grab a drink, a good book and a few minutes of peace. Audrey had silently opened the door and now stood just inside the room watching him. Reggie was about to draw the cork when he looked up. He set the bottle down on the blotter with a bang.

"Drinking again, heh?" Audrey clucked sadly.

Reggie did not throw the bottle. Instead, he walked around

to the front of the desk and straddled one corner. "Now, be Jaysus, if it isn't the Duchess of Peter, the duck of Drake."

"Your Irish accent stinks."

"So does the audience, right through the rafters."

Audrey's eyes flashed. She walked over and sat on the other end of the desk. She clunked her bag down, hip-stepped herself to comfort, crossed her legs, adjusted her skirt for effect, set her arms akimbo, elbows thrown back, bringing the breasts up and forward. "I don't know why I've tolerated you all these years, Reggie."

Reggie bowed, offered her a cigar from the desk humidor. When she refused with a glance of scorn, he shrugged, took one himself, bit off the end. He deposited the end in the bowl-like brass ashtray, then grabbed Audrey's bag and examined his lips in its mirror. Apparently satisfied, he dropped the bag back on the desk and picked up a brass and green leather lighter.

He looked about at the forest-green leather decor of the lovely room, then at Audrey's green suit and accessories. "All this green rather washes you out," he commented tentatively. He studied her bosomy profile. "Sort of flat, like a billiard table." That brought nothing. "A shade sickening, too, isn't it?" When she continued to ignore him, he lighted the cigar with a flourish, inhaled deeply and destroyed his smile of satisfaction with a racking cough which brought him to his feet.

"Hah," laughed Audrey contemptuously.

Reggie examined her loftily, inhaled again, did not cough, showed his pleasure frankly, replaced the lighter carefully and resumed his own place on the desk. "There are always compensations," he said philosophically. Then more sharply, "You'll never have to tolerate me again. And after all you've suffered, you'll be able to fully appreciate your escape."

Audrey pricked up her ears. There was a foreign note here. "What do you mean?"

Reggie jammed the cigar out in the ashtray, got up and moved away. Audrey immediately grasped one knee and leaned back a little on her spine. When Reggie turned to face her, he was halted by this further exhibition of allure. There was little left to the imagination, just enough. He pretended to ignore it. "I mean that, in spite of all your bitchery, you've always held top spot with me. But you've been knocked down now for good and all and I hope to God I never see you again as long as I live." He looked down at the smooth flesh of the thighs above the silk stockings. "And don't show me most of what I don't want any of."

Audrey flushed and sat up. She had forgotten her position as she listened to him. "But you don't really mean what you're saying, Reggie."

"I've never meant anything so much." He was standing some distance from her, standing on both feet, his eyes angry. "It's not just what you've done to me. It's the hurt you've done everyone. You don't know what real hurt is. But there's no excuse or forgiveness in that."

"You *are* serious, aren't you?" There was a little awe-struck tone to her voice. "I've never known you to be serious before."

"That isn't because I haven't been serious."

He was too far away, altogether too far. She got up and crossed to him. But he was still far away. She must get him back. She looked into his eyes pleadingly. "Don't desert me now, Reggie. I need you now, more than ever."

"What makes you think you need me?" He fired the question at her.

"I need you because I love you," she fired back, "most of all because I think you love me."

"I did."

"Then you still do. You can't just suddenly stop that way."

"One wouldn't think so but you've made it possible. Anyway, what would you know about it?"

"I just told you that I love you."

"I heard you," he almost shouted, "and I'm thinking among other things, that I don't believe you."

"Oh, but you do." She was close to yelling, too.

"I know how much I want to believe you. That's why I don't."

"Then I was right. You do love me. And you won't desert me, no matter what reasons you may think you have, will you?"

They paused for breath. This had gone beyond anything either had expected. Audrey was thrilled and frightened. It had dawned on her so suddenly that she loved Reggie and that it was of first importance that he should love her. And he had said he did! When had this happened? And when could it be confirmed? There must be no doubt. It was the most wonderful thing ever. There was no doubt where she was concerned. But there was always that shadow of doubt, now a haunting doubt, where Reggie was concerned. Even how he was frowning, looking right through her.

Reggie was thinking that, Heaven help him, he did still love this girl, perhaps could never free himself of that obsession, for 'obsession' was what she was. He had made the final mistake of admitting his love. Regardless of what he said or did after this, she would always know. She might be a little doubtful from time to time or even most of the time. But with her sure feminine eye she would be looking for, and be sure to detect, those fatal signs which must inevitably give him away. Well, he reflected candidly and with no little courage, it could not matter now. As of this hour, it must all go one way or the other. And with his knowledge of the unused mind of the girl he loved, he could have only forebodings. Never mind. It might well be for the best that it should go the wrong way. There was much in life which he adored, much which might be neglected through subservience to one particular passion of questionable merit. There was an unadorned side of Audrey which, if she really loved him as she claimed, she would grant full recognition as their lives melded. She was maleable in that she would not oppose the natural results of getting what she wanted. Then all would be well. But did she love him? Could she *love* anyone?

"Are you trying to tell me that last night was a mistake?" he asked cautiously.

"I've been rotten to you, Reggie, in loads of ways," she confessed eagerly. "I know that now."

"Never mind that," he continued doggedly. "Do I understand that if I'm prepared to forget it, you're ready to drop Peter, and all your other delicate ambitions?"

"What *are* you talking about, Reggie? I'm to marry Peter. Today. I thought you knew that."

"What?" He gasped the word in spite of himself.

"Of course. That's all part of it. If you loved me, you'd understand."

"But you said you loved me." He was still dazed.

"And it's true. I do," she said defiantly.

There is ugly surprise in even expected shock. Reggie managed to down it with a sort of bitter amusement. "You love me and you're going to marry Peter?"

"My love for Peter is different."

"Different?" This was really rich stock stuff. "My dear Audrey, you can't be in love with two men at one and the same time unless they're one and the same man."

"Don't be silly. Of course I can. All great women have." She saw Reggie throw up his head and snort. Just like a horse! "Peter's sweet but, well, he just doesn't understand. Not as you do, Reggie."

"I see," he said, smiling quietly, a bit grimly.

"I've got to have a certain kind of life," she explained with wheedling impatience. "It's essential to me. You've always known that. And I'm going to have it now." She curbed her spoiled irritation, injected the soft, seductive quality. "But it won't be any good unless I can have you, too."

Reggie drew a hand across his eyes, then looked back at her. The lines around his mouth hardened. "Audrey, I thought I'd seen you as cruel as you could be. If anyone had told me this, I wouldn't have believed it."

"Why? What's so awful?" She was poutingly truculent as the bewildered child which would hide its alarm.

Reggie stepped free of her and walked to the desk. Audrey pivoted to watch him. He went around the desk. With one well coordinated movement, he scooped up the bottle, drew the cork and poured a half tumbler of whiskey. He recorked the bottle, returned it to the drawer, kneed the drawer closed. He picked up the glass, examined it, took a deep breath and drained it. He gasped, set the glass down, started to cough, controlled it, screwed his features to the point where it looked as though his face might fold up and disappear. Through clenched teeth and loose lips, he made blubbering sounds. He grasped the edge of the desk, compressed his lips and breathed deeply through his nose a half dozen times. That did it. He straightened and shook himself, then exhaled with a sigh. It stayed down.

"You drink too much," said Audrey.

He heard her, looked for her through the pleasant visual fog, found her. No, it simply could not be. The sardonic twinkle appeared. "You have a discovered talent for farce," he said. He waited for the warmth to race through his entire body, then walked slowly back to her, looked at her squarely. "My God, but I'm sorry for you, sorry as I've never been for anyone in my life. Through all your vicious tricks, I've always thought I could see sweetness. Believe that if you can. Sweetness. Yes, and light, for me. That's funny, I know. And that isn't all that's funny. I still think I was right. But somewhere along the way, I lost you. That isn't the bad part. The bad part is that somewhere along the way, you lost yourself. You're a dead wench, Audrey. And there's no Messiah around to call you back. That's why I'm sorry for you. That's all I can say. And there's nothing I can do."

Audrey forgot to be angry. There was real panic clutching at her heart now. She stepped close to him. "Reggie, if I lose you now, I *will* die. Please don't be so serious."

"Don't say any more." Was there no stopping this woman? "It couldn't be worse but when you know it was over, you'll be sorry you said anything."

This was too much for Audrey. Action was the only solution. She reached up and took his head in her lovely, frightened, red-clawed hands. "Don't say it's over, darling. It must never be over."

"Stop it, Audrey." He grasped her wrists, tried to draw her hands away. Those soft hands were very strong at that moment. "Can't you see how ugly this is? Can't you see we're through?" Genuine distress and disgust were unmistakable. "Good God, even you should be able to see that."

She pulled his face to hers. "Reggie, please. I love you."

He tried to avoid her kiss. It was useless. She shoved her tongue between his lips, in and out, in and out. Her moist panting mouth sucked loosely, avidly, on his. One hand slid to the back of his neck, the other went gropingly to his thighs, then around to the tip of his spine. She pushed her body in against him, rotated her hips slowly, with slowly increasing tempo, now spreading her legs a little, now bringing them together, a knee forward, now relaxing the pressure of her body, now increasing it. His arms went around her. He returned her kiss.

Peter dropped his bag in the hall, gave a preoccupied, farewell look around and caught sight of the tableau in the library. He walked over to the library door and stood watching. Here was the damnedest thing.

At last, Audrey pulled her mouth away. "Please, please, Reggie. Someone might come along."

Reggie looked up, saw Peter, looked back at Audrey and released her. "You see," he said flatly. "Even that's gone." Then he looked up again. "Hello, Peter."

Audrey, adjusting her suit and scarf, smiled knowingly at this practical joke, turned her head to look at the doorway, then spun around.

"Peter!" she ejaculated aghast.

Peter came into the room

Audrey thought of her makeup, then remembered that she had meticulously applied liquid rouge to her lips that morning in anticipation of a long series of romps with Peter as the day wore on and glamour must not wear off. She was prayerfully grateful. "Peter, I hope you don't think what you just saw was my idea?"

"I was just going to the living room to see George for a minute," he said absently. No one had told him that Reggie was in love with Audrey. He would not want to do anything to hurt Reggie.

Reggie cleared his throat. "I'm sorry if my swan song offended you, Peter. All sentimentalists say good-bye."

Then Reggie *had* cared for Audrey. But perhaps it was over. Peter had so much on his mind, it was impossible to tackle a fresh problem. "It doesn't matter," he said.

"Well!" said Audrey indignantly. "That's a gallant reaction, I must say."

"I think it is," said Reggie with quiet appreciation. "Thanks, Pete."

Audrey turned on him. "And you," she stormed with attempted sarcasm, "for someone who claims to be through, disgusted and what not, you do behave very strangely!"

"Oh, that?" asked Reggie innocently, then answered his own question. "That was just a little amorous rigor mortis. Surely, you understand?"

Tears springing to her eyes, Audrey stamped her foot, turned from one to the other in futile, inarticulate rage, went to the desk, snatched up her bag and marched into the hall ahead of them.

XVII

ONCE AGAIN THEY WERE ALL GATHERED IN THE LIVING room. George had not moved. Henry sat in the armchair opposite him. Lesley was on the divan. Audrey leaned against the cabinet bar 'Western style.' There was only one way to take a ridiculous situation and that was to kid it. Thus Audrey. Reggie, vaguely seeking effacement, stood at the garden door, his back to them. Hands in jacket pockets, Peter stood squarely before the fireplace. He and George had said 'good morning.' The urge to get away made Peter's attitude slightly rigid. There was an embarrassed silence. They could hear the two tall clocks ticking in the corner and in the hall, ticking time away. Outside, the birds, flashing color, swooped and chattered and did not seem to care. Mickey and Mike lay at Peter's feet, muzzles to the floor. They followed speech and movement only with their eyes and ears. George wondered why the others did not leave him and Peter together. Perhaps Peter wanted them there. Or perhaps they were fearful. They need not be fearful. His spirit was strong and calm. So much so that he did not even find their continued presence too awkward. He had, thus far, survived the greatest emotional crisis of his life. There was no room for lesser concerns.

Peter made an impatient gesture with his shoulders and was surprised to see George's head jerk involuntarily. "There's little else to say, I'm afraid, George. Except 'good-bye.' " Again George's head jerked in that crazy way. It was very disturbing. Hank may not have exaggerated at all, even through unconscious anxiety. The man certainly did not look well.

George moistened his lips. He supposed he was cutting a sorry figure. But that was unimportant. He felt an indifference of the sort he had enjoyed when drunk. "Peter, I'm sorry, deeply sorry, about last night."

"So am I." Peter's shy utterance was packed with feeling.

Relaxation swept over George. He realized that he was the one who had been fearful, fearful of what Peter would say and do. This sort of admission was new and rewarding to him just as was his effortless unselfconsciousnes. "Then we can shake hands and forget it?"

Peter started to accept the invitation and remembered that he could not. He spurred his mind to quick excuse. It must be right. Truth was best. "Certainly, George. But let's have it clear. We'll never meet again. There's no forgetting."

George knew he must not shake this way. The old spirit of fight had been replaced with thought. This was a new kind of fight which took thought of other thought. He must say something to hide his misery. "Time, time," he muttered.

"No, George. If it's touched you, there is no time."

The boy could not mean that he had really loved Lesley? But never mind. He might, he might. Ten thousand devils spun and hopped and jabbed. He must keep his chin up even if it trembled. He heard himself talking. "And how am I to give you up after all these years, Peter?"

"We won't forget. Anything." Peter was watching George apprehensively now, reaching out for the moment of divine release.

A dream-like terror had settled into George. Katherine's boy was leaving him. There was no mistaking that. They were all leaving him. Even Reggie had unexpectedly informed him that something had come up and he had to go that very day. Lesley would be back but she was not close to him. He was alone. Peter would not be back. He spoke throatily. "Then perhaps through the work. That may be the way. You will go on with your work, Peter? You will vindicate your mother?"

"We'll see," said Peter embarrassedly, noncommittally.

George looked imploringly about him as a lonely man will. "Lesley, Hank, can't you help me? Can't you make him see how wrong he is? You must."

Both Lesley and Henry warningly gestured silence. There was nothing they could say. Like Peter, they wanted to be away.

Peter gathered up the moment with clumsily hearty juvenility. "I've got to be on my way, George. Audrey and I are going to New York. Then we're headin' South for matrimony. That makes for a very full day with no ten-minute breaks."

The old George came to the surface fast. He gripped the arms of his chair. The chin jutted firmly. The vitality of anger gave him a transient full touch of life. "Peter, I know you must be seeking some out. I understand that. But use reason. This sort of thing, this moral suicide, is no answer. Believe me, it isn't."

"Aren't you forgetting to be sweet, George?" asked Audrey acidly.

Peter was happily angry, angry with himself for having been duped. "George, Audrey and I are to be married. When you insult her, you insult me." Surely he could not want to quarrel again? Enough harm had been done already.

Audrey chimed in again. "Thank you, Peter. I told you what to expect."

George went on. "No, wait, Peter, wait. I won't quarrel. I'm trying to be calm. Matter of fact, I've been quite ill as a result of all this and I've got to be calm."

"I told him to expect that, too." Audrey was relentless.

George ignored her. "You're going through with this?" he asked Peter.

"I'm not going to fight with you again, George, ever. But get this and get it straight. Audrey and I are happy in our own silly fashion." Nice unction crept into his speech. "Audrey's been very kind and sweet and generous. About everything. And I'm going to marry her. Can you understand that?" He might be commanding troops, the way he said it.

George's blood went hot. He was nastily sarcastic. "You've been away for a long time, Peter. It's conceivable that you don't know Audrey. She's been 'kind and sweet and generous,' as you put it, many times since she grew up, and with no accountable discrimination."

Reggie came away from the garden door. "That's pretty lousy, George."

"And true or false, it's nobody's business but Audrey's," amended Peter sharply.

George tried to reel away from his inconsequent rage. He must make sense, real sense. Now was the time. But divorce was not easy. "Well, that's the lay," he said stupidly. "Audrey's out for two things, money and revenge. Money comes first, I'm sure."

Peter grappled with the weird problem of George, spoke incoherently. "In a wrong sort of way, you're trying to help."

Audrey cut in. "I think I've proved to Peter that I love him. And he's proved that he loves me."

"Don't defend yourself, Audrey," pistoled Peter. "It's quite unnecessary."

"I suppose you'll hate me for it, Peter. But it had to be said."

Audrey was breathing spittingly through her teeth. The damage was on the table. Her eyes were frightening. She stepped into the group. "So you were fool enough to do it after all?" Looking at George, she addressed Peter. "I'd like to confirm part of what our ageing cavalier has just told you."

"I wish you wouldn't," from Peter.

"So does he. The man George has a lot of nasty talents you don't know about. While you were away, he trotted them out. And it seems he's just as promiscuous as he's dirty. It turns out that his lechery's an old companion and in his dim and distant youth, he managed to seduce your mother and thereby become your father, which accounts for all the pleasant tragedy which surrounds your birth and life."

George was shaking again, violently. "Don't believe her, Peter. Don't believe her."

Wildly disturbed, Peter spoke simply, clearly. "I don't. But I'd like to."

Audrey was agape, George unbelieving. He stopped shaking. There was a long silence which seemed short. "What?" he whispered.

Peter sprang to inspired lies. It was all unreal. But it demanded action. The hell with whether it was psychic or not. Do it. "Through the years, I've come to know Mother a lot better than you think. Through all I've heard of her, the pictures of her, the things she liked. But most of all, through the music she composed." Now the jump. "And the letters she wrote me before I was born. They came with the first small part of the legacy." He studied the ceiling furtively. He must play it true, not overdo it. What was he afraid of? Come on. He was suddenly and inexplicably, an actor who had learned his part. "They're beautiful. Through them, I know, as she knew, that you loved, tried to help her, to make her happy. And you succeeded oftener than you'd believe. And so, I can honestly say we'd both be glad to know you were my father."

"Are you being funny, Peter?" But Audrey's poor little question carried no conviction.

George was quite overcome, prayed, for the first time in

his life, that he might be granted retention of his dubious grip of living until this greatest passage should be completed. He garnered a vocal output. "Peter I—I don't know what to say. You make me happier than I ever thought—And perhaps you understand a little now that, I've always felt, somehow, you see, that I really was your father."

"Of course," said Peter hoarsely.

George knew he was punch-drunk, punch-drunk and deliriously happy. Through all his ecstatic confusion, he told himself that he must act rightly now, if ever. This was his sole visit to eternity. "You won't discover gratitude in what I believe to be duty, Peter, not at first, anyway. I'm going to risk losing everything. I've got to do one more thing you may think cruel, the last, I hope, I'll ever have to do. Some time, some way, I pray you'll forgive me." He wanted a cigarette but that would look too bad, too callous. "When you entered the Army you returned full control of your estate to me. Right?" As Peter nodded, he plunged on. "No more of it goes to you as long as a marriage with Audrey is maintained."

This switch to worldliness brought Peter close to vacant laughter. "Surely you don't think that can make any difference?" he asked disarmingly.

"I think you'll find it will make a great deal of difference." George was consciously definite.

Audrey felt she should be more furious than she had ever been. She was not. Reggie was mitigation. But no matter. George had beaten her. But she would beat him down before she would let him know it. "The loving father at his best. It's kind of you to plan to starve us out, especially since Peter will never work again."

George was infuriatingly complacent. "You'll be able to support him very nicely, I think."

If Audrey supported anyone, it would not be through pressure but rather a man of her own choosing. She gunned George pleasurably. "Do you know why he'll never work again?"

"I know that once he's free of you, he will work again."

Audrey was contemptuous. "How smug you are. How well you deserve what I'm going to tell you."

Sure alarm hit Peter. "Audrey, you promised!"

"No, Peter," she whipped the rejection at him, returned to George. "He'll never work again because he's crippled." The word crackled as she said it—'crippled.' "Crippled, do you hear?" Oddly enough she was screaming, touched more than she knew. "Have you seen his right hand this morning? Did he shake hands with you when you asked him? No, no, no. He can't use it. He'll never be able to use it. He had to defend himself against you, you, his loving father, and now he'll never play the piano again as long as he lives. And you did it. You, who would have him fulfil his mother's destiny!"

Peter went limp. George became a powerless maniac as he slowly grasped the full significance of Audrey's shouting. He became red, pale, red, pale. His eyes were sightless. He uttered the terror of his speech croakingly, heavily. "Peter, Peter, is this true? Tell me. Tell me it's a lie."

Peter talked harshly. "You know it's a lie, don't you?"

"But the hand, Peter. Your right hand. Show me your right hand, Peter. Peter, let me see it. Hank, you know. Look at Peter's hand. Tell me it's all right, Hank."

Henry spoke swiftly, hollowly. "Peter has told you."

George gasped for breath. He was almost inaudible. His chair shook the room. "Then it's true. It's true. Katherine, I—" he drooled what else he might have said.

Peter was instantly alive. In one flashing movement, he was kneeling beside George, gripping his arm, his shoulder, left-handed. "It's a lie, George. Listen to me, listen. It's a lie." George was near death. Peter did not question how he knew that. "God damn it, I— Wait, just wait. I'll show you. I'll prove it to you." Peter was on his feet and in the hall in a breath. One road to love.

Henry never used voice. Everyone jumped when he did. "Peter! What are you going to do? Peter, don't use that hand. Don't!" He had bounded out of his chair only to come face to face with an equally quick Lesley.

"Let him alone."

There was supreme command in Lesley's poise in strength which stilled his fraught panic. "But it's true. Audrey's telling the truth. He mustn't use it. If he does, he may never use it again. Never. Do you understand?"

"Let him alone."

Henry sank back into his chair with an insistent fatalistic resign. What more could he say? What could anyone do? Lesley remained standing. Mickey and Mike sat up slowly, their tawny coats twitching. She turned her head from side to side, despair ridden. She narrowly escaped high hysteria. More melodrama. And horrible. Her mind was numbed and incredulous. Hideous dream quality again. Such misshapen accidents did not occur to life.

Music, of a sort, filled the air. Peter had found his way to the tawdry music room. Pain was an old story. He ground his teeth, chipped them. He had done that many times. Grinning madly, he forced that right hand to the keyboard. It would work or he would chop it off. The bass was clear, definite. There was no treble. But there would be. Cutting misery here. The treble came in, spasmodically discordant. It was weak, then strong. It faded. It joined the bass again. Then the treble assumed form. With a kind of wild joy, defiance, upper bracket, Peter played the main theme of his symphony, found his way into the development, went into the secondary theme. It was terrific. Without perfection of technique, but with great courage, feeling and warmth, he rode it through to a stirring conclusion. And he joyfully grasped the bright beauty that he was riding high. And there were no air pockets.

As he stepped back into the living room, he faced a spellbound group. Even Audrey was obviously moved. She was losing a hell of a man. Lesley was at the highest emotional tension. With blind faith, she had banked everything and won. No, Peter had won. He was pale, unsteady, drenched with sweat. But his eyes were shining with the brilliance of lightning.

He stood beside George's chair. "How was that?"

George, who had been mouthing 'God help me, God help me,' had, strangely enough, gained control of himself as Peter gained control of his playing. Now, sadly weakened but alert, he was the proudest man in the world. "That—it was—we always knew." He was choking in such an absurd way but that was of no consequence. His boy had risked everything to prove him wrong, to save him. "But your hand?" He touched it gently. "Hank, Hank, will you, will you see?"

Henry examined Peter's wrist dexterously, anxiously. It was possible. It need not be what was fondly known as a miracle. He preferred to think that it was just that. "It's amazing. It's all right, George. It's fine." Recovery could be accomplished through force, that way. But when had it ever happened other than to, say, a gangster?

Peter looked around him as though he were six and had just talked to Santa Claus. His eyes stopped on Lesley. He could see nothing else, would never be able to see anything else. She stepped unconsciously, uncertainly, toward him.

"Peter. Peter, it was so beautiful."

His arms went around her. They were one person. Her breasts, her arms enveloped him. His grip was brutal, eternal. He was in her, through her. It was all so natural.

Instinctive fury in his veins, George half rose from his chair. A sharp, deep pain in his side sent him back. He was set for a second attempt when he caught Henry's eye. This was more effective than the pain. He was out of character, new character. He tried to think. Now was another moment. What was the right thing to do? The answer was simple, really. All right, admit it. He knew Hank must still be watching him. He glanced in his direction, found he was right, grinned sheepishly.

Audrey broke it all with a contemptuous snort. She was getting weepy, silly. Over slush. "Of all the saccharine slices of sentimentality it's ever been my misfortune to witness, this is quite the most revolting." Why was she swinging into trite, well-exercised phrases? The hell with it. The hell with everything. It was all a lot of sap. "I know you'll excuse me. I'm going to vomit." With tigress speed she was at the hall doorway. "And it's a sad commentary on the times that the only man in our set, worthy of the name, has nothing else to offer! Come on, Reggie." She flounced out of the room, out the side entrance, broke tradition, handled her bag from Peter's car to Reggie's.

Reggie, drunken, walked out into the hall, came back. He was sweetly bewildered. Then he caught himself. He shrugged and smiled. "Some of us seem born to this sort of thing." Lesley and Peter were looking at him with rare affection. He shrugged again. There was no taking too much of this, not easily. "Maybe it's not such a bad fate after all."

Lesley made a little gesture with her hands. She loved this boy just as Peter did. "You'll come to see us, Reggie? Often?"

Reggie smiled like an old man. "That'll be wonderful. If you won't object to my wife." And he was away.

Quiet settled over the room.

George was impressed, deeply impressed and had got himself in hand. There was new authority in his voice. "Peter, I think you and Lesley ought to leave us now. You must want to go to town or be together or something."

"And what about you?" Peter was clearly solicitous.

George wanted to cry, could not, was glad he could not. "I have some plans to think over," he said slowly. "I need a little time."

Henry spoke up out of his wonder. "You would have plans. Just like that. Why don't you relax?"

"Oh, these are very simple plans," said George scoffingly, "but they do require some thought. I think a month or two at sea might be very sweet just now, very sweet indeed."

Henry was back with George again. "Going to take me along?"

"I am not. I don't even want to see you again until you've had yourself psyched. I never knew a psychiatrist yet who didn't need that."

"We love it. That's why we go in for it."

George looked at him with kind, open admiration. "Hank, it's the toughest thing I've ever had to say. But I've got to tell you."

"What's that, Georgie?"

"You've been right. *All the time."*

Henry flushed violently. "Now you really embarrass me. If I've been right once, I've established a record."

George went on with listless but vital indifference. He felt a glow. "But through all your preaching, through all the years, there's one thing you never told me. You might have told me, I think."

"Well?"

"That without accepting any of the accepted theories on the subject, I could still believe in God."

Henry was not humble, he was, in attitude, abject. "Then I never told you anything at all," he said softly.

"May be, may be, Hank," muttered George, "but I doubt it." He dragged himself away from his old friend to recall Lesley and Peter. When his eyes travelled Lesley, his heart did a flip. "That cruise," he said limply, "of course, I won't leave until after the wedding. I can't miss that, I must wait for that. In fact," he addressed Peter, "I'd like to be best man, unless you have other ideas?"

"I haven't."

"That's great." George let his head sink forward, closed his eyes.

Lesley and Peter hesitantly waved good-bye to Henry and tiptoed away. Mickey and Mike scrambled to their feet and shot to the side door. Lesley's bags were ready. Fulton stacked the luggage in Peter's car as he and Lesley dashed up to tell a delighted Mrs. Williams the news and give her their promise to be back in a few days. Plumes awag, the dogs flanked the car as far as the road.

At 'Stoneleigh,' Audrey, Garden, Yvonne and Celeste had kept the 'phones hot—New York newspapers, a gigantic cocktail party that afternoon. She would be married on Thanksgiving Day, an anniversary for a man to remember. She joined Reggie in the great hall. He was broodingly sprawled on the divan. She fixed him a drink, gave it to him, lightly touched his cheek with the back of her right hand, sat beside him. "It's going to be the best wedding ever!" They would be called for lunch any moment. "Reggie, I think you could design a super, super car, if you really tried, couldn't you?"

"It would be a Laurens car."

"I know. It would dress the line."

Reggie was bitterly happy. He was going to earn his keep. Among Audrey's many interests was stock control of a popular car which rolled off the assembly line at the rate of one every split second. 'It would dress the line.' Sure it would. "I'll design it, not sell it."

"That's all I want."

"Is it?" He looked her over very slowly. "Do you know what I'd like to do to you, butch?"

Audrey's lips parted gradually. "I think so. I hope so."

"Is there time?"

"The hell with lunch, darling," she croaked and waited hot-eyed.

Peter's car slid down the Post Road headed for Route 80, New Haven, the Parkway and New York. They would grab a bite on the way and be in the city early enough for a good rest before it was time for cocktails. His thinking paused. Mr. Ed had always said, 'Quit when you get a head.' It had been a big, the poorest, head ever. It could repeat. He decided he would go easy on the cocktails. Faith, work and Lesley were all the exhilaration he could use at top capacity. He would never go on the wagon. He would never fear the stuff, nor love it for the sake of itself. He would never give it that much importance. He might go for months or years without touching a drop. But he would never go on the wagon. As long as he lived, he would take a drink wherever and whenever he felt like it. But, in trenchant gratitude for infinite favor, he promised himself that never again would he drink too much. And he knew he never would.

Lesley's mind was busy, busy, busy, singing away—visions of their home. They would have a wonderful dinner that night, probably at Chambord or Henri Soule's Pavillion, and then they would talk about it. Peter must have a whole floor, all his, most attractive, bedroom, bath, sitting room, and, most important, the studio. He would never be disturbed unless he wanted to be. His meals would be served to him quietly. He could hole in for a month or however long he liked. Or if he wanted suddenly to travel, to London, Berlin or the Bowery or Quebec or Tucson, with her or without her, that would be all right, too, bless his heart. She would make his linen and prepare or supervise those meals. And socially, they would see only those people who were right for him at the time. She would take on the others who had to be seen for one reason or another. That would be hard to handle on concert tours but she could quickly learn if love and instinct were clear. And they were. She adored this man for all his sweetness and strength and the breath of Heaven in him.

Peter looked at her, looked back at the road. "Darling," he whispered deeply.

George lifted his head. Henry stood gracefully before the fireplace smoking one of those mellow cigars. George sniffed the odor gratefully. It had been a very satisfying nap. He would go back to it presently. He was wistfully happy about the way Hank was looking at him, waiting for him to come awake.

"Would it be all right if I had a cigarette, doctor?" He had it. Hank was so deft, so quick. "And a drink?" The drink was his. He was glad Hank was so strong and sure. "The kids are gone?"

"They're gone."

George stole a contented glance at Hank, back at his fireplace stance. This was no good. It might be a last moment. And there was no argument. How could they have fun unless they were arguing, unless he was ribbing this brightest of all men? Well, maybe he was not so bright as all that but that was the way he felt about him. Here was a friend, a friend. Here was much more, too, and it failed to frighten him. He hoped Hank understood that. And he thought he did. Hank would always be standing by, always. "Hank, I guess I won't be here, and that's oke with me, but there's going to be another war, you know."

"I *don't* know."

"There is. It's coming fast. And it's going to get Peter and Lesley—and you. It spells complete destruction for all of you. Where's the sense? Everyone going around scared crazy." He leaned forward. "This thing has just hit me out of nowhere, hit me hard. What's the answer? You teach me a philosophy, I learn to accept it. The moment I do, I know it's useless."

Henry was richly pleased, came back, Henry style. "It's because you know it isn't useless that you accepted it."

"Yes, but what good will it be in a crisis?"

"The same good it was a minute ago. We're not dead yet. And we never will be. That's the purpose of it all, to overcome. The maintenance and furtherance of beauty is your job and mine and everyone's. That's why we're here. That's why we think and feel. And as long as we know nothing can stop it, nothing will stop it."

Hank was really plugging. George was delighted. "Then how can wars go on?" he asked.

"How do we know they do? How do we know they don't just seem to, horribly? And that we can stop them if we will? Peter knows. Man hasn't reached his perfect state yet. When he does, they won't happen."

"Meantime, we die."

"No. You don't listen. You live. Work, live, give, fully, that's all. Work and love. Yes, love fully, as Peter and Lesley do. That's the joy of life. That is life. That's why we have music, philosophy, painting, all sincere and artistic work, to help Man toward his perfect state. When he reaches it, he won't need help. There won't be any sculpture, poetry or painting as we know it. Life will be the perfection of beauty." Metaphysical preaching was illogical, divergent. That was of no moment now. It was the kindred moment of yearning that counted. Henry swung on. "There won't be any music because there'll be nothing but harmony. There won't be any philosophy because there won't be any problem of life. There won't be any plays because there won't be any conflicts."

George put his cigarette out, set down his drink, threw up his hands weakly. "You win. You win."

Henry plunged on. "No, maybe not for awhile. But I will.

So will you. So will we all. It took two children to make us see that. And that nothing can kill it. Nothing!"

George stopped him again, one hand this time. He raised it firmly, dropped it back to the chair arm. He sat back. His head sagged a little. He lifted it sternly. He would have none of that. Henry's eyes did not leave George as he threw his cigar back of him into the fireplace. Here was the miraculous, mysterious drama he had witnessed so many times and would never understand. Piercing pain crossed George's face and body and was gone. Henry saw flames as distinct as candle flames in George's eyes. Flames of purest happiness. The first which had ever burned there. As they tapered slowly away, George knew a pang of joy as sharp as a steel barb. In instant dream, his life went by. The glassiness which followed the flames dissolved. He could see his dear friend. He grinned derisively. There was no malice. Rather was it the derision of the schoolboy who was telling his best friend that he talked too much.

"Eyewash," said George and quietly died.

FINIS